SCARLETT FINN

Also by Scarlett Finn

GO NOVELS
GO WITH IT
GO IT ALONE
GO ALL OUT
GO ALL IN
GO FULL CIRCLE

EXILE
HIDE & SEEK
KISS CHASE

WRECK & RUIN
RUIN ME
RUIN HIM

**THE BRANDED
SERIES**
BRANDED
SCARRED
MARKED

**FORBIDDEN
PREQUEL DUET**
ALL. ONLY.
ONLY YOURS

TO DIE FOR...
TO DIE FOR TRUTH
TO DIE FOR HONOR
TO DIE FOR VIRTUE
TO DIE FOR DUTY
TO DIE FOR LOVE

**LOVE AGAINST THE ODDS
STANDALONE COLLECTION**
SWEET SEAS
HEIR'S AFFAIR
RESCUED
MAESTRO'S MUSE
GETTING TRICKY
THIRTEEN
REMEMBER WHEN...
RELUCTANT SUSPICION
XY FACTOR

NOTHING TO...
NOTHING TO HIDE
NOTHING TO LOSE
NOTHING TO DECLARE
NOTHING TO US
NOTHING TO SAY
NOTHING TO GAIN
NOTHING TO YOU
NOTHING TO THIS

THE FORBIDDEN NOVELS
FORBIDDEN DESIRE
FORBIDDEN WANT
FORBIDDEN WISH
FORBIDDEN NEED

KINDRED SERIES
RAVEN
SWALLOW
CUCKOO
SWIFT
FALCON
FINCH

THE EXPLICIT SERIES
EXPLICIT INSTRUCTION
EXPLICIT DETAIL
EXPLICIT MEMORY

MISTAKE DUET
MISTAKE ME NOT
SLEIGHT MISTAKE

**RISQUÉ & HARROW
INTERTWINED**
TAKE A RISK
FIGHTING FATE
RISK IT ALL
FIGHTING BACK
GAME OF RISK

LOST & FOUND
LOST
FOUND

ONE

UNTIL THAT WEEK, Shyla Bellamy had never been to a single job interview.

At that moment, she was on her way to her third. Her baptism of fire would continue until she acquired a job. Tough as it was to be optimistic, she had to keep going. Without work, she wouldn't be able to secure an apartment or pay her bills. She'd be homeless and destitute. She had to keep going.

As pep talks went, that wasn't the most inspiring. Every interview had been a bust, so believing the next would be any different wasn't easy. But there was no alternative. Anyone who'd agree to see her was a potential employer. All it took was one person willing to take a chance. Just one.

Shyla didn't make the best first impression. Knowing that didn't do much for her anxiety. If anything, that made it worse. At that moment, relaxing was all the more difficult because she was on her way to interview for the role she wanted most.

Walking through the entrance into the glass lobby and seeing the valet parking intimidated the hell out of her. While travelling up in the elevator, she reminded herself not to be nervous. Nerves meant rambling and that was unprofessional. She would nail this. Nothing but potential.

Nobody rewarded a quitter.

With few vocational skills, and no formal education beyond high school, Shyla wasn't a catch for any employer. But time was of the essence, she needed a job and had to believe that it would happen. Succeeding in the next interview would put an end to her problems. That was easier to focus on than the opposite.

Losing her job and home had happened almost overnight. Caring for the elderly could be that way. Three years ago, her grandfather's sudden death hit her hard. One minute he was there, the next he was gone. Adjusting to being without him took time, she'd been caring for him since her teen years.

The person responsible for getting her through that loss was her grandfather's best friend, Stanley Sedgwick. Caring for him and her grandfather, Bernard, had given her purpose. The three of them had lived together in Stanley's home. If it wasn't for Stanley, Shyla wouldn't have known what to do with herself after her grandfather died. In the years since, Stanley had been her crutch. They'd leaned on each other.

Five days ago, Stanley passed in his sleep. Life as she'd known it was over. Shyla was out in the world on her own, really for the first time.

While in the midst of grief over losing the only person she could count as a friend, Shyla was also coping with being evicted. Stanley's good-for-nothing son wasted no time in storming into the house to announce that he was selling. Being a generous type, he'd given her a week to vacate.

There were three days left on the clock.

The elevator didn't ding, it just came to a stop. After a moment of anticipatory silence, which Shyla speculated may have been programmed in for maximum suspense, the gleaming silver doors opened.

As the view was revealed, it took her breath away.

On the opposite side of the room, a glorious vision of the gleaming blue ocean was laid out before her. It wasn't like she'd never seen the ocean before, but at this elevation, she got a real sense of its vastness.

She stood there dumbfounded for so long that the elevator doors began to close. Inhaling her panic, Shyla grabbed one to hold it in place while bounding out onto the gray ash floor that spread through the sleek modern space. One wall, to the right, was smoked mirror. The wall on the left was a warmer brown color. A low marble shelf, around knee height, ran along that wall and around the corner.

Between her and the view that had first captured her eye was a large square lobby area with a dining table beyond and a terrace on the other side of the full height windows.

The residence was incredible. The ad for a housekeeper said the job included room and board. It said nothing about the room being in an amazing condo. Jumping to conclusions could lead to disappointment. Maybe she was wrong and wouldn't be living there at all. Shyla didn't want to get her hopes up. It could just be a business premises used for interviews. They might be miles from the location of the job.

She tiptoed forward to take in more of the open plan space. The living space opened out to stretch far to the left. The terrace wrapped all the way around, as far as the eye could see.

Her mouth dried.

The gleaming white marble kitchen next to the dining table was separated from a hallway by a wall. Contemplating where that hallway might lead, she peeked at the light glowing from the end and wondered if the terrace wrapped around that side of the apartment too.

"Miss Bellamy?"

Caught in her pondering, she whipped around, her anxiety cresting again. Someone appeared at the other end of the apartment. Figuring there had to be another hallway or room down there, she was sure no one had been sitting in either of the two separate seating areas of the living space.

"Yes," she said to the well-groomed, if somewhat frantic, suited man hurrying toward her. "Sorry, I wasn't sure where to wait."

It was a sad state of affairs. At twenty-nine, she was less experienced than most nineteen year olds in how to conduct herself at interviews.

"No, my fault; I was using the restroom. It's been an insane day, I have to apologize," he said, coming toward her, his hand outstretched.

Hoping that he hadn't been too rushed to forget washing his hands, Shyla shook his hand because it was the polite thing to do. She didn't expect him to tug her toward the closest seating area, guiding her in his haste. More than once, she almost lost her footing. Face-planting hadn't featured in her interview experience… yet. That would be a brand new low.

Winding around the end of the couch that had its back to the dining table, he let her go and spun around. "Will you sit down," the businessman said, gesturing to one end of the couch as he sat at the other. "Please."

Sitting on the edge of the couch with her knees tight together, Shyla clutched her purse in her lap. The heavy chess board in the middle of the central glass coffee table snagged her attention. The pieces appeared to be hand-carved wood. Shyla was impressed. Bernard, her grandfather would be elated to see such craftsmanship.

Frantic Man shifted an inch closer and opened his hand. "Do you have your resume?"

This was the part of the interview process that she hated. Not that she'd found an enjoyable part yet. Most online vacancies required her to attach a copy of her resume. So far, not one of those employers had got back to her.

Opening the front pocket of her purse, Shyla slid out a folded document that she handed over. "Uh… sort of."

He unfolded it and began to read. Just as she expected, his optimism began to fade fast. "This is…" He turned it around to show her what she'd given him. "Your birth certificate."

"Yes," she said, trying to make her smile seem genuine. No matter how hard she tried, her anxiety must have been obvious. She pushed her interlinked fingers together and raised her hands, pulling and twisting at her fingers as she did. "It is… I… I did try to make up a resume, but after I got past name and date of birth, well… things get a little… sparse."

"Did you graduate high school?"

Shyla grinned. "Yes!" Nodding, she squeezed her twined fingers around each other. "Yes, I did that. I did graduate high school."

"Okay," he said, nodding too like they were making progress. "That's good, that's… something. College?" Wincing, Shyla kept working her fingers and shook her head. He sort of cringed, but was polite enough to try to hide his reaction by glancing down at her birth certificate. "According to this you're… twenty-nine."

"Yes," she said, showing her teeth in more of a grimace than a grin. "I am twenty-nine. I did graduate high school. I didn't go to college… and I've never had a real job."

"Let me guess," he said, folding her birth certificate and handing it back to her. "Knocked up by your high school boyfriend, married young, pushed out a couple of kids, and now he's split… probably dumped you for another teenager."

"No!" she exclaimed, pointing her index fingers to the ceiling in firm disagreement. "No, I have never been married. I don't have any kids."

The businessman frowned at her. "So what the hell have you been doing for the past decade?"

Inhaling, Shyla held her breath for a minute. She shouldn't be disappointed, it wasn't like the interview had ever been on course to go well.

"Caring for my grandfather and his best friend," she said. "He just died last week."

"Your grandfather?"

"His best friend… My grandfather died three years ago. He raised me," she said, twisting and squeezing her digits again. "And my brother…" Her next admission had a tendency to cause her to hyperventilate. "Who's in prison…" Taking a shot at laughing it off was her go-to maneuver. As always, she got nothing from the blank person seated in front of her. No one ever reacted well to that part. Her desperate, last-ditch effort was begging. "I can cook, and clean, and sew… I know how to get red wine out of soft furnishings and blood out of bedsheets…" Rubbing her lips together, Shyla kept working her fingers and raised her shoulders. "I work hard. I work long. I can do anything that's required of me.

Anything… All I need is a safe place to sleep, that's it… and maybe an allowance for food and medical. I can take care of everything. I live frugally. I don't drive, so there's no expenses there. I don't smoke or do drugs. I don't have any addictions… I…" The guy hadn't stirred, even his expression was static. "I'm not getting through, am I?"

She sighed, coming to terms with the truth. The interview was another waste of everyone's time. All she needed was for someone to give her a chance, but she didn't blame anyone for being hesitant. Anxiety was not her friend. When she was fidgety and rambling, she might not give herself one.

"Hire her."

The deep voice came suddenly from the recesses of the apartment.

It was so unexpected that even the man opposite her jumped. "Jesus, Score, do you have to loiter like that?"

Twisting around, Shyla didn't see anyone. Only a slight movement in the mouth of the hall she'd been peering down earlier proved there was someone there. The wall between the kitchen and that passage created an angle of shadow. This Score had used that cover to his advantage.

With his arms still folded, he moved into the light at the end of the hall, and propped a shoulder on the wall. Shyla was stunned by the picture he presented. Her wide eyes couldn't remember how to blink. The view of him didn't even compare to that of the ocean. She forgot about the watery dullness in a flash.

At least six foot four or five inches tall, the broad man was wearing jeans and a tee-shirt that didn't seem to know how to contain his biceps. His hair was thicker on top than at the sides, and he had stubble across his jaw. Nothing about him appeared forced; nothing about his look or manner gave the impression he'd made any effort at all.

Shyla kept her lips clamped shut to ensure her tongue didn't roll from her mouth. How could a guy look so mean and dangerous just standing there, leaning on a wall?

"Where's your brother at?" Score asked, his expression registering nothing.

He was talking to her; he'd asked a direct question. His eyes weren't wide like hers, but Shyla guessed he was looking at her too.

After a couple of false starts, Shyla got her tongue to respond and forced her reluctant mouth to open. "Raiford," she inhaled the word in a desperate breath.

"Florida State."

"Haven't had the pleasure, have you, Score?" the businessman opposite her asked.

Staring was rude, but Shyla couldn't tear her attention away from the man at the end of the hallway. So tall and dominating, so powerful and so… unlike any man she'd ever seen in real life. Though real life for more than a decade had featured men enjoying their retirement.

"No," Score said, though she didn't see his lips move.

His response was more like a sound than a word.

Amusement bled into the businessman's words. "Of all the things she said, how come the only word you heard was prison? Her brother could be a rapist, you know? A kiddie fiddler. Don't other inmates pound on guys like that? You want to cut some slack to the sister of a pedophile?"

"Oh no," Shyla gasped, turning back around to address the businessman. "It's nothing like that. He would never… It was just burglary, he got a seven year sentence and…"

Twisting to ensure Score could hear her too, she stopped talking when she discovered he'd vanished.

The businessman sighed. "Okay, well, I guess you're in…" Suffering whiplash, Shyla was still trying to orient herself and barely registered his false smile. "I'm Amos Beeks, Score's lawyer…" He continued by muttering, "Among other things." Before Shyla could react, he returned to his smile. "Everyone just calls me Beeks, so Beeks will do… What do we call you?"

"My… my name is Shyla Bellamy."

"Well, I suppose, that's, uh… what we'll call you then."

Which he would know because he'd read her birth certificate; Shyla wanted to kick herself. He was asking about nicknames and preferences. She'd done what she always did and said a stupid thing by opening her mouth without thinking first.

With Bernard and Stan, it hadn't mattered if she'd spoken without thinking. Even if she said something shocking or ridiculous, the pair laughed it off. Shyla had lived quite a closeted life; she knew that. Being on call required her to be at home night and day in case either of the elderly men needed her. They came first. Shyla's primary responsibility was to them.

That meant no social life. No nightclubs. No boyfriends or lunches with friends. Shyla had dedicated herself to caring for the men who'd always been there for her. Stan had been like an uncle, and had been there as often as her grandfather for school shows or life events. Losing him was going to be a difficult thing to get over.

"Miss Bellamy?"

Beeks leaned closer, giving her a whiff of his cologne.

Only then did Shyla realize she'd lost herself in her thoughts. "I'm sorry, were you saying something?"

Already he'd be regretting the decision to hire her. After promising to be a hard worker, she'd zoned out only seconds into the job.

"I asked if you have many things to move in? We have a storage area on one of the lower floors if you have larger items. All of your bedroom furniture and linens will be provided… unless you have special requirements."

"No, I don't have any special requirements or large items," she said, shaking her head, almost unable to believe this was actually happening. "Is this where I'll be living?"

Beeks retrieved a phone from his pocket. "Yes. You'll be on call twenty-four seven for whatever is required. You will have to do the cooking and cleaning. All of the errands, including grocery shopping, etc. We'll give you a credit card… Just keep your receipts for anything household related, I'll collect them whenever I'm around." He was typing into his phone. "There won't be anything too strenuous, the building has maintenance for household repairs. You can dial the concierge from any phone or intercom."

"Concierge?" she asked.

Beeks looked up from his typing. "Yes," he said, lowering his phone to his knee. "There are ten units in the building, one on each floor. We'll have your fingerprint added to the system so you can use the elevators, and access the apartment from either of the two stairwells. There's a pool and lounge area downstairs, as well as a bar and a restaurant too. We have valet—"

"Oh, I don't drive."

"Okay, well, there's a gym. You'll have full access to that… Everything you need is right here."

"Laundry?"

He pointed to where Score had been. "Laundry room's second right in the hall. This place has all the mod cons, built in coffee machine in the kitchen, everything you could need. We can control all of it from the smart panels dotted around."

Standing up, he seemed more at ease when he put his phone back in his pocket. "Come on, I'll show you around."

***

THE APARTMENT WAS BREATHTAKING.

Shyla learned there *was* a second hallway at the far end of the living space. From there, they had access to one stairwell, a powder room, and a third bedroom. Oh, and it turned out that the terrace did sweep around every side of the apartment.

The trash chute was first on the right of the longer hallway. A small offshoot after that led to the second stairwell as well as their full-stocked laundry room. Beeks took it all in his stride, but she was overwhelmed.

At the end of the longer hallway, two doors faced each other. Two bedroom doors. To the left, the master suite. Beeks didn't take her in there; she supposed because Score was home. If she was going to be looking after the whole place, she'd have to go in there sometime. Stripping the beds and cleaning the bathroom would be tough if she wasn't allowed in the master's bedroom.

Beeks took her through the door opposite Score's and revealed that bedroom was hers. The view from everywhere in the apartment was amazing and her bedroom didn't disappoint. It had the same full height windows that she'd seen everywhere else. They even slid open to allow her access to the terrace.

The bed was huge with a black padded headboard taller than her. It contrasted to the crisp, sumptuous white linens. Amazed, it was almost unbelievable, shocking even, that she was going to live in such a gorgeous place.

Shyla stood at the window for the longest time, gaping at the view and wondering if she should be thanking karma for placing her so gently on her feet.

When she didn't return to the living area, Beeks came back to usher her through. He sat her at the dining table and they started to go through paperwork and contracts. The man's ability to multitask was impressive. Without missing a beat, he asked her to fill in various details and sign dotted lines all while he typed furiously on his phone.

Once they were done with documents, Beeks gave her instructions for the following day. Shyla was to pack whatever she needed and be ready for noon. He took down her current address and told her that someone called Russell Tench, who everyone apparently called "Fish" would come to pick her up. He asserted that all her moving in should be done that weekend. Obviously, he didn't understand that she didn't own much.

Beeks gave her a cellphone and added her fingerprint to the system at the smart panel in the kitchen. It was official. She had a job. She had a home. She was going to be okay.

TWO

SHYLA SPENT THE NIGHT filling bags and suitcases with clothes and knickknacks. Stan's son, Mick, wouldn't let her take any items from the house. Being the sentimental type, the odd ornament or picture would've been appreciated. As it was, she was relegated to pack only things from her bedroom.

It was sort of pathetic that her whole life could be reduced to half a dozen suitcases, gym bags, and trash bags. But that was it. Her life in a heap by the door.

Before moving in with Stan, her grandfather rented a furnished house. They didn't have any precious heirlooms. The picture of the three of them on her nightstand would have to serve as enough of a memento.

To her, it didn't seem right that a man who'd done so little for his father in life got to dictate so much of his death. Even the funeral wasn't being held until it was convenient for Mick. So, Stan's friends and family were on pause, waiting for Mick to authorize the man's burial.

Shyla was kneeling on her bedroom floor sorting through the stack of letters she'd been telling herself to deal with for months. Figuring out if there was anything worth keeping was the last thing on her to-do list. She'd just finished when a car horn blared outside.

The whole street was residential and occupied by the elderly. There wasn't a lot of noise or hubbub, so even a car horn would stir attention. Leaping to her feet, she read the time on her wall clock: ten after noon.

Guessing Tench was responsible for the horn, Shyla grabbed her heaviest case and pulled it out of her bedroom and down the stairs. When she got to the first floor, Mick came running down the hallway from the kitchen.

"Hey! Hey! Hey!" he called out. "You have to open that up."

Just the question felt like a violation. Shyla didn't have anything to hide but didn't want Michael Sedgewick rooting through her underwear and private possessions either.

"I have to… what?"

"I have to make sure you didn't take anything that belongs to the house."

"I didn't," she said, certain her face was flaming.

Her first reaction wasn't offense, it was embarrassment. That anyone could think she was capable of stealing was upsetting in the first place. But someone believing she could steal from the man she'd cared for and loved like a second grandfather devastated her.

"I won't know unless you show me," Mick said, gesturing at the case and taking a short step back. "Open it up."

Shyla liked to think she could get along with most people. Although gregarious wasn't a word that could be used to describe her, she could talk to people when their paths crossed—as long as she didn't have to ask them for anything… like a job. But "*people*" didn't tend to make invasive requests. Despite her discomfort, she wasn't sure that she even knew how to object.

As she was about to acquiesce, the doorbell rang. Both she and Mick turned to look at the oval glass panel in the front door. On the other side was a young man with dirty blonde hair. He cupped a hand against his face to peer through the non-distorted part of the etched glass.

Just seeing his disarming smile brought one to her face too. When he waved, she almost laughed. Shyla had never seen him before in her life but could tell that she liked him already.

"Who is that?" Mick demanded, stamping the few steps to the door to pull it open. "Who are you?"

"Russell," the guy said, thrusting a hand toward Mick.

At six foot tall, the guy was no slouch; even though he'd been hunched over when they first saw him. Without the door in the way, Shyla could see his impressive physique beneath his pristine white tee-shirt.

"We're not buying anything," Mick barked and tried to close the door.

Fish, as she was supposed to call him, slapped a defined forearm flat on the door to prevent it from closing. He maintained his smile, in spite of startling Mick with his abrupt action. Picking his wraparound shades from his floppy hair, he dropped them over his eyes.

"I'm not selling," Fish said, patting his front pockets. "I'm not carrying..." He pointed at her. "I'm Shyla's friend..." His head tilted in her direction, away from Mick. "Right?"

Her smile grew as she nodded. "Yes... Yes, this is my friend."

"Your friend?" Mick spat out the words, but was too stunned—and probably too scared—to object when Fish stepped up into the entryway.

Just by moving forward, Fish managed to get Mick out his way without ever touching the guy. "This to go?" he asked, pointing at her suitcase.

Shyla's smile faltered. Her fingers slid between each other, a sure sign of her anxiety. "Uh... yes, but—"

"I have to check that before it leaves," Mick said.

Holding the top handle of the case, Fish rocked the suitcase back at an angle to look at it. "Check it for what? Looks secure to me."

"I need to check inside," Mick said and tried to edge closer.

Fish stepped between him and the suitcase, blocking his way. "Does it belong to you?" he asked. Mick was too dumbfounded to respond. At only five foot eight, and without having seen a gym maybe ever in his entire life, Shyla doubted that he wanted to take Fish on. "Does anything inside it belong to you?"

"That's what I have to check."

"Oh," Fish said and looked to her. "Everything in this suitcase belong to you?" She nodded, so he grinned again. "Great! Problem solved."

Picking up the case like it weighed as much as a pillow, he started for the door.

Mick hurried after him. "I can't take her word for it," he protested. "I have to check."

Fish put the suitcase down, then lifted his glasses back onto the top of his head. "You got a warrant?"

"A… a what?"

"A search warrant," Fish said. "I've got this friend. Beeks. He tells me to always read the warrant and to, you know, only let folks search what it says on the paper… If there's a warrant, I should go along with it he says, you know, and he'll fix the problems they find later. So…"

Opening a hand to Mick, Fish was patient about waiting for the paperwork.

Given that it didn't exist, Mick began to bluster. "I… don't have a search warrant. I'm not a police officer."

"Oh," Fish said, slapping his shoulder in a friendly, but firm, gesture before returning his glasses to his face. "If it's not a legal problem, then Beeks' rules don't count, Score's do."

"I… What does that mean?"

Fish raised both shoulders in a contrite shrug. "It means you don't got no rights over me or Miss Bellamy." Attempting to take another step, Fish stopped when Mick had the audacity to grab his elbow. Her protector's gaze moved slowly down to the point of contact and then up to the man at his side. "You don't wanna do that, man. Score's rules in non-legal situations are pretty much the same as Beeks' in legal ones. I do what I've gotta do in the present… He'll take care of the problems later… You don't want Score coming all the way over here to take care of you… Trust me, you don't… But it's your call… are you gonna be a problem?"

Mick's hand fell away, so Fish strode out with the suitcase, down the path to the pick-up he had parked on the curb.

"Did he just threaten me?" Mick demanded. "If he threatened me, I'm calling the police... I had no idea my father's carer associated with criminals!"

To be honest, neither did she. Well, other than the one she was related to who was doing his time in prison. Although Shyla was still in shock over Fish's cool and capable approach, she did wonder at Mick's attitude.

Mick's mother had divorced Stan when their son was a child. After that, Mick lived with her. Stan hadn't seen much of him. Shyla spent more time with him and knew him better than his own son. Still, there had been enough contact that Mick wasn't ignorant to the care needs of his father. Despite knowing for years that Stan needed care, he hadn't increased his visits or sent any aid.

So, in that time, Shyla could've turned the building into a whorehouse or a crack den. Mick wasn't around enough to have noticed.

Fish came bounding in before she could respond to Mick. "Where's the rest of your stuff?"

"Upstairs," she answered, stepping back to get out of his way. "First bedroom on the right."

Mick rushed over, but stopped at the bottom of the stairs Fish was vaulting up. "He can't go up there."

"I'm sorry about your father, Mick," Shyla said, picking up his hand to stroke the back. "He was a good man. I cared a lot about him... I know that you're hurting. I feel the same way... I can't quite believe that he's gone."

Fish came lumbering down the stairs laden with the rest of her things. Somehow, he managed to carry everything at once. She would've needed a bunch of trips. Her new friend was a blessing. The quicker they could get away from Mick, the better.

Shyla hurried out of Fish's path. As she went forward, Mick was forced to leap back, which gave Fish a clear shot out the front door. Although it hadn't been her intention to circumvent Mick, she couldn't deny being happy that he wasn't going to search her things.

"If I find anything missing, you will be hearing from me," Mick said, going to the door, probably to watch Fish.

Opening the closet at the bottom of the stairs, Shyla slipped her feet into the only shoes left in there that were hers. It was sort of sad to take her cropped denim jacket from its hook for the last time. As she put it on moisture dripped from her lashes to her cheek.

The building had been her home for almost a decade. After she walked out, there would be no reason for her to come back. Taking the long strap of her hippie purse, she slung it over her head and straightened it between her breasts before turning around, closing the closet door as she went.

Scanning the stairway and the hall, through to the living room, she closed her eyes and let herself breathe the air for another few seconds.

"I will need a forwarding address," Mick barked, breaking her reverie.

Fish was on the porch, waiting for her, wearing a smile.

Dipping a hand into her purse, Shyla flicked open her sunglasses case and retrieved her oversized shades to cover her eyes. The last thing she wanted was for either of the men to see her crying over something as silly as moving out.

"If she's forgotten anything, we'll come back," Fish said.

Going to the door, Mick acted as a barrier between her and the exit. "I'll need one anyway."

Something about Fish's ease relaxed her. Shyla's new friend extended an arm to offer a hand. With that arm, Fish pushed the door further open, away from Mick, giving her a narrow space to reach for the proffered hand.

As soon as he had her in his grip, Fish gave her a tug, pulling her past Mick who was forced back.

"We'll check with Score, get back to you," Fish said, guiding her across the porch. "Later, man!"

Dragging her down the path, Fish lifted her into the truck and then ran around to get in his own side. Even after they got on the road, Fish maintained his smile. He caught one look at her and then another.

"So, you're Russell Tench?"

"Fish," he said, offering her a hand so they could shake. "And you're Shyla… Just Shyla?" She nodded wondering what people expected her to say instead. Did everyone in the world have a nickname except her? "Would you prefer Miss Bellamy? Beeks told me to be respectful like."

"Shyla is acceptable," she said, smoothing her skirt down her thighs. "You're young."

"Twenty-three. Not that young."

"And you're friends with Score?"

Amusement sparkled from behind his smile. He caught another glance at her. Shyla wasn't sure about Score's age, but he'd seemed older than twenty-three, maybe she was wrong, she'd only seen him for a brief minute.

"I don't think I'm friends with him," Fish said. "But I'm working on it… Beeks is my friend. Well, he's my lawyer, and I guess we're tight. I trust him, you know? When he found out Score was coming down here and needed someone to have his back, he called me… Guess you could call me Score's assistant. I do his running around. His flunky."

"I'm sure he doesn't call you that."

"Could call me worse," Fish said, his smile still broad. "So, I guess you and me will have to get used to each other. I do all his business running around and you're going to do all the household stuff. Some of the personal will overlap, Beeks said. We've to not get under each other's feet."

"I have no interest in starting on the wrong foot," she said and slid closer. "We could exchange numbers… maybe we could be friends."

His smile widened. "Really?" She nodded. "Man, I don't have a lot of pretty friends, you know?"

That was flattering enough to make her lips curl too. "You think I'm pretty?"

"Are you kidding? You're flat out hot," he said. "Is that how you got the job?"

That was funny. Fish was being sweet, so Shyla didn't want to laugh in case she offended him. "Score told Beeks to hire me… Beeks implied it was something to do with my brother being in prison."

His smile became something more serious as he bobbed his head in understanding. "Score knows it's tough to get a fair shake when you've got connections like that. Folks are quick to judge, that's why us ex-cons have got to stick together."

"You… did time in prison?"

He nodded and showed her a tattoo on his forearm that meant nothing to her. "Sure did, last stretch was three years. Went in just before Score got out. We were in the same pod a few weeks together, didn't get close or nothing… He had a rep…obviously. Not many could get close to him… He was on death row two years before Beeks got him down to life without parole…" When he next glanced her way, something, probably her lack of response, made him push his sunglasses to the top of his head. Although she was gaping in the direction of the windshield, she caught that he was frowning. "You do know who he is… don't you? Are you close to your brother?"

"No," she said. "Not since we were kids…" Shaking herself out of her shock, Shyla twisted to face him. "I don't understand, who is he?"

"Phoenix McDade," Fish said like it should mean something to her, but she was at a loss. "You've gotta have heard of the McDades."

The name was familiar, but she couldn't place it until… Shyla gasped when she recalled a documentary Stan made her watch a couple of years ago. He was into a lot of crime stuff and watched all those cop shows and re-enactment things. Shyla usually only half watched or went to her room to read when he was engrossed in the TV. But the McDade documentary had stuck with her.

"The East Coast McDades?"

His smile was joined by a nod. "Yeah! That's it. Irish. They control half the import and export of knock off goods. Have interests in every drug sold on the streets and run a countrywide prostitution racket. If it's illegal, and profitable, they're making money."

The documentary went into details of the family's

crimes and their wealth. The three main Irish families battled against each other for a piece of the illegal-turnover-pie that was somewhere in the hundreds of millions. The speculative figure was likely higher these days. It also didn't account for what the families made from their apparently legitimate businesses.

"Score is the second of Burl McDade's four sons; Burl's the head of the family." Yes, Shyla had a vague recollection that Burl McDade was the father and that the boys' mother was dead… if she remembered it right. "Parker McDade is the oldest, he runs some of the company now, Burl relies on him. Zaiden McDade, Razer, he and Score were tight. He probably visited prison the most, I guess. Doran, the youngest, he's snorting and riding his way through life last I heard; there's nine years between him and Score."

"Why do they call him Score?"

"'Cause settling scores is his bag. Street calls Parker The Biz, 'cause he was always into running things. If there was a mess or someone disrespected the family, Biz called in Score and it was dealt with. Was the same in prison. Even on death row, if you could get word to Score that someone had fucked you over, he'd find a way to even the score. Hearing his name scared the shit out of people, but you'd rather him be on your tail than Razer… Razer's an actual psychopath… that's what they say. Never met him. Would be cool though, right?"

To meet a psychopath? Shyla wasn't sure she agreed with that. Razer was less her concern than the man she'd be expected to live with.

The documentary had mentioned one of the McDade sons being in prison, but Shyla couldn't remember the details. "How did he go from being on death row to being free?"

Fish laughed. "How can you not know this? I thought everyone did. Guess it's all about the circles you run in," he said and took a big breath. "Score was in Texas, running with a girl he'd been tagged with for a while. Don't know much about that, 'til one day she goes missing and next thing you know, there's a hotel manager claiming he saw Score beating on the girl and dumping her in his trunk. But there's no body see. Still the cops are trying hard to pin something on him, then there's a fire and they find some corpse that matches her dental records." He took his hands from the wheel to clap them together so loud that she jumped. "So they got him."

"Their theory is he beat on his girlfriend, took her to someplace else and then set her on fire?"

"They said he kidnapped her and fuck knows what else, I don't know," he said. "But here's the thing…" Fish hunched his shoulders and lowered his volume, like they were discussing salacious gossip. "Score sits in jail for a year and a half or something while they build the case. He's sentenced to death, sits on death row a couple of years, Beeks gets it down to life without parole 'cause, you know, I guess there's no proof he really kidnapped her or something. Beeks has connections, you know? So, Score does another three years just living the life, you know?"

Shyla didn't really, but she nodded anyway. Life in prison wasn't something she needed a run down on to understand it wasn't a barrel of laughs.

But Fish didn't elaborate. Shyla prompted him on. "So…" He glanced her way. "How did he get out?" She gasped and straightened. "He's not on the run, is he?"

"Man, you've gotta open a newspaper once in a while. So, he's been in prison for like six and a half years until, boom, who walks into the police station with a story to tell?" One glance, then another, Shyla just raised her brows in expectation. "Siobhan Kelly! The woman he's supposed to have killed. She wasn't dead at all!"

"Oh my God!" Just trying to wrap her head around the idea was almost impossible. With wide eyes, she stared out at the road ahead. "Oh my God! But who was the woman in the fire?"

He shrugged. "They never bothered to do DNA, because the dental records matched. I mean, who thinks that the murder victim isn't the murder victim, you know? They had a body, a witness, a suspect… They did the DNA after Siobhan showed up. Turned out she was some co-ed who'd OD'd and been buried the week before, same build as Siobhan. They screwed with her teeth, but yeah, total accidental death."

"But wait," Shyla said, turning to him again. "That's no accident."

The co-ed's death might have been accidental, but setting Score up hadn't been. Someone had to match the dental records and support Siobhan who must have been in hiding.

Shaking his head, Fish looked so proud of himself. He might think she'd been living under a rock, but he was definitely pleased to be telling the story. "It's all intrigue, right? That's what Beeks says… turns out Biz paid Siobhan to fuck off to some place south of the border. He set the whole thing up. Siobhan was pissed Score wasn't putting a ring on her finger, and wanted the whole gangsta life, you know? Biz just wanted his brother out the way, so their dad couldn't, you know, decide he liked him better or something… So, Score went to prison for a crime he never committed, not even that he didn't commit, but that never even happened. The media was all over it. They awarded Score like a record figure in compensation or something. I don't know, he doesn't talk to me about money…" Closing his mouth, Fish puffed out his cheeks before parting his lips to let the breath out. "He doesn't really talk to anyone… 'cept maybe Beeks."

"What about his family? His dad? His brothers?"

Fish caught a glimpse at her, but shook his head. "He cut all ties. He didn't hear hardly nothing from his dad while he was in prison. Think Razer kept in touch. Doran, Score's youngest brother, only went to see him a few times in the later years. That's all Beeks said… Don't think Score likes to talk about it."

"He must be okay talking about it if he told you."

Fish snickered. "He doesn't tell me shit. I knew 'cause everyone knows. Death row, man, that's no fucking joke… He had a rep before he went inside, now he's not only mean and dangerous, but he's bitter too, got something to prove… I know all this stuff 'cause it was all over the news, and Beeks told me some when he set me up to work for Score… But I don't push Score on nothing. No one does."

"Have you been working for him long?"

Checking the junction at a stop sign, Fish was a

careful driver and she appreciated that he took the time to obey the rules even though the streets were quiet. "A week," he said. "He's opening a club, we're getting the place ready. It's a lot of responsibility. It's a big deal."

"I can imagine."

At least she had a better idea who she was working for, though she didn't know what to make of the whole mess. If Shyla had been told that her employer spent time on death row without knowing the surrounding story, she might have been reluctant to work for him. But after learning the truth, her heart broke for him.

If this Siobhan had been upset in their relationship, she could've ended it. Instead, she'd conspired with Score's own brother, another person who was supposed to care for him, and ruined his life.

Death row must have been terrifying. Prison in general was probably terrifying. Score had lost six or seven years just wasting away for something he didn't do.

She must have been thinking about it for a while. By the time Shyla snapped out of her reflection, they were approaching Score's building.

"I have to check out this other club tonight," Fish said. "Score wants me to get the skinny on the competition... Want to come with?"

"A... a nightclub?" Her mouth opened as she shook her head. "I... I've never been to a nightclub."

While trying to determine if it was a good idea, they pulled up to the valet. Fish got out to give the guy his keys. Her things were in the back, she assumed they'd have to unload them. But Fish's question had left her two steps behind. Shyla was still trying to decide whether or not to accept the invitation when Fish startled her by opening her door.

"Come on out," he said, offering his hand to draw her out of the truck. "They'll bring your shit upstairs... You can unpack, grab some food, and I'll pick you up about ten... Unless you want me to take you for food first... We're on expenses, I have a card, so you know, we're good..."

His brow wiggle made her smile. They went toward

the entrance of the building as the valet drove the truck inside.

"Food first might be nice."

Shyla didn't have a safety net anymore. For years, she'd lay in bed thinking about what she might be missing out on. That time shrank to nothing as she anticipated learning more about the world and who she was in it.

Fish was a nice guy. She was pleased to have a friend. Other than her grandfather and Stan, she couldn't say she'd had a real friend since high school. The city was daunting, but Fish seemed like the kind of guy who'd look after a girl. Sure of that, Shyla decided that nothing could go wrong.

THREE

BOY, HOW SHYLA came to regret that thought.

Dinner was great fun and drama free. Learning more about Fish and his upbringing was enlightening. Fish wasn't born a criminal. Life hadn't dealt him the best hand. He talked about his parents being into drugs and disappearing when he was a teenager. After that, there was no one to guide him. He was an only child, so got sucked into hanging with the wrong people and dealing drugs.

He'd been in and out of juvie for trivial offenses as a minor. Jail followed, but his last stint of three years inside was enough to scare him into kicking his shady friends. That's what he said anyway. Since his liberation, Beeks was the stable influence keeping him on the right track. Fish had nothing but praise for the lawyer. Her impression of Beeks was all positive too. He seemed to be a good guy who got attached to the lost souls he took under his wing.

In her turn, Shyla told Fish about her brother, Wyatt, how her parents had been killed and how that led to her grandfather becoming their guardian. Fish listened and absorbed what she was saying.

After enjoying the food and conversation at the restaurant, they went to the nightclub. Shyla's mood was high.

Her confidence brimming. For an hour, she stuck to soda, and spent all her time on the dancefloor. The atmosphere left her soaring. At some point, while feeling invincible, she decided to try one of the fancy cocktails.

Three drinks later, she couldn't stand up.

Her memory was sketchy. Wherever she was, the whole room was spinning. She had a vague recollection of falling over something or someone before being picked up off the floor. After that, she sort of lost track.

Shyla had no idea where she was or what was going on except that everything seemed to be moving. Her feet weren't on the floor, so it wasn't her... or maybe... was she being carried?

Bright lights hurt her eyes. On a hiss, she buried her face against the person carrying her, whoever it was. Something made her stomach jump, which she figured was odd because they weren't moving forward anymore. The bright lights faded when something metallic whooshed.

"What the fuck did you do to her?"

That was a deep voice she didn't recognize. Whimpering, Shyla thought maybe she should be scared. Except holding down her dinner was taking all her effort; flailing or panicking was beyond her.

"I don't know, boss. I don't know." The terror in that second male voice was obvious. A flare of recognition made her frown. Was that Fish? "I didn't know where else to take her. I didn't know what to do. We were at a club. She was dancing, she was fine, and then she was falling all over the place. It was like super fast. She just lost it."

"Give her to me."

Her weight transferred from one body to another. The movement quaked her sensitive stomach. She rose higher, so high it felt like she was being lifted into orbit. Alarm shot through her. On instinct, she grabbed for the new person holding her. Except she couldn't reach the back of his neck, so instead of locking her fingers together to hang on, her nail dragged down what felt like flesh.

"I'm sorry, boss. Shit... I shoulda taken her to the hospital, right?" They were moving again. Her senses were all out of whack. Giving in to exhaustion, Shyla closed her eyes and went limp. "I think she was spiked."

"Shit," the deeper male voice said. In a primitive response to someone shaking her, her whole body braced. Confused about what was going on, all Shyla could do was yelp when he lifted her higher. "Where the fuck did you take her? Why the fuck were you together?"

"She wanted to be friends," Fish said. "We went to The Tropics, just like you said."

An arm moved higher on her back, rearranging her into a more seated position. The prone one worked better for her, but she wasn't really in a state to complain. Her opinion changed fast when her cheek came up against warm fabric, wrapped around a hard body. Too tempted to ignore the opportunity, she rubbed her face against it.

The act released an arousing masculine scent. Bathing herself in it, Shyla moaned. "Mmm, you feel nice."

So nice that she was provoked into arching her body further into the security of the solid form holding her. For a minute, she forgot about her disorientation and nausea and gave herself over to pleasure instead.

"Great," the deep voice grumbled.

"This is not good, right? You know, we're two felons in a bedroom with a spiked babe," the weaker male voice said.

Yeah, that sheepish voice belonged to Fish, she was pretty sure.

Were they in a bedroom? Shyla guessed so, but didn't care while rubbing herself against the enticing body holding hers. Forgetting that her ears were ringing, and her head spinning, she opened her mouth to drag her teeth on the cotton beneath her face.

"Is she biting you?"

"Get out of here, Fish," the deep voice snapped, impatient to the point of anger. "Get out. Go!"

Still unaware of what was going on and unable to open her eyes, Shyla whined in disappointment when the arms receded from around her. They'd laid her on something so soft it might have been a cloud.

Rolling over to her back, she tried to take some deep

breaths. Her stomach was rebelling again. Someone freed her feet from her shoes. As nice as it was to wiggle her toes, she couldn't contain the stirrings inside her.

Sucking in a breath, she sealed her lips for a second before forcing herself to talk. "Oh, I'm going to throw up."

"Wait a second. Hold it for me, Little Lamb."

Shyla didn't think she'd be able to. But whoever he was, he was a man of his word. Just a flash later, a hand slid onto her waist to pull her onto her side, and she threw up. Someone was stroking her temple, but she couldn't make herself open her eyes until her stomach was empty.

Once she was done, Shyla tipped up her chin toward the cool towel soothing her forehead. Only then did she realize she was hanging off the edge of a bed, upchucking into a bucket that was being held by…

"Score?" she whispered.

The dark scowl on his face didn't go anywhere, he couldn't even look at her.

He just kept pressing the towel to her head. "Close your eyes, Shy," he said. "Close your eyes."

She did exactly what he said; she wasn't capable of anything else. Shyla tried to roll onto her back again, but Score wouldn't have it and pulled her onto her side. He held her there, somehow telling her to stay in that position.

Movement and sounds of water in the bathroom preceded the toilet being flushed. Her first night on the town had been a bust, but that wasn't even the worst part of the night. The worst part was, the adventure had probably cost her the only legit job she'd ever had.

***

WAKING UP THE NEXT morning, Shyla felt worse than she ever had in her life.

Even though the blinds were closed over all of her windows, the light that was breaking through made her head ache. Trying to remember where she was and how she'd got there, Shyla groaned and dragged herself up into a seated position.

The gorgeous room reminded her of what was supposed to be her new home. After her display the previous night, she doubted she'd hold onto it.

Licking her dry lips, she bent her legs in an attempt to get out of bed. It was then she realized something was touching her neck. Raising her fingers to the fabric, she felt around it to learn it was a collar… She was wearing a white shirt, a man's shirt… that she hadn't been wearing last night.

Peeking inside behind the buttons, it was a relief to see her underwear still in place. Other than her aching head, the rest of her body was more stiff than sore. So she didn't suppose that she'd been violated. Just being uncertain was horrifying. She'd never considered herself a lush, but had never had the chance to prove otherwise… until last night.

Shyla had no idea what time it was, but took one last liberty in the form of a shower. Given that she'd moved out of Stan's and was probably going to be kicked out of Score's, she needed to take advantage of a last chance to wash.

The shower made her feel worse. Not because it *didn't* help her head or her body, but because it helped both. The sumptuous steam got her oriented. The pressure and the warmth of the glorious water only made her more aware of what she'd screwed up.

Waking up to such an invigorating shower every morning would be a dream. Although she hadn't enjoyed the pleasure yet, Beeks' mention of a coffee machine in the kitchen played on her mind. A luxurious shower and a cup of high-class java, life couldn't get more perfect. She probably shouldn't be surprised that she'd screwed it up.

Messing it up before it had even begun was just like her.

In a nod to her reluctance to face her employer, she took her time drying her hair and getting dressed. Even though she had only just started to unpack the previous day, Shyla began putting everything back in the cases and bags.

All she was doing was delaying the inevitable and being rude. Others in the apartment could probably hear her moving around. They'd be wondering why she hadn't gone out to address her terrible behavior. Thoughts about that plagued her until she got to her feet, deciding it was time to face the music.

Except she had no idea what to say. As a teen, Shyla hadn't so much as missed a curfew. She'd never been disrespectful and didn't even know how to begin apologizing for such a shocking display.

Staying in the bedroom, acting the coward, only made her feel worse. So, setting her shoulders back, she raised her chin and opened her bedroom door to stride out. Traversing the hall, she marched into the main living area of the apartment ready to grovel, except… it was empty.

There was no one in the kitchen, no one in the living room, even the powder room door was open, the room vacant. The digital clock on the microwave revealed that it was lunchtime. Figuring everyone must have left for the day, it was excruciating to know she'd have to wait until they returned to apologize.

Just in case anyone was there, waiting for her to grovel, she decided to check every corner. In the laundry room, she found towels and a tee-shirt in the washer. She couldn't be sure, but there may have been a vague scent of puke in the air. Her stomach roiled again, in embarrassment rather than sickness. Learning that someone must have cleaned up after her was humiliating. She decided that doing the laundry before she left was the least she could do. It seemed only right.

To make up a load, she collected towels from the powder room and kitchen. She also grabbed the shirt she'd slept in the night before. Shyla stripped down her bed to wash her sheets too. Score would have to hire a new housekeeper and they wouldn't want to sleep in her dirty sheets.

Next on her list was the hamper in the master suite. After emptying her arms in the laundry room, she strode into Score's bedroom, set on her task.

What she saw stopped her in her tracks.

The bathroom was to the left, but her attention was drawn to the right. How could it not be when he presented such a mouthwatering sight? Him. Yes, Score, her employer. Sleeping in the middle of the bed on his chest, his arms were wrapped around the pillow bunched under his head.

Squeezing her eyes closed, her lips moved to mouth, "Oh God."

Startled and frozen to the spot, Shyla couldn't stop studying him. The bedsheet over him stopped just beneath his hips. The top of his muscular ass was on show making it clear that he was very naked.

His tanned skin stretched over his defined form that was lit by the sunlight streaming through his windows that weren't even covered by blinds. Her bedroom and his shared the same part of the terrace. If she'd gone out that way, she'd have been able to see him, but still, her gawping felt like a violation.

In spite of that, she was tempted to move closer to explore the black ink on his back. Spread on his shoulder blades almost like wings, the tribal design curled around in the direction of his collarbone and down his upper arms. It was all part of the same motif and related to the almost birdlike head on his spine in the center of his back. The figure descended toward his ass in a curled tail that matched the tribal black ink above.

Tilting her head, she examined it as closely as she could from a distance. When Shyla realized what it was, she smiled. "It's a phoenix," she whispered.

Speaking out loud was a mistake. His next inhale was louder than the previous. Hit by panic, she backed up to slip out of the room. To remove the temptation, she closed the door without making a sound.

Score was still in bed, which implied he'd stayed up through the night to check on her. As if she wasn't going through enough shame… Shyla clutched her stomach, the weight of guilt ate her up. In an attempt to distract herself, she went back to the laundry room and put on the first wash.

The distraction didn't work. Shyla was still fretting about the previous night when she left the laundry room and found Fish coming from the direction of the elevators.

"Hey!" he said, smiling and holding up a bunch of dry-cleaning bags in one hand and some tickets in the other. "I picked up the clean stuff."

Going to meet him, she took the hangers from around his finger and the tickets from his other hand. "What are these?"

"The tickets for the stuff you have to pick up tomorrow." Peeling them back, he showed each one. "That's your dress, that's Score's stuff, mine, and Beeks'… You don't mind picking up Beeks' stuff, do you? He'll pick it up from here, you don't have to take it anywhere… He's here like every day… and I'd get mine, but I never know what Score will tell me to do, you know?"

Done with his explanation, he left her side to go into the kitchen and open the fridge. Fish was a sweetheart, but she didn't think he was really the brightest crayon in the box. He had obviously forgotten about last night.

"Uh…" she said, joining him in the kitchen, still holding the clothes and the tickets. "I made a fool of myself last night." Fish took a carton of juice from the fridge and began to drink straight from it, but he twisted enough to show that he was listening. Shyla laid the dry-cleaning and the tickets out on the white marble island that separated the kitchen from the dining area. "I don't think I'll be here tomorrow."

Frowning, he took the carton from his lips and wiped his mouth with the back of his hand. "Why not? You got vacation time already? Oh…" Putting the carton on the counter and leaving the fridge open, he came over, digging something out of his pocket. "Beeks said I should give you this. He's on his way over, but he gave it to me just in case."

Taking the piece of paper Fish had retrieved, she unfolded it, expecting it to be a demand for her to vacate. Instead, she discovered a credit card wrapped inside a list of chores. Next to that was what appeared to be a grocery list.

"When did he give you this?" she asked.

"This morning."

Score probably hadn't had time to tell his lawyer about last night. Fish would be too polite to spread stories. Shyla couldn't tell the story because most of the details were foggy. In truth, she was sort of grateful for that, the clues she'd left weren't encouraging.

She'd obviously been sick. If her dress had to be dry-cleaned with such urgency, she'd probably made a mess of herself. She couldn't remember leaving the club or arriving at Score's, but there would be only one man to thank for that.

"Fish," she said. "Thank you for looking after me last night."

"I didn't do nothing," he said, laying a hand on the counter. "Boss took you from me minute I got you through those doors." He side-nodded toward the elevator. "Kicked me out after you bit him… I don't know what he did after. I got a text this morning saying we weren't to mention it again." Leaning closer, he was smiling when he whispered. "You're not making that part easy."

She'd bitten her boss? A lump formed in her throat that could only be mortification. She couldn't begin to figure out why she'd have done something like that. Where did she bite him? Was she afraid? Shyla didn't remember fear, but couldn't think of another reason she'd take a chunk out of someone with her teeth.

"Oh my God," she whispered, edging closer. "Why would I want to hurt him?"

One side of his mouth curled higher than the other and his eyes slunk toward the window like he was trying to contain the amusement dancing in them. "I don't think you were trying to hurt him, not by the way you were whining and rubbing yourself all on him."

Heat rushed to her cheeks. Her mouth opened in shock at her own impudence. "Oh my… I was…" She'd thought she was embarrassed that morning. That was nothing to what she felt listening to Fish. Her jaw stayed slack as her hand slipped under her bangs to support her forehead. "I was…"

Fish rubbed her forearm for a second then went back to his carton. "I don't think the boss minded that much. It's not like you were trying to kiss him or grabbing his junk or nothing… Least not while I was around."

He closed the carton and put it back in the fridge.

While her other hand joined the first to cradle her forehead, Shyla bent over the counter, sinking her elbows into the plastic wrapped clothes. Being bold with a man wasn't in her repertoire. She'd never spent any time with Score, they weren't friendly. Yes, she'd been aware of him in the brief time she'd seen him, and he was attractive, but he was more man than a woman like her could handle.

Jumping into something with a man like him was definitely off the cards. Her lack of experience with the opposite sex was something she'd always regretted, but it wasn't an easy thing to remedy while stuck in the suburbs surrounded by people who were fifty and sixty years her senior.

Maybe she could build up to a man like Score. Start with someone simple and uncomplicated, like a store clerk or a bank teller. A wrongfully convicted felon from one of the country's most infamous crime families was not a good first step into the world of romance.

Squeezing her eyes closed, her hands descended from her forehead to her eyes. What was she thinking? Score wouldn't look at a woman like her. It didn't matter that her saliva glands went into overdrive whenever he was near. Being attracted to him was a natural female response. He had to be used to it.

Admitting to her attraction wasn't easy. She couldn't be sure that's what it was. She only had two clear memories of being around the guy. Once from across the room, and the other time was… Shyla was ashamed of her intrusion. The image of him more than half-naked in bed was imprinted on her mind.

Score had more experience with her than she did with him. He'd remember what happened after taking her from Fish. Shyla had no recollection of it. He must have changed her dress and removed her shoes. She couldn't even remember being undressed. Someone was responsible for the towels in the laundry room too, and she'd definitely thrown up. There hadn't been a mess on the bed or floor, so either he'd been at her side to take care of her, or he'd cleaned up afterwards.

Either way, her boss had gone above and beyond for her. She had no idea how she'd ever repay his kindness… or look him in the eye again.

FOUR

THE SOUND OF THE elevator doors opening straightened Shyla up. The delight of the blue ocean beyond the windows enraptured her for a few seconds delaying her finding out the identity of their newest guest.

"What you doing in there, boy, making a mess?" Beeks' voice came from behind her. He walked around to pull out a stool and sat down in front of her. "Where's the food? Miss Bellamy?"

"Hmm?" she asked, dragging her attention away from the windows to look at the scowling lawyer. "Oh, I… I haven't made any food, I… I haven't been out."

"There's some food in here," Fish said, going back to open the fridge up. "Might be able to make something… Score will be hungry when he wakes up… he's always hungry when he wakes up."

Shyla was still trying to figure out if she was fired or not. "Mr. Beeks—"

"Just Beeks, Shyla," he said, retrieving his phone from his pocket. "And Fish is right, you'll want to rustle up something for your boss…" He lifted his eyes over his phone to give her a pointed look. "Something that says he was right to take a chance on you, given that you're not making the best impression so far."

"Hey, I gotta ask," Fish said. "How come Shyla gets a day off tomorrow and I ain't had one yet?"

Beeks dropped a hand to the counter. "A day off? What day off?"

By the way the lawyer had just looked at her, Shyla assumed he knew what transpired last night. "I thought I was fired," she said, getting no hint of understanding from him.

His judgement could have something to do with the lack of lunch rather than her drunken idiocy. Going to the fridge, she checked what was inside and then explored the cabinets.

"Boss said not to mention last night," Fish said. "So I figure we're not mentioning it."

"I can make French toast," she said and began to pull out the ingredients.

If Score wanted to fire her when he woke up, food wouldn't stop him. In the meantime, cooking kept her busy with something other than obsessing.

"Last night?" Beeks said as she began to crack eggs. "What happened last night?"

"Nothing," came a gruff voice from the end of the hallway.

Everyone turned. Score stood there, his hair damp, his tee-shirt clean, and his gaze narrowed on her. Shyla shivered. Just being snared under his scrutiny changed the way she breathed. It wasn't easy to remember her name or what day of the week it was when he was treating her like the only person on the planet.

Score wasn't an easy man to read. Shyla couldn't tell if he was angry or annoyed or if the intensity of his laser-precise focus was trying to tell her something else. Sliding the bowl further onto the counter, she spun away from the stove at the center island and busied herself with washing her hands.

Except that didn't save her from being inspected by the men in the room. The sink was central in an inset section of the units. The splash back and wall around it were mirrored, which was great for giving the illusion of space, but not so great for a woman who needed time to compose herself.

After washing her hands, she grabbed a clean towel from the drawer to dry them. No one had said anything. Score was still fixated on her, standing there by the wall that separated kitchen from hallway.

She wasn't sure what Fish and Beeks thought of his examination, but she sure felt the weight of it.

Curling her lips into her mouth, it was time to face the inevitable. "Could I talk to you a minute? Please, sir?" Shyla asked, doing her best not to sound desperate.

Sir had seemed appropriate given that he was her boss. It just came out and no one corrected her. She was grateful they hadn't, another misstep might have ended her. Although Shyla had never considered herself an elegant soul, she couldn't remember ever being quite so inept.

Score nodded once, but didn't move, meaning it was left to her to lead the way. Leaving the kitchen, she gave Score a wide berth, going around him to head down the hallway. At either side of the end of the hall were their bedrooms. Shyla didn't want to take the liberty of walking into his or remind him of the previous night by going into hers, so she slipped into the laundry room instead.

Almost immediately she realized her mistake. Shyla leaned over the washer to pause the cycle and spun around only to be reminded of just how big Score was compared to her. He'd just shut the door, trapping them in there, in the confined claustrophobic space.

There was no reason to catalog that his arms were solid and his jaw strong and square. She shouldn't have noticed the scent of his soap and his deodorant or the way they mingled to create the most alluring aroma.

Shyla had been aroused before, but never in that way. The potency of her visceral reaction was brand new. The tightness of her chest grew, so it became harder to breathe. The tingling between her thighs was unnerving too.

Everything about him caused sensory overload and they weren't even doing anything. There wasn't even the suggestion that they would. They were just two people standing in the same space. That was all. Yet, Shyla could feel the intimate core of her body responding to him like it had an expectation of his attention.

"That it?" he asked.

Realizing that she'd just been standing there, saying nothing, kind of staring toward his abs, Shyla's anxiety picked that moment to remind her that she'd bitten him.

"I'm sorry," she said, the words rushing out.

Locking her fingers in front of her abdomen, she pushed her digits as deep together as they'd go. When she was nervous or stressed, she didn't know what to do with her hands. They always just tangled and tensed of their own accord.

"For what?"

Was he asking if she remembered what she'd done or to which part specifically she was referring? From what she picked up in the brief glances she stole up at him, there was little expression on his face. If anything, he appeared bored. Looking him in the eye was just impossible while she was so mortified.

"For everything. For all of it."

"I said nothing happened," he said. "Nothing happened."

The terrifying thing was she had no idea what had actually happened, so she had no idea what he was giving her a pass for. If only half of what Fish relayed was true, then Score should be kicking her out on her ass. Shyla dreaded to imagine what a fool she'd made of herself after Fish left.

Just then she caught sight of an angry red mark on Score's neck. From the side around to his throat, it looked just like a scratch. Horrified, she gaped at her fingernails, which were long enough to have injured him.

"Oh my God," she gasped, stepping forward to reach up. "Was that me?"

Before she could make contact, he twisted himself out of her reach. His scowl grew deeper. Of course it did! She chastised herself for ever thinking of taking the liberty of touching him, especially after hurting him. Shyla locked her fingers together again and tried to steady her breathing. Hyperventilating wouldn't improve his impression of her.

He wasn't making this easy, but he had no reason to.

"If you want me to leave, I'll leave," she murmured, her heart thumping against her ribs. It was so fast and so loud, she feared that maybe he could hear it. "I won't make trouble… I won't embarrass you anymore… I'll understand."

"You wanna leave?"

"No!" she said, losing her battle with desperation. "No, I don't. I want to stay. I want to make it up to you. I want to show you that I'm not the fool I made of myself last night. I'm a serious person. A quiet person. I would never… I have never… I…"

Dragging in a ragged breath, Shyla closed her eyes and tried to erase the horrible possibilities that were filling up her mind. She pictured herself doing what Fish had said. Maybe she had tried to kiss her boss. Maybe she had touched him inappropriately.

If he'd changed her clothes and put her in bed, they must have been in the bedroom together. It was possible that she'd propositioned him. Maybe he hadn't been the one to take off her dress at all. Shyla had no idea that she could be a floozy. She'd never been loose before.

Apologizing for biting him and for rubbing her body on his seemed the least she could do. Except the words wouldn't come. Just thinking of them conjured more images of what she might have done or said to him. She couldn't handle the heat of shame. Biting him! That meant her mouth had been on him somewhere. She couldn't even remember touching him with her hands and yet, her mouth had…

Pressing her palms to her cheeks, Shyla hoped her color hadn't risen too high. Though there was no way to disguise her disgrace whether she was blushing or not.

"Shyla," he said her name in a monotone. "Look at me." Compelled by instinct to comply, her chin rose until her eyes met his. "Nothing happened."

The weight of those words made her swallow hard. Although there didn't seem to be a change in the way he looked at her, she got a better understanding of that gaze. Something had done it, she didn't know what, but somehow the translation had been slipped to her. It was nothing to do with her getting drunk or puking, she couldn't pinpoint what it was. Yet, in an odd shiver, she felt him. Even without touching, he got inside her.

Score said nothing else and turned to exit. Shyla stood there trying to figure out what had just happened. The previous night alcohol was an excuse for her actions, but she didn't have that excuse anymore. Lightheaded, she felt tingly and sick in an excited way, like she was anticipating a treat or a holiday.

Something odd was going on in the apartment. She didn't know what it was or how she fitted into it. Until she figured it out, her job would keep her occupied, and unless she was told otherwise, she'd try her damndest to do it well.

***

BY THE NEXT AFTERNOON, Shyla was only just beginning to breathe normally again.

"What's it supposed to be?" Fish asked from his place on the stool at the end of the kitchen island.

Shyla scored her dough. "What do you mean what's it supposed to be?" she asked, slipping the two trays into the oven. "It's bread. You've never seen bread before?"

Sitting up from his slouch, he glittered with excitement. "No way! Bread? You're making bread?"

After wiping down the counters, Shyla went to wash her hands. Catching the eye of his reflection in the mirror wall, she nodded just as another figure moved into her view.

"Good morning," she said to Score who went to sit at the kitchen island.

It was nearly two in the afternoon, but she figured it would be rude to point that out. The previous night, Score hadn't come home until after she was in bed. His routine was unusual, work at the club kept him out late. Beeks told her Score would return home late most nights. In her slumber, Shyla hadn't even heard him come in, so she had no idea when he'd got to sleep.

"Hey, boss, guess what?" Fish asked. Bouncing on his stool, he leaned over to swat at Score's chest. Their boss blinked unimpressed eyes down at the spot Fish assaulted, but the youngster was too excited to notice his boss's disdain. "Guess what? Shyla made bread! She's actually making bread? You ever hear that shit?"

"I hear you swearing in front of a lady," Score mumbled, taking his phone from his pocket.

Shyla laughed. "That's okay. Stan swore like a trooper when he had a drink in him… I've never seen someone so excited about bread before."

"I never knew a person who could actually make it," Fish said.

Shyla poured coffee and juice and took both to the island for Score. He looked from one to the other and picked up the coffee. Ah, a man after her own heart.

Before she thought too much about how mortifying it would be to say that aloud, Shyla retrieved eggs from the fridge. "I was thinking eggs benny or a Denver omelet?"

Score didn't even look up. But she'd been told he was always hungry so decided to go with the omelet and left the eggs out while she gathered the other ingredients.

"Is Stan the guy who died?" Fish asked.

They'd talked some about him at dinner before the club, she had a vague recollection of that. "Yes," she said, retrieving a chopping board and a knife.

"Did you tell Score about the asshole at your old place?" Fish asked.

Score lowered his phone.

Shyla hadn't actually looked at him and his head hadn't moved, yet somehow, she could tell she was the target of his focus. Ridiculous as it sounded even in her own head, she could feel him looking at her. That wasn't the first time either. Even when he didn't talk to her, she could feel his attention whenever he gave it. It made her squirm and pant at the same time, neither of which was easy to conceal.

"I don't think he cares about—"

"Beeks said we should always tell him or Score about assholes," Fish said, dropping forward to rest on his forearms, mimicking Score's position. The young man idolized his boss, it was easy, and sort of sweet, to see. "Asshole wanted to search Shyla, you believe it? Thought she was stealing or some shit. You ever see a person look less like a thief than Shyla?"

"No, I haven't," Score muttered like he was considering something.

Grateful to have a task to concentrate on, Shyla ignored the words he aimed her way. Without daring to peek, somehow she was aware of Score's every nuance. She wished she'd worn a thicker dress; her nipples were starting to peak and there wasn't a draft to blame.

"My brother is in jail for burglary," she said, compelled to fill the silence.

"You think stealing's in your genes or something?" Fish asked and turned to address Score's profile. "That the way it works, boss? Your whole family's in it."

Score hadn't taken his attention from her. "No, that's not how it works," he said. "What kind of search?"

"Her bags and shit," Fish said and snorted as he shrugged. "Though I'd bet if I hadn't showed up when I did he'd have gone for the strip search too. He looked the type. You know the type, boss. We see 'em all the time."

"Yeah, we do," Score said. "Were you gonna tell me, Shy?"

Shaking her head, she finished beating and put on her stove. "Fish was incredible, forceful but polite, Mick got the message."

"Mick?"

"Stan's son. He'll inherit the house. He didn't want me to take anything that wasn't mine."

"You lived there a long time."

"Almost nine years," she said. "But I don't need things… The only thing I regret leaving is the clock in my bedroom. Stan gave it to me for my sixteenth birthday, so I guess he purchased it. That means it's not mine, right?"

"A gift's a gift. That's yours, you should've brung it," Fish said and grinned. "Oh, hey, you mean that cat one with the eyes and the tail. Yeah. Yeah. I saw that. That was cool… I've seen 'em in movies."

"Anyone puts pressure on you, the first thing you do is dial me," Score said, diverting her interest from the exuberant Fish.

The minute her eyes met his, her lungs began to shrink. She'd have to learn how to avoid being ensnared by his intensity.

"Yeah, all our numbers are in that phone Beeks said he gave you," Fish said. "You call anytime you need us. She's one of us now, boss, right? Beeks says we gotta watch each other's asses close."

"She's one of us," Score said.

Shyla still couldn't regulate her breathing. She had to open her mouth to get more air. "Thank you," she murmured. "But I don't get in a lot of trouble."

Fish laughed. "That might change now you run with us, you know? You're gonna have people want to talk to you about the boss. People want to know about the club. All sorts of folks in the city and all of 'em want something."

"I'm discreet," she said, struck by a need to reassure Score.

"Can't share what you don't know, Lamb," Score said, returning his focus to his phone.

"Lamb?" Fish asked. "Oh, hey, I get it. Bellamy, right? That's cool."

Fish thought a lot of things were cool. Although he talked a little funny sometimes, Shyla really liked him. But Score was the one she kept stealing glances at while she cooked. Declaring her as one of them meant more to Shyla than Score could know. They'd only known each other a few days. Beeks was still wary of her. In a way, she was grateful for that because it proved how much he cared about Score and Fish.

Living there was easy, Score made it easy. Shyla didn't have a clue why he'd taken so many chances on her, but she was grateful he'd taken the risk, and wasn't going to let him down.

FIVE

LEARNING SCORE'S HABITS took up the majority of Shyla's time over the next two weeks. Until beginning her new job, she hadn't realized the value of routine. Knowing his schedule gave her the chance to set her own. Once she had that, the apartment began to feel like home.

Being around Score didn't feel like home yet, it probably never would. Her senses just couldn't process being in proximity to a man like him.

Concentrating on her work instead of her crazy attraction to her boss, Shyla mastered what was expected of her. So far it was guess work as to whether or not her work was adequate. No explicit praise had come her way, but no one had reprimanded her either. Though the latter was likely related to her sobriety. Since her screw up on the first day, she hadn't dared go to a nightclub or touch alcohol. From that low, she supposed her employers estimations could only go up.

Score liked to sleep until around two in the afternoon. He'd get up, eat, drink coffee, and work on his computer or go out until around eight p.m. The evening meal was required to be on the table by then. He'd eat, usually with Beeks and Fish, then the three men would go to Score's club, which, funnily enough, was called 'Score.'

His peculiar schedule made sense for someone who owned a nightclub. Most nights he'd be out until three or four a.m. In case he wanted a snack, Shyla would make something and leave it in the fridge, though he only sometimes ate it.

Score didn't expect her to be awake when he returned from the club. Sometimes she'd hear him moving around and got the impression he enjoyed having the time to himself; he was never in a hurry to get to bed.

Usually he'd listen to music while doing things with paper and the computer. Often it would be six or seven by the time he went to bed. She didn't like to think that she was obsessed or nosy, but she could listen to him for hours. Just knowing they were alone in the apartment agitated her. On the nights that she did fall asleep, her senses would wake her of their own volition in time to hear him going to bed around five or six.

At eight, she got up to run her errands. To minimize the chance of bothering Score or interrupting his sleep, Shyla was as quiet as possible in the condo while he slept. Most days she stayed out until closer to his breakfast time. She never went far and kept her phone on loud, in case he woke and needed something.

Their building was great. Every day she would swim or use the gym. If she was done early, the pool lounge was a great place to work or chill while she gave Score privacy and peace to sleep.

That night, Shyla was on the terrace leafing through magazines. Even though the time approached midnight, she wasn't tired enough to sleep yet. Looking at the glossy pictures, she assessed different hairstyles, trying to figure out if she might suit any of them.

A noise in the supposed-to-be-empty apartment made her turn. Score was over at the closet by the elevators. He hung up his jacket then crossed to drop onto the couch that backed onto the dining table.

Typical that he should come back early on the night she'd made a mess. Earlier, Shyla had spent time leafing through recipes she'd printed out. The papers were still spread out on the floor and on the glass table by the chess board.

Leaping up, she ran into the living room to begin tidying. They didn't address each other, but that was normal. Score was a man of few words, so it was actually a positive not to hear his voice. Fish once told her that if someone forced Score to speak, he wouldn't say anything they'd want to hear.

Living with her formidable boss was a life experience in itself. She'd never lived with a man like him, never before felt how she did when he was around. The way she became hyperaware of her femininity when he was in the room perplexed her. Shyla felt all kinds of new things around him, things she hadn't felt in the past.

Score was conscious of what he did to her. Somehow, even without the words being said, Shyla knew it. He didn't acknowledge it or humiliate her by putting her on the spot, but something had given her away. Trouble was, she couldn't stop doing it because she didn't know what it was. Maybe it was the way she often stuttered or forgot her words. Maybe it was the way she stole glances at him when she thought she could get away with it.

Energy buzzed between them and it was messing with her ability to function. It wasn't going anywhere either, it only seemed to be getting stronger the longer they existed in the same life.

Sitting on the couch, with his arms stretched along the back, Score didn't say a word. Shyla could feel him watching her as she gathered up the papers and piled them on the edge of the table with the magazines.

All that illuminated them was the yellow light from the lanterns outside mixed with the muted recessed lighting in the kitchen. It felt intimate… almost romantic. Just thinking the word made her self-conscious. She cursed herself for not putting on more lights when she'd come in from the terrace.

The room was suddenly hot… humid… her skin ticked and itched. It didn't help that her heart was pumping faster than she could count the beats. In its haste to keep the blood flowing, the organ demanded too much space in her chest. Her lungs couldn't expand enough to allow her a full breath. She couldn't breathe this close to him, yet she'd never felt so alive.

His intensity had been one of the first things she noticed about him. Even when he wasn't saying a word, he was aware of everything.

They were complete opposites. To her, he was a puzzle, one she wanted to solve. That could explain why he occupied so many of her thoughts. Figuring him out would take a lifetime; even then she wasn't sure she'd succeed.

Nothing in their backgrounds matched. Shyla grew up with safety and security. She'd been sheltered and cared for. Her upbringing spared her hazards that would've been part of Score's daily life. She wouldn't deny being naïve, but never having to apologize for who she was gave her a strong sense of self.

In contrast, danger and darkness had been a part of Score's life since birth. Beeks filled in some blanks for her, Fish too. Both cautioned her that Score wasn't vocal about his history.

Being born into a family who thrived in the organized crime world, Score must have seen every depravity society had to offer. Drugs and prostitution would've been part of his day to day life. His babysitters were probably hookers and drug dealers.

For McDades, fighting was a hobby, bleeding was the norm. Deception and duplicity lurked around every corner. Score learned the hard way that even trusting his family was a mistake. He'd also learned to be quiet, to monitor, to watch and listen, and never offer any hint of weakness.

Shyla's experience taught her not to hide her emotions or be afraid of her vulnerabilities. In Score's world, emotions and vulnerabilities could get him killed.

"Do you need anything?" she asked, fearing if she didn't break the oppressive silence that she might stop breathing altogether.

Through narrow eyes, he assessed her, giving nothing of himself away, showing no expression. "Come help me with my boots."

Leaving the magazines and recipes in a neat pile, she crawled over to kneel at his feet. As she unlaced each of his boots, he didn't move. After taking his boots from his feet, she intended to get up to put them away in the closet.

Before she rose, he spoke. "Loosen my belt."

Shyla let herself breathe in before rising a little higher on her knees to do as he asked. She was used to taking care of old men who couldn't do things for themselves. Something like a belt or buttons could be difficult for arthritic fingers to take care of.

Score wasn't old and his fingers were deft. Still, she did as told. "Would you like me to undo your button?" she asked, blinking up at him through her bangs.

He nodded once, so she unsnapped the top button on his jeans. "Bring me a scotch."

"Yes, sir," she said and picked up his boots as she stood.

Taking them to the closet by the elevator door, Shyla put them away, then turned around to head back the way she'd come. The bar was her goal, but she didn't get that far.

As she passed the couch, Score spoke again, using the pet name she'd heard from his lips many times. "Lamb."

Shyla stopped to face him, assuming he had another request. If it meant going to the kitchen or the bedroom, she'd have to turn back. "Yes, sir?"

His position was the same, his expression as aloof as when she'd been kneeling in front of him. The only thing different was the angle of his head, which she guessed gave him a better view given how his gaze was sliding over her.

"Take off your dress."

Her throat twitched and began to tingle. She'd never known a man to be so direct and didn't know what to do. Didn't know what to say. Having never been in official employment, she didn't know what was normal, what was expected. Shyla doubted that a boss could ask an employee to strip. But it was late, they were alone, maybe this was less of a professional order and more of a personal request.

Denying that she was attracted to him would be crazy. Despite never admitting it out loud, her desire wasn't in doubt. She'd never been able to breathe right when he was in the room and struggled to look him in the eye without blushing.

It terrified her to think he might see straight through her into the insane and wild fantasies she cast him in. Until meeting Score, Shyla hadn't known she was capable of having such vivid carnal dreams.

She struggled to claim each shallow breath. "I… I don't think I should," she said, sensitive to the pace of her chest rising and falling.

Her own panting filled her ears. Sealing her lips in an attempt to stifle the sound forced the air through the narrower passages of her nose, amplifying the noise.

"I'm not suggesting we fuck… Just take off the dress."

Parting her lips took some time, if she relaxed too much there was a good chance a whimper could escape. Being so overwhelmed while ten feet of space separated them was crazy.

She was near a phone and had a clear route to the door. If she wanted to run screaming, she could.

No part of her, not one single cell, wanted to escape. Without realizing it, Score was feeding her a new fantasy, one more alluring than the rest because… it was real.

"I… I need this job, Mr. McDade."

"Shy, look at me." Until he requested she look up, Shyla hadn't even noticed her gaze was fixed on the floor. Peeking up, she found he was intent on her. "You are never in danger when I'm around. Do you understand?" She nodded. "Tell me you understand."

"I understand."

When he rose from the couch, she held her breath for a good half minute. With every step he took in her direction, she grew tenser. Shyla didn't know what he was going to do, or what she'd do if he did it.

Their height difference was ridiculous. Her body was a splinter compared to the muscle he carried on his. Being all alone in this private space, he could do anything he wanted to her and no one would ever know it.

But Shyla wasn't afraid when he came to a stop in front of her. Even when he slipped a broad finger under her chin and she began to tremble, it wasn't in fear. Squeezing her eyes closed as he urged her chin higher, she predicted spontaneously combusting if their eyes were to meet while they were in such close proximity.

"I choose my women carefully these days, Miss Bellamy," he murmured, the bass of his voice shaking her bones. "And I protect who I choose with my life because they're precious. You're precious." She stopped breathing again. "Open your eyes, Lamb." Her eyes popped open. When they fixed on his, her lips parted in a short gasp that was almost a squeak. "Could be you're the most precious."

The need in her belly warmed and weakened her simultaneously. The intoxicating sensations had a shocking effect on her words. "Are you saying I'm… your woman?" she whispered.

"Taking off that dress will be our first step toward finding out."

Oh, that was almost a promise, and one that tore at her. Shyla wasn't adventurous and had little experience with men. Trying to figure out how she might handle one like Score confuddled her.

If he was disappointed, she could lose her job, and that would put her back where she started. "You're my boss."

Closing his eyes in a slow blink, his head moved a fraction to the side and then back in a sort of semi shake before opening his eyes. "Not me. Beeks pays you."

So Score wasn't her boss? That was something.

Her strong attraction to him was screaming at her to capitulate, but another voice in her head said she'd be too timid for him. "I… I don't know."

Score was so cool, she wondered if he cared either way. "We take this up a notch or leave it alone for good…" He was giving her the choice. Shyla had to decide. "I see the way you look at me… I know what you want, Shy."

Mortified, she considered just falling down dead right there at his feet. Nothing explicit had ever been said about what they might feel or want. Score was telling her the moment for advance or retreat was upon them. Either she opened herself to him or shut down the possibility forever.

"You… you do?" she asked.

"Anything you do for me that crosses the line from business to personal, you do because you want to, not because you're being paid."

"And if I refuse?"

"You refuse," he said, sliding his finger away from the underside of her chin to brush the back of his index finger down her jaw on its descent to his side. "I take my time, Miss Bellamy. I won't rush you or pressure you. But I am bold. If I want something, even if it's something that might shock you, I won't be subtle or discreet about asking for it."

That much was obvious given his opening gambit was asking her to take off her dress. First date stripping wasn't something she'd ever experienced. Though this wasn't their first meeting, it was the first time they'd addressed this. Whatever "this" was.

A positive thing about his candor was it forced her to gather the courage to respond in kind. It took her time. The adrenaline circling her heart was so potent that she could taste it in the back of her throat.

Shyla had to be bold if she wanted an answer. "Are you attracted to me?"

"Yes."

Why use ten words when one would do? Shyla had a feeling Score wasn't the type of man to wax lyrical. Writing, or even reading, romantic sonnets probably wasn't his style. But that was no surprise and wasn't what she expected from him.

The raw animalistic air that hovered around him gave the impression he could snap at any second. He intrigued her. It felt like he was always on, whether it be for sex or a showdown, Score was ready.

After caressing her jaw, his finger had dropped to his side and he hadn't touched her since. Without his direction, her chin descended until she found herself staring at his tee-shirt.

"I don't have a lot of experience with men," she confessed. Her hands slipped around her back to cling at each other. "I might make mistakes."

When his body moved away, she assumed he was

retreating. It wasn't until his breath warmed the top of her ear that she realized he'd bent down to whisper to her.

"Everybody makes mistakes."

He eased back and she let her attention rise. They locked eyes and Shyla knew that trusting him wouldn't be one of them.

SIX

SWALLOWING HER SELF-CONSCIOUS anxiety, Shyla gathered every thread of confidence within her. Score was a strong, enigmatic man. He might like her innocence, but he'd also appreciate her rising to a challenge. That's what this was, a challenge.

Behind her, beneath the built-in faux fireplace, a shelf ran from the elevators all the way to the powder room by the third bedroom. That shelf, just behind her knees, prevented her from retreating as she fumbled for the zipper beneath her arm.

Not that Shyla wanted to run away. No, she just thought that distance might calm her rattling nerves. She kept on believing that right up until the moment Score stepped back.

Further away might make her less aware of his intoxicating masculine scent, but it broadened his view. It allowed him to take in more of her at once. Her nerves quaked; Shyla had no idea what kind of picture she made. Trepidation affected her speed. She tried to stretch out the moment. To gather her wits. To prepare herself. Unfortunately, there was only so much zipper on her dress and eventually, it reached its base.

This was it. She'd gone this far. Score's neutral expression was fixed on her body, not her face. His expectation weight heavy. Pulling down the zipper implied she was going to comply.

He'd said when something crossed the line from business to personal, she should only do it if she wanted to. Terrified of being exposed, Shyla reminded herself that wearing a bikini on the beach was normal. On days out with Bernard and Stan, even on the pool level downstairs, she wore a bikini and didn't think twice about it.

But this was different. Intimate. Shyla closed her eyes and held her breath while easing the dress straps from her shoulders. Scooping the material down her body and over her hips, she let it drop to the floor.

Shyla wasn't sure what to do next. Had he seen enough? Should she pick her dress up? Scurry away? She hadn't thought beyond the achievement of actually taking off the dress.

Score took care of that. "Turn around."

With her eyes still closed, she managed to take tiny steps and move in a circle, coming to a stop when she faced away from him. For some reason, having him behind her was easier on her breathing. At least, it was at first. The longer the silence stretched, the more her pulse began to creep up again.

"Score?" she whispered.

"Let your hair down."

If she let her hair down, it would take time to tame it back into a curled chignon. Didn't matter though, it wasn't like she was known for having the tidiest hair even when she tried her best.

After pulling the pins from the knot, she bent to put them on the shelf beneath the fireplace. Shaking her hair loose and combing her fingers through it, she worked out some of the tangles. It fell around her elbows, down her back and over her breasts.

Something snagged the back and it took a second to realize Score was touching her. At first, she figured an errant pin was the culprit. But the gentle pressure left and rose again, like just one of his fingers was testing the depth of her locks near her spine.

The moment she realized it was there, it disappeared.

"Wear it like this at night. Once your chores are done and your work day is over, let your hair loose."

She appreciated that his request didn't include daylight hours. When running errands out in the sun or in the heat of the kitchen, it could get in the way or overheat her.

Shame she had to point out a problem. "My workday is never done. I'm on call for you twenty-four seven."

Beeks had told her that on the day of her interview.

"We're going to teach you about what you shouldn't say to men, 'specially when you're standing in front of them in your underwear," he said. "Go pour two glasses of scotch."

The task distracted her from her apparel, or lack of it, and gave her a chance to consider what he'd meant. Avoiding looking his way, Shyla went to the bar on the other side of the opening to the second hallway and poured the two drinks.

All she'd done was state fact. It wasn't easy to know which were work hours. From the start of her day, she worked for Score, but he wasn't awake until the afternoon. Shyla was always there to prepare his first meal of the day, and to help him with whatever he needed in the afternoon before making his evening meal.

This was the first night he'd come home early. Although she was curious about why he'd returned, it didn't feel like the right moment to ask. It wasn't really her business anyway. His professional life was nothing to do with her.

By returning, he proved that she wasn't off the hook even in the dead of night. If he came back late and needed something, she'd be working again.

Except, this wasn't work. Wasn't that what he was trying to communicate?

Picking up both glasses, she went toward the living room where he was seated on the same couch as before. Instead of sitting back like earlier, he was propped on the edge, leaning over the glass coffee table that he'd pulled closer. She noted that her dress was no longer on the floor and had no idea where it was. Again, Shyla thought it best not to ask; that would mean drawing attention to the fact she wasn't wearing it.

On her approach, Score took care of reminding her. He looked up and the first thing he did was fixate on her body.

She held both glasses toward him. He didn't take either of them and just kept on scrutinizing her figure. "You're all natural."

"Yes," she said, touching her Achilles tendon with the front of her opposite big toe. Self-consciousness was beginning to creep back in. As much as she tried not to squirm, with him sitting and her standing, she felt even more exposed. The corner of the coffee table was between them, but still, he sat there just looking at her. "I've never even considered cosmetic surgery."

"Don't," he said, taking one of the glasses from her. "Can you play chess?"

The board on the table had been one of the first things she'd noticed in that particular space.

Shyla hadn't considered playing. "Yes," she said. "My grandfather taught me."

"Good. Sit."

He nodded at the opposite side of the table and shifted to get more comfortable. Only then did he drink from the glass she'd handed him.

"I…" Shyla was confused. "I thought we were going to have sex."

His head tilted and his glass dropped an inch. "You're impatient," he murmured like the characteristic intrigued him. "Good. That will make this more fun."

Going around the coffee table, she sank onto the floor, folding her legs beneath her. "What's *this*?"

"The wait," he said. "Drink your drink."

Wondering how long the wait would be, she squinted at the glass in her hand. "I don't do well with hard liquor."

Something he should probably know from what had happened on her first night. After their conversation in the laundry room, no one mentioned her drunkenness again. Shyla wasn't even sure Beeks knew what happened. Score had given her another chance; she'd promised herself not to waste it.

"Pays to have a tolerance," he said. "You never know when you might need it."

Shyla wasn't really sure what that meant, but she screwed up her face and took a sip. The liquid stung her lip then burned on her tongue. Taking just a little spared her the embarrassment of coughing or choking on it.

"I never learned how to drink."

"You'll only do it when I'm around," he said. "Shy, look at me." She did. "Only when I'm around. Understand?"

"I understand," she said.

"Good girl."

All this time she'd thought they were ignoring what was between them. Score was a man of so few words and she hadn't wanted to push. It wasn't possible to push him anyway, Shyla wouldn't have known where to begin. Though his requests sounded like orders, she was grateful for him taking the lead and being direct with her.

She wanted to explore what he made her feel, but didn't really know how to do it without making a fool of herself. Shyla had been too self-conscious to even broach the subject knowing there was a high chance she'd read his intense stares wrong. It was sort of encouraging to learn that she hadn't.

"Did you learn about chess in prison?"

Score turned the board around, presenting the white side to her. She put her drink on one of the glass coasters in the corner of the coffee table.

"No," he replied. "My father made my brothers and me play when we were kids. Said it was civilized."

Shyla hadn't expected such an open and honest answer; he could've stopped after no. Unsure if she should or not, she let her eyes ascend. Her hair was in the way, but she could see he was looking back at her.

"I'm sorry," she said. "I… I didn't mean to assume…"

"Your questions are honest, Shy," he said. "I don't volunteer information. Most people are too afraid to ask anything straight out. Even when they do, there's an ulterior motive behind it…" His eyes narrowed again. Although he didn't move, she felt his attention probing her, trying to peer deeper into her. "I doubt you've ever had an ulterior motive for doing anything in your life."

Resting a forearm on the table, she boosted a little higher to share her secret. "I used to go across town to this deli that did these crullers Stan loved," she said, drawing out the last word. "He'd make such a big deal of being grateful I made the trip." She grinned and lowered her volume further. "Truth is, they did this coconut iced mocha that was just…" Rising just to sag, she breathed out her bliss. "Oh, it was to die for."

"Wow," he said. For a second, she was sure sharing that made her sound like an idiot. That was until, to her shock and delight, one side of his mouth rose a fraction. "I take it back, you're a real hustler, Lamb."

Just seeing him attempt a smile was enough to make her grin. Laughing at herself helped relax the mood… for a few seconds anyway. The air began to crackle again when their eyes met. The light was so soft and her clothing so sparse…

Tucking her hair behind her ears, she cleared her throat, then shifted onto her knees and laid her hands flat on the table. "Okay, who goes white?"

He'd turned the board toward her, but it didn't seem right that she should get the first move for nothing.

"You go first, Shy," he said. She intended to object, but he spoke again. "You'll always go first, baby… In everything we do."

A zap of electricity shot down her spine. If she wasn't already sensitive to the evening air on the silk covering her crotch, he'd just ignited her awareness. Her thighs began to tingle; she squeezed them tighter together.

Taking her time over her next inhale, Shyla tried to calm herself. "I love how you can do that," she whispered, corkscrewing the end of her index finger into the point at the corner of the coffee table. "How you can touch me without touching me."

"Easy, baby," he soothed. "I said slow, didn't I?"

Shyla didn't know anything about the proper pace of seduction; she didn't know what was fast and what was slow.

"Sorry," she mumbled.

"Make your move." That seemed like a mixed signal. A spear of fright went through her. What the hell kind of move did she know that might impress him? When her gaze leaped to his, he must have read her terror because he nodded at the board. "Chess."

SEVEN

RIGHT. THE GAME. They were playing chess.

Leaning over her forearms, Shyla moved her pawn. They each took a few turns without saying a word. Playing in silence felt like a missed opportunity. Since beginning her work, she hadn't had many chances to get to know Score in his own words.

Still on the edge of the couch, his elbows were on his knees, his fist propped under his chin. It was a pose of concentration, though she didn't think they would really be competing for the win.

"There's something I've been trying to build up the courage to say for two weeks," she said as he assessed the board and then made his move. "If you'll let me?" He didn't take his eyes from the board, but nodded once. Bracing herself, she cringed so much that one eye closed. "I'm sorry that I bit you... and for being a lush, if I was a lush." His attention rose. "I... I've never done that before, any of it actually, going to a club, drinking cocktails... biting men... I'm really very sorry."

One of his fingers curled up over his mouth. "I told you nothing happened."

Forgetting the game, she rose higher, pressing her

hands to the table to push up and get more height on her knees. "But something *did* happen…" Shyla heard herself pleading. "And I haven't been able to stop wondering about it… I thought I didn't want to know. I thought it was better not to, but the not knowing is worse. Please… Please tell me what happened that night. Please, Phoenix."

His head jerked up at the sound of his name on her lips. For the first time, she read surprise on his face. Could be that she'd crossed a line… again. She sucked on her lower lip, praying he'd oblige her and not get mad.

After considering her for a moment, his brow relaxed into its usual hood over his eyes. "You're right, something did happen." Sucking harder, she waited; anxiety pounding in her belly, her palms sweating. "I made my decision to have you that night."

Having not expected something profound or romantic, Shyla was taken aback. Her elbows bent, so she sank back to sit on her feet. "You… you did? Because I bit you?"

"Because no one has ever let themselves be that vulnerable around me. You weren't afraid. You needed me. You let me give you what you needed without any fear. You didn't fight me or question me or accuse me. You trusted me."

In her defense, she'd been drunk and unable to fight anyone. Still, in her current position and state of undress, someone else might be afraid or dubious, Shyla was neither. Again, she'd opened herself up to being vulnerable.

"If you knew you wanted me two weeks ago, why didn't you act on it then?"

Nodding at the board, he encouraged her to take her move. "You needed time to settle in. To get over the death of your friend and find your feet… And it's not my nature to take anything at face value."

"You thought I might be conning you?" she asked on a laugh. "If I knew how to do that, I might have done more than bite you."

Horrified, she slapped a hand over her mouth. Her attention flew to the liquor. She'd only had a sip, yet the words had tumbled out like her inhibitions didn't exist.

"Shyla—"

"I'm sorry," she said, her hand only just leaving her lips. "I'm so sorry. I've always had a habit of speaking before I think, but to say something brazen like that and you told me to be patient. I—"

"Shyla," he said, obviously trying to calm her. "Stop apologizing. You don't have to apologize to me, not for anything."

So far, he'd proved that through his actions. At interview when she babbled about her lack of experience, he'd given her a chance. After getting drunk and screwing up, he'd given her a pass. Even when she made mistakes, he didn't expect her to grovel.

"Did Siobhan ever apologize or Parker?"

A deeper frown set on his face. His concentration fell to the game. "We're not getting into that tonight."

It was a major topic, and a personal one; too much to broach this early in their path. He'd never mentioned anyone from his past around her. But he wouldn't be surprised that his history wasn't a secret. Even though most of her knowledge hadn't come from the media, he probably assumed that she'd done some research. The details were all out there, that's what Fish had said.

"Sorry," she murmured.

His eyes jumped to the top of their sockets, surprising her. "No is an acceptable answer, for either of us. It doesn't have to be followed by an apology. This will only go as far as we want it to."

Agreeing with a nod, Shyla was pleased that he wasn't mad at her for asking.

Getting away with that question prompted her to ask another. "What exactly is… this?" she asked, wondering how far he wanted them to go.

Straightening up, he took a breath. "I won't know until I know how far you want to take it."

With certainty, she confessed in a rush. "I want to have sex with you."

As soon as the words were out, she wanted to snatch them back, but settled for rolling her eyes and cringing at her own idiocy.

"Good," he said. "But I wasn't talking about sex."

Again he left her confused. "I… I don't understand."

"If I want sex, I can get it on any street corner or in any club… This should be something different, or, to be honest, it's not worth my time."

So she wasn't worth it for sex alone? Shyla could understand that. She wasn't the hottest woman in the city and didn't have any special moves.

"What will make it worth your time?"

"I want you to share everything with me, Shyla. Everything."

Nodding, she was compliant. "I can do that."

"No," he said, slowly shaking his head. "You don't get it. There's a reason I'm taking this so slow. It might frustrate you. Might frustrate me too. But I have to know you'll give me all of yourself before I'll let this complicate our lives… What I want us to build is a trust deeper than either of us have had before, deeper than people have after a lifetime together. If it doesn't happen, we're both better off leaving it alone."

After what Siobhan had done to him, it was no surprise that he wanted to be sure about a woman's character before jumping into bed with her.

More than that, from her point of view, it was an incredible opportunity. A powerful, enigmatic man who enflamed her hormones was offering her the chance to get closer to him than anyone else had ever been.

"I'd like that."

Peering closer, he seemed to be trying to read her mind. "Do you understand what that will involve?"

"I think so," she said and then smiled. "I trust you to guide me… Like I said, I don't have much experience with men; I need you to lead."

He considered her for another moment, giving few hints about his thoughts in the way he scrutinized her. "Good," he said and took his turn. "I'll just listen while you tell me everything you can about your life, from the very beginning."

Shyla took a deep breath. "That's not a lot," she said.

"My brother and I were raised by my grandfather after my parents died. When I was sixteen, Bernard, that's my grandfather, he fell and broke his hip. I had to do everything for him while he recuperated. It was one health issue after another until I was about twenty. That's when Stan had a stroke. We couldn't afford the house we were renting, so Bernard and I moved in with Stan and I cared for them both. My grandfather died three years ago, Stan three weeks ago.

"As for my brother, Wyatt, he got in with the wrong crowd. Went to prison for the first time when he was nineteen, just before my grandfather broke his hip. He'd already moved out by then. Really, that's it, my whole life."

They made another couple of moves before he stopped to relax against the couch, laying his arms along the back. "I didn't think you understood what I meant by everything. Now I know you don't."

"I do… I think," she said, running a finger along the edge of the board. "Why don't you give me an example?"

He raised his chin a fraction. "When did you have your first orgasm? When did you start menstruating? What event made you cry hardest? I want to know what you're afraid of, what you fantasize about. I want to know what you think about when you can't sleep. I want to know what makes you relax, what pisses you off, what cheers you up. Facts and dates are great, baby, but they're for small talk in the doctor's waiting room. You don't want me close enough to know the most intimate and private things about you… then I'm not interested."

Leaving the couch, he went to the bar to refill the glass she hadn't noticed was empty. Stunned, Shyla had difficulty processing. One thing she couldn't fail to process was his last sentence.

Leaping to her feet, she rushed over just as he put the scotch bottle down to replace the cap.

"You were there for the most embarrassing night of my life," she said, standing so close to his side that her breasts almost touched him when he began to gulp the liquor she could barely sip. "And the only thing I've fantasized about recently is you."

Gasping in a breath, she sealed her lips by sucking them into her mouth again. When he angled his head to look at her, there was such feral satisfaction in his eyes that blinking was the only response she could come up with.

"Now we're getting somewhere," he purred. "Start talking."

"I…" Pushing her linked fingers towards the floor, she feared her panic had led him to believe she was braver than she actually was. "I've never talked about… my fantasies with anyone."

Curling a finger under her chin, he urged her head back so she'd look at him. "I don't want to be just anyone, Shy." He didn't tell her that in anything close to a sweet or gentle tone. He was vehement, almost angry in his tone. "You want me to tell you how I've dreamt about bending you over every piece of furniture in this condo and sinking my cock into you? Would that make you feel better about sharing?" Putting down his glass, he kept his finger under her chin and started walking, forcing her backwards one slow step at a time. "Maybe you wanna hear about how I jerk off in the shower, just minutes before I come through to the kitchen and look into those emeralds of yours." Sucking her lip harder, Shyla didn't dare move her gaze; she was too mesmerized by the depth of his brown eyes drilling into her. She came up against the second hallway wall hard. When she stopped, he did too. Their bodies didn't touch, but his finger kept going, gliding down her neck to her throat and descending toward her cleavage, where it stopped just short. "You want me to tell you how I've dreamt about possessing this body? About owning you? About dominating you? How I decided that night you lay helpless and vulnerable before me that I was one day going to be the only man allowed even close to that fuckable body… You're transparent, pristine… uncorrupted in a world I was through with." The curiosity in his gaze drew her deeper. "Can I take what I want from you?"

"Yes," she said without even pausing for a heartbeat. "Yes, please."

Assuming he'd kiss her, she tried to reach for him, but he backed off, coming up against the opposite wall.

"Not sex, Shy. Sex is the easiest thing in the world. We could do it and be just like every other relationship either of us ever had. I want to know if you can be something else."

She couldn't be anything other than herself, but was more worried about what he'd said about her other relationships. Her previous relationships equaled exactly nil. It didn't feel like the time to dwell on that truth. Score had shared with her, so she felt it was right to reciprocate.

Though she tried to flatten her hands on the wall, they didn't stay put. In their need to fidget, they slid toward each other to tangle at her back, meaning her hips rose from the wall.

"I… I dream about what it would be like to lie with you," she whispered, unable to look at him. "About what it might be like to wake up next to you instead of in the next room."

"Not sex?"

A smile twisted her lips as her fingers coiled tighter around each other. She caught a glimpse up at him. "I've thought about that too."

Pushing off his wall, he loomed over her, planting a forearm high above her head to support his weight. With that anchor, his body didn't come into contact with hers. "Tell me."

"I've thought about kissing you," she said, twining and loosening her fingers, her body rocking in time with that toying. "About what it might be like to…"

"To what, Shy?"

"To be allowed to touch you," she confessed, even though the mortification made her dry lips crack. "Sometimes when you're eating, I think about how I'd like to let you taste from my fingers or how I'd like to…"

His voice grew softer though there was an unfamiliar rasp to it. "Don't stop, baby."

"Feed you," she mumbled, squeezing her fingers tight.

"Keep talking."

Something about just releasing the words into the air caused her skin to prickle. "I want to touch you under the table… Like that time you told me to sit and eat when Beeks and Fish were here. Your knee brushed mine under the table… I wanted… I thought for a minute you might have meant it."

"I did."

Her heart slammed against her ribs.

At dinner, Score always sat at the head of the table. On that particular night, he'd ordered her to sit perpendicular to him facing the windows. In their usual places too, Beeks had sat opposite with Fish beside him. Score hadn't acknowledged the brief contact; he hadn't even been looking at her when it happened.

Shyla didn't often eat with him. Her lunchtime came before Score woke up. He ate his first meal of the day at the kitchen island while reading news and emails on his phone. Beeks and Fish were usually around then too, so if she interacted with anyone, it was them.

At night, she ate dinner before the three men sat down. It just seemed right to do it that way, given that she was there to serve, not to participate. No one had ever made her feel unwelcome. In fact, the only reason she'd eaten with them that once was because Score had ordered it after learning her doctor's appointment had taken the place of her usual mealtime.

"You're going to start eating dinner with us every night," Score said. She nodded. "We will build up to everything you just said… Tell me, have you pleasured yourself while you've been here?" Anxiety wouldn't let her speak. Her lips stayed shut, but she nodded. "You think of me?" She nodded again. When she started to avert her focus, he caught her chin to raise it. "No apologies, no embarrassment. I want to know it all…. what were you thinking about, baby? My mouth? My hands? My cock?"

Although it seemed he wanted her to pick one, she parted her lips to answer. "All of the above."

It was nice to see the side of his mouth rise. He didn't often smile. It was flattering to think she might make him happy.

"You're gonna get them all, Lamb, all of them."

Her throat narrowed. Never once had she really believed fulfilling her fantasies with him could be a reality. She'd wanted Score to notice her, but had assumed he'd never let himself be curious enough to explore any interest he did have in her.

"Which part of me is it that… that you like?" she asked.

Dipping down, he let his breath warm her ear. "All of you." Her eyelids sank down as she whimpered. It felt so good to have him close. Boosting himself away from the wall, he didn't seem to realize that he'd turned her insides to soup. "Let's finish the game."

Score didn't leave things undone, when it came to chess anyway, but Shyla couldn't tear herself from the wall even after he was out of sight.

EIGHT

ROLLING HER HEAD on the wall, Shyla caught sight of the third bedroom, where Fish slept on the nights he wasn't crashing at the club or at Beeks'. There was a bed right there. If she'd been thinking and capable, she could've taken a swing at coercing Score into it. The thought proved her to be a liar. After earlier claiming not to be a lush, there she was considering seducing her boss in another man's bed.

"Come, Shyla," Score commanded in a stern voice.

Trust him to say that word in the moment she was visualizing them being together. Her new fantasy gave her the strength to push away from the wall. Score coughed to get her attention up.

"What?" she asked, returning to her place on the floor opposite him. "Sorry…" But she wasn't supposed to apologize. "Sorry."

His slow blink was almost an eye roll. "Why were you smiling?"

Was she smiling? Yes, she was. Her fantasy had the potential to become reality. Score had done that for her. Just by telling her to take off her dress.

He'd also asked her to tell him everything. While it wasn't habit to be completely open with him yet, there was only one way to change that. It was in that second, and in respect for all the liars he'd had in his life, Shyla vowed to always answer him with the truth, even if it was embarrassing.

"I was thinking about having sex in Fish's bed," she said, then paused with her fingers poised over the chess piece she'd been about to move. "With you... I was thinking about having sex with you in Fish's bed... not with Fish."

That was a sickening thought. Fish was the sweetest guy who was always happy, but she'd never once had a sexual thought about him, not once.

"Good to know," Score said.

Although he was dry, she might have heard a strain of sarcasm in there.

She took her shot. "There's nothing wrong with being clear."

His curled fingers found his chin again. "No, there's not, baby."

"Sometimes I babble or say stupid things," she said. "I did as a kid, like with my fingers." Raising her hands over the board, she twisted them together and stretched them out to highlight her point. "It's a nervous habit. If I'm uncomfortable or awkward, I have to do something." With a renewed expression of interest, he propped his chin on his knuckles while studying her. "What? What are you thinking about?"

"How I might help with that."

Shyla didn't know what he meant, but she'd never take the word 'help' in a negative way. Not from Score.

"Already tonight I've talked about sex way more than I ever have before in my life. You're already helping with something."

"Are you using birth control?"

"Am I?" His questions were so direct. He'd stated up front that he wouldn't pull his punches, that didn't mean some of the questions wouldn't blindside her. "No... no, I'm not."

"Any reason?" She shook her head; it wasn't like she had any allergies or moral objections to it. In her history, there had never been any need for her to consider contraception. "Are you on any medications?" She shook her head. "Good.

It's your move."

Wondering if his dull tone was a reflection of her talking about sex too much, she focused on the game. Shyla had stated that she'd follow his lead. He'd need to be in control or else they'd never get anywhere.

The game went on for another few moves before she shifted onto her knees to make a final move. "Checkmate," she said, squeezing her hands in between her thighs. Rubbing her lips together, she winced. "Are you mad?"

Though he was examining the board, he muttered, "Men who get mad about losing are insecure." When he opened his eyes after a blink, they were fixed on her. "Do you think I'm insecure?"

One thing older, physically incapacitated men did a lot was play board and parlor games. There wasn't a card game she hadn't at least tried. Dominoes, darts, even charades were typical in Stan's house. Chess and checkers were played almost every day.

"No, you don't, sir," she said, feeling an odd retreat when her skin began to prickle again. Her first instinct was to look away. Except Shyla wanted to make progress with Score, to show him that she was eager to be with him. So, bundling up her courage, she fought against that instinct. "Do I... do I get to pick my prize?"

Almost suspicious, but with a hint of amusement, he sank back to stretch his arms along the back of the couch again. "What would you like, Lamb?"

Asking for what she really wanted was too brazen. More brazen than she was capable of yet. Dropping her weight to her hands, she crawled around the table, watching him watch her as she came to a stop by his leg.

Rising to her knees, she shuffled as close as she could without touching him and opened both of her hands, presenting her palms to him. "Your hand."

The corner of his eyes twitched in curiosity. In spite of any misgivings he slid his hand from the back of the couch and laid it over hers. Shyla drew it forward, curling her thumbs against his palm, forcing him to sit forward.

Guiding his hand to her face, she closed her eyes and

rubbed her cheek against his rough palm. Unable to stop herself, she parted her lips to taste him for the first time. As she pressed her mouth deeper against the heel of his thumb, the sound of his inhale encouraged her.

"Time for bed," he said, taking his hand away from her face to stand up.

Shyla couldn't quite figure out the quick turnaround. When it became clear he was waiting for her, she bounced onto her feet. Score strode away from the couch toward the hallway, which led to both of their bedrooms.

Suffering a little whiplash from the quiet intimacy of the moment suddenly becoming a rush of movement, Shyla had to hurry to catch up to him. Following in his wake, she was a little disappointed when he turned his back on his own bedroom. For some reason, she wanted their first time to be in his bed. That upset was quickly forgotten. Seeing his purpose while he stood there at her bedroom door infused her with happiness instead.

He didn't open it, he just waited for her, like he was respecting her private space. Shyla went around him to push open the door and then faced him, wondering if she should say anything. Wrapping both of her hands around one of his, she crept backwards, trying to draw him inside, but he didn't move.

"Phoenix?"

His gaze travelled down her body. "No," he said, slipping his hand out of hers. "Go into your bedroom and take off your underwear. From now on, you sleep nude."

Something she'd never done before. At Stan's house, there were times she had to leap up in a hurry if one of her dependents needed her.

Shyla swallowed hard. "Okay."

Score nodded at the bedroom door. "Leave your bedroom door open."

She was quick to reassure him. "It's never locked."

"No. Open, Shy," he said.

There wasn't a hint of shame or equivocation in his voice, but she couldn't stop herself thinking about how vulnerable she'd be.

Edging closer, she whispered. "Anyone could walk in on me."

"No, they couldn't," he said. "Because to get to you, they have to walk past my room... I'll be leaving my door open too."

She already knew that he slept in the nude from her first day fumble. Just the idea that he'd leave himself open like that, open to her, made her mouth begin to water and her heartrate climb.

"Oh, boy," she said, blowing out a breath.

"Knowing you're accessible to me... that you're so close and exposed... It'll drive me wild, Shy."

Finding his gaze, she was desperate to taste him, desperate to have his arms around her. It might be slower than she'd like, but he'd explained why he was taking his time. This was what he wanted, this pace, these steps, and she wasn't going to refuse him.

"I am accessible to you, Score," she said. "And I trust you."

"Good," he said. "And you won't touch yourself."

Her inhale was almost a gasp. Although they'd touched on fantasies, she hadn't expected him to be direct about something so intimate. "Score, I... I wouldn't—"

"You will," he said, matter of fact about it. "When I tell you to... This is the man I am, Shy. I like control. If you don't like it, you have the power to end this any time. I give the orders, but you're in charge. Don't forget that."

Having him in control sounded like an adventure. His leadership and support were already arousing her fantasies. He talked to her in such a way that even the simplest requests sounded like both suggestions and commands at the same time.

Submitting to him was her ultimate fantasy, though she wasn't strong enough to admit it out loud yet.

"Just... be gentle with me... I'm a rookie."

He touched his knuckle to her jaw. Moving against him, she closed her eyes to appreciate the gentle contact.

"Beeks thought it was the mention of prison," he murmured. "It wasn't... A safe place to sleep. That's what you said. That's why I hired you… As long as I can provide it, that's what you'll get from me."

Opening her eyes wide, Shyla was grateful for the light of the city illuminating her bedroom or else she might not have seen how deeply he looked into her. She felt adored. Appreciated. Valued. Score offered her so much that she felt inadequate in comparison. He was so much and she was so little.

His hand fell from her face. "Go to bed, Shy."

Nodding, she slunk backwards, past her open door and into her room. Her thumbs slid up her back and she loosened the clasp of her bra. Before she could take it from her arms, he turned his back and walked away.

So, he wanted her naked, wanted her under his power, wanted her door open so he could come to her at any time… Yet, he chose to drive himself wild by resisting.

This was becoming the affair of a lifetime and they hadn't even kissed… yet.

NINE

THE NEXT MORNING, Shyla was icing a cake, listening to Beeks and Fish discuss some sports team when Score came around the end of the hallway.

Beeks was spread out on the table doing paperwork. Fish was lounging in his usual spot, the stool closest to the elevators. Score didn't say anything as he passed Fish to sit on the stool nearest the windows.

Going to the coffee machine, Shyla poured coffee for Score like she would on any other day. Except for her, that day was different. Her boss wasn't just her boss anymore. He'd seen her wearing nothing but her underwear, he'd demanded to see her like that. She'd slept naked because he wanted it that way.

The fizz of excitement in her belly felt so naughty. They might not have slept in the same bed, but they'd both slept with their doors open. That morning, when she'd left her bedroom, she'd loitered outside Score's open bedroom door, teasing herself with the idea that she could slip in and watch him sleep or maybe even slip in beside him.

But he hadn't asked her to do either, and she'd said she was going to follow his guidance. That meant behaving herself. Playing with the idea didn't mean she'd do it for real anyway. It would take more courage than she had to get into bed with a naked man.

Seeing him that way in bed had been an accident. Although the image of him had saturated her thoughts ever since, she doubted she'd ever be brave enough to confess her invasion of his privacy.

Though their new open door policy clouded the rules, she wasn't exactly clear what she was and wasn't allowed to do.

The coffee quaked as she took it from the machine. Her hand was shaking so bad that ripples hurried across the top of the liquid. The porcelain was hot; it burned her opposite palm when she tried to steady it. Knowing spillage would bring everyone's attention to her, she decided to take the heat.

With two hands, she lowered the cup to the island. At least her need for concentration meant she could avoid looking him in the eye on the walk over there.

"What team do you like?" Fish asked.

Shyla was smiling at her achievement and shaking the heat out of her hand when she realized he was talking to her. "Me?" she asked, her eyes widening.

Fish got up to go over to the fridge. "Yeah. You've got to be into something."

"Not sports," she said, noticing that Score was focused on his coffee and hadn't acknowledged her. Fish retrieving the juice from the fridge diverted her thoughts fast, she jumped to action and ran to him. "Ah!"

Putting one hand on the pitcher, she used the other to open a cabinet and take out a glass.

"Right," Fish said as she poured the juice into the glass.

Handing him the drink, Shyla urged him away from the fridge to put the pitcher away. "Thank you for obliging me."

Fish raised the glass and went back to his stool. "How do you make this juice anyway?"

"I juice fruit," she said, looking past Score. "Mr. Beeks, would you like more coffee before I cook?"

"Please," he called out.

"You don't got to call him Mister," Fish said.

Shyla poured the coffee. When it was for Beeks, her hand didn't shake. Score still hadn't looked at her. Maybe she'd just dreamt up their chess game and all that came with it.

"I gave up telling her that," Beeks said as she put the cup down next to him.

"When can we eat the cake?" Fish said, looking at the dessert laid out on the counter. "It looks so cool."

"After dinner," she said. "The frosting is still wet, please don't touch it." Going to Score, she paused at his side, trying to remember how she'd acted every other day after he'd woken up. "I was thinking bacon and pancakes, sir?"

He raised his eyes without lifting his head and acknowledged her question with a bob of his brows, then his focus returned to his phone. Shyla didn't know why she expected that day would be different from any of the others. Somehow, she had woken up feeling different and thought he might too.

Forcing him to make any acknowledgements that he didn't want to make wouldn't be smart. Leaving his side, she considered that he might have changed his mind. Maybe he'd walked into her bedroom while she was sleeping and seen something he didn't like.

Going about her cooking, she tried to figure out what she could have done to put him off. At breakfast on other days, he'd look at her, watch her. Not constantly, but once in a while she'd catch him just sort of monitoring her. That day there was nothing.

"Hey, Score, can I have Friday night off? Beeks says I've got to ask you."

"No," Score muttered.

"Oh, man," Fish whined. "I met this babe who wants to climb up on me, man… I figure since it's almost a whole week away…"

Given that it was Tuesday, she'd forgive him for saying a whole business week, but it wasn't a full week.

"Where did you meet her?" Shyla asked, working on

the pancake batter while the bacon was sizzling.

"At Score's," Fish said, proud of himself.

"You can't date the dancers," Score murmured.

"She's not a dancer," Fish said. "She's a dancer's mom." Shyla stopped stirring at the same time both Score and Beeks looked at him. "What? She had Chardonnay when she was like fifteen. She's only the boss' age."

Shyla glanced between Fish and Score, who was reading his phone again. "I… I don't know how old the boss is."

"Thirty-five," Score responded, propping his chin onto the heel of his hand.

Her smile spread. "That's twelve years, Fish… You like older women?"

"She's not that much older," Fish grumbled, flicking at the edge of the glass.

Beeks laughed. "Ah, you're looking to bag yourself a momma!"

"Oh, don't tease him," Shyla said, pouring the pancake batter into a pan and flipping the bacon. "I think it's cute."

"Can't be that much difference between you and me, Shyla," Fish said and she thought she saw Score's jaw twitch. "How old are you?"

"Twenty-nine."

"You want to go out with me?" Fish asked.

Shyla deliberately ignored the shift of Score's jaw. "No, thank you, honey," she said, turning around to retrieve plates. "Drink your juice."

Beeks laughed again. "Shot down, boy… Shyla is your momma. She feeds you and washes your clothes. You'd be lost without her."

She flipped the pancake. "I wouldn't want to ruin our friendship."

Fish twisted in his stool to look to Beeks. Shyla glanced at Score and was surprised to find him looking at her. So, another man showing interest made him notice her? If that was what he needed to keep him interested, their relationship was going to be short-lived.

As soon as he saw her eyes, he flicked his back to his phone.

"You think it's 'cause I'm a con?" Fish asked, hooking his elbows on the island to better see Beeks.

"I think Shyla needs a man who can look after her," Beeks said, distracted by his work. "She doesn't want a boy who can't look after himself."

"I can too look after myself," Fish said. "Can so. I've been out on my own since I was twelve." That truth broke her heart so much that she paused while slipping the pancake from the pan. "Only had foster homes before that."

Pouring more of the batter into the pan, Shyla couldn't imagine what it would be like to be on her own. Except Stan's death brought her to that point. Maybe that was part of the reason she'd thrown herself into looking after Bernard and Stan. They were all she had, and their time together was finite. Even after her grandfather was gone, she didn't let herself think about how she'd lost the last of her blood family.

"Going from prison to prison doesn't count as looking after yourself," Beeks said. "What would Shyla do if you went back inside?"

"You'd look after her," Fish said.

Though this was an intellectual discussion more than an actual possibility, she couldn't help but draw comparisons with Score. What would she do if he went back to prison? Although he hadn't committed the crime he'd been convicted of, she would assume—given his upbringing—he'd probably been involved in other crimes.

"Great, thanks," Beeks said. "So I get your girlfriend and none of the sex… what's in it for me?" Leaning forward, Beeks looked between the two men at the island. "I'm making a point here, Shyla, honey. You know I'd see you right."

Pleased to hear that Beeks wasn't ready to abandon her, she smiled, until she noted Score's complete lack of interest in the conversation. What if they got together and broke up? What would she be left with then? Beeks would look out for her because, as Fish had put it, she ran with them. But if she and Score broke up, he wouldn't want her working for him anymore. Shyla wouldn't *want* to work for him, what if he brought home other women and she had to hear him…

Fish and Beeks continued with their hypothetical discussion about Beeks caring for Fish's prospective girlfriend if he went to prison again. Shyla focused on her cooking, making enough for all three men.

"Okay," Fish said and thrust an arm to the side. "What about Score? What if he had a girl and went back to prison?"

"What's he going to prison for?" Beeks asked. "Man's never committed a crime in his life."

Fish lost his bluster, Beeks relaxed, and they both began to laugh at the same time.

Guessing that answered her speculation, Shyla left the last pancake to cook while she delivered Score's food to him and went to retrieve flatware.

She was serving the last of the food to Fish and Beeks when Fish spoke again. "What about Shyla's man?" he asked, his mouth full.

"Who?" Beeks asked, probably not understanding the youngster.

"What if she had a guy and she went to prison? Would you look after him?"

"If she couldn't find herself a guy who could look after himself, Score and I would make sure he wasn't her man for long."

A weird double standard lived in that statement somewhere, but Shyla just fixated on the idea that she might go to prison. "What would I go to prison for?"

"You wouldn't," Score said, cutting his food.

"Yeah, I'd get you off," Beeks said and then frowned at his turn of phrase before shaking off his reflection. "You're a first time offender. You don't have a record."

"We'd get her out of the country," Score said.

He hadn't paid an iota of attention to the previous conversation, but the new tangent engaged him for some reason. His statement suggested he'd look after her. Might be tough to do that when he wouldn't look at her for more than three seconds.

"I always wanted to see South America," she said in a tease.

None of the men laughed. "You want somewhere without an extradition treaty," Beeks said.

"Montenegro," Score said, putting down his fork to pick up his coffee.

"Beautiful there," Beeks said.

Fish laughed. "Now we got a plan to get you out, what crime you want to commit?"

"I thought about sunbathing topless, does that count?" Fish dropped his fork; even Score raised his head. "Or not."

Beeks laughed. "Might be indecent exposure… though not in this town. There are tits everywhere… naked maybe… if you went walking down the street… If you were playing with yourself on the patio downstairs or having sex… then you'd be in trouble."

"What about on the terrace?" she asked, noting in her peripheral vision that both Fish and Score were focused on her.

Shyla pretended not to see either of them and went about her cleaning up.

"That's private property; I guess you're safe to do either out there," Beeks said. "Though we do have other apartment buildings nearby."

"This whole place is glass," Fish said. "You do anything, even inside, and some dude is out there with binoculars…"

"I don't think anyone is using binoculars to spy on us," she said, laughing off the idea. Fish obviously wasn't so sure. He actually glanced from Score to Beeks, who weren't amused either. "I use tinted moisturizer… better for you than the sun anyway."

"Then you need a new crime."

"You need to do some work," Beeks said. "You've got a bunch of stuff to do before tonight."

"We all do," Score said, sliding off his stool and putting his phone in his pocket.

None of the men had finished their food. Fish

worked hard to clear his plate while Beeks gathered up his paperwork.

"Oh, okay," Shyla said, wiping her hands on a towel. She moved with them to the end of the island and watched them head for the elevator. "Have a good day!"

She called it out like the wife saying goodbye to her family. A moment later they were gone and she was left alone. Turning around to look at what was on the island, she decided to concentrate on her own work.

Most days Shyla was happy to get on with things. That day was different. Maybe because Score had blocked her out. All morning she'd anticipated him getting up. The idea of seeing him again excited her; she'd thought he might feel the same. To say reality had been a letdown would be an understatement.

She didn't understand why she'd become invisible all of a sudden. Questions swirled in her mind. Did he want to be with her or not? Had they started something or had he changed his mind?

It would be hours before she saw any of them again. All she'd have was time to wonder. Was she going to be Score's girl or was their relationship over before it had started?

TEN

DINNER WOULD BE READY, that's what Shyla was thinking while singing along to the song playing in her earbuds. Rushing out of the laundry room after folding a bunch of towels, she ran straight into someone in the hallway.

"Oh," she said, jumping back, but sighed and pulled out her earbuds when she saw it was Score. "You scared me. I didn't think anyone was back yet."

Retreating a step, he gave her space to walk down the hall toward the living room. She anticipated finding Beeks and Fish except no one else was around. The clock revealed it was a few minutes earlier than normal.

Putting her phone and earbuds on the kitchen island, she figured it was time to set the table. But when she turned around, Score was right there behind her, up close.

When Shyla laid a hand on his arm to try moving him aside, Score didn't budge. "Were you good?" he asked.

She blinked up through her bangs. "Was I… I don't understand."

"Last night," he said. "Did you do as I told you?"

All afternoon she'd been preoccupied with how he'd ignored her and disappeared from the condo without a word. In sharp contrast, she felt anything but ignored as he examined her up close.

"You mean, did I…" Dropping her chin, the flames of awareness crept from her chest to her neck. "I didn't… please myself, if that's what you're asking."

The confession felt odd on her tongue. It wasn't the kind of thing she'd discussed with anyone in the past, and yet, it was what it was.

"Were you naked?" his deep voice queried, arousing her in all sorts of stimulating ways.

"Phoenix," she whispered. He touched the underside of her chin to hold it up, showing he was serious and wanted an answer. "Yes, of course I was." He eased away, but Shyla had her own question. She laid a hand on his forearm to stall him. "Why did you ignore me today? I've spent all day thinking I did something wrong."

"You did nothing wrong."

Simple answer to him, though it didn't alleviate her confusion. He retreated to the fridge to fill a glass with water.

Shyla went to the table to lay out the place mats and flatware. On her return to the kitchen, Score stepped into her path and held up the glass of water between them.

"Thank you," she said, mystified by the offer.

Once the drink was in her hand, he turned, forcing her to do the same. Backed up against the counter, she was trapped when he planted a hand on either side of the island behind her. Shyla had no idea what was happening or why his attention was so intent on her.

From one extreme to the other, she considered that maybe he was making up for earlier. In a straight choice, she'd take having him up close over being ignored every time.

Though he still wasn't actually touching her, so he wasn't quite as close as she'd like.

"Open your mouth."

His unexpected command was so lascivious that she smiled. "Score," she whispered, fighting her urge to squirm. "Beeks and Fish will be here any second. Dinner is in the oven—"

"Open your mouth." Her excuse hadn't swayed him, and she wasn't supposed to refuse orders. Letting her lips part for a second then close, she licked them before opening them further. "Show me your tongue."

Closing her mouth, Shyla breathed out a laugh. "I feel stupid."

Score wasn't laughing, in fact, he appeared to be getting annoyed. "Do it, Shy."

"Okay," she said, rolling her lips together and clearing her throat in an attempt to scare away her urge to laugh. "Okay, sorry."

This time she closed her eyes as her mouth opened. That made it easier to poke her tongue out. Anticipating that he'd kiss her, her head fell back. Instead of his mouth, the brush of his fingertip grazed her tongue for the briefest of moments.

Her eyes popped open when she realized he'd left something small and cylindrical behind.

Score stepped back and nodded at the glass of water. "Swallow."

It was a pill. Taking the glass to her lips, she couldn't begin to guess what he'd given her, but she swallowed as instructed. Score took the glass and leaned over her to put it on the island.

While looming over her, he leaned down to murmur above her ear. "When I move inside you, there won't be a damn thing between my skin and yours."

His body ebbed from hers. Stunned, still draped against the counter, Shyla was in a daze, so it took a second for her to figure it out.

"A birth control pill," she whispered. "It's birth control."

"Yeah, the rest are in your vanity," Score said, standing behind his seat at the dining table, holding the back. "Why are there only three places?"

"I wasn't sure if you'd changed your mind."

After how he'd been earlier, she assumed he wouldn't want her to eat with him. Trying to seem as normal as possible, she took water and glasses to the table.

"Set your place, Shy."

Score sat down. She took the food from the stove

before grabbing another one of everything to set the place to his left. As Shyla was about to go back into the kitchen, something stopped her. Something like the question he hadn't answered. Studying him, she tried to figure out what had changed between her going to bed and him waking up. What was the difference between the current moment and the ones earlier on?

She couldn't put her finger on it until boom, it hit her. "You don't want them to know," she whispered, more to herself than to him, but he looked up. "You're ashamed of your attraction to me."

"What?" he said just as the elevator doors opened.

Beeks and Fish came across to the dining table engaged in another of their debates. More than half the time, she didn't know what they were talking about. Still, it was nice they had each other to spar with. Shyla went into the kitchen to retrieve the food. The men always ate family style, she preferred that to dishing out portions for them.

"Hey, you're gonna eat with us," Fish said, taking his seat. "I always wondered why you didn't."

"She's not less than us," Score said, wearing a scowl as he pointed to her chair. "Sit."

Her revelation made things awkward. It wasn't like she expected him to take out a full-page ad declaring what had happened between them. Especially when in the most technical of definitions, nothing had actually happened. Except, to her, everything had. Maybe she was facing a symptom of her naivety.

Slipping into her chair, she coiled her fingers in her lap. Her mind was on anything but food. To her surprise, Score stood up with her plate to serve her meal before anyone else got anything. He dropped it down in front of her and moved on to fill his own.

Only after he sat down did Beeks and Fish serve theirs. Score's knee bumped hers beneath the table, but she couldn't bring herself to look up. Taking her fork, Shyla scooped up some food and kept herself hunched over her plate.

All his talk of wanting trust and them being

something different didn't erase the differences between them. A man of Score's experience couldn't think about a long term relationship with a woman like her. She couldn't be a gangster's moll. What did she know about organized crime? Nothing. She didn't even know how the girlfriend of a nightclub owner was supposed to act. Shyla's singular experience of going to a nightclub ended in disaster.

Maybe Score was a step ahead and had come to realize they were incompatible. That would be a reason he didn't want to claim her in public. If it wasn't for the birth control pill she'd just been fed, Shyla might even assume he'd decided friendship was the most they could have... Being the only woman in his apartment, maybe proximity was all she had going for her.

Her mental speculation continued through dinner. It was still going on after the trio disappeared into the elevator to return to the club.

Being upset was ridiculous. Her disappointment was completely her own fault. After one evening together, she'd turned their prospective relationship into something it could never be.

She went through the motions of cleaning up from dinner, then turned off all the lights except the recessed lighting in the kitchen. That was left on so Score didn't come home to a dark apartment.

With nothing else to do, Shyla slunk down the hallway to her bedroom intending to take a shower and get an early night. The last thing she expected to find was a gift. But there it was, a large flat box on the end of her bed.

Tilting her head, she crept toward the black and ivory box. Getting closer to it, she noted the small rectangle of cardboard tucked beneath the bow in the middle.

Plucking it out, she opened the card. Her curiosity stayed on the box until she dragged her eyes to the card to read the handwritten words. *Be ready tonight* —P. Be ready. Laying the card on the bed, she bent over to take the lid from the box. After putting it aside, she unfolded the delicate paper and inhaled in wonder at what she saw beneath.

A balconette bra in the same deep jade green color as

her eyes lay atop of a matching pair of panties. Letting her fingers trail across the soft fabric, she didn't know whether to be awe-inspired, touched, or overwhelmed. Some part of all three swirled within her.

The card wasn't explicit about what Score expected, but it sent her a message all the same. Shyla picked up the card to touch the letters he'd written for her. Asking her to wear his gift implied he'd be home early again.

Biting her lip, she looked to her shower, wishing for a bathtub instead. His invitation gave her notice to prepare for him. Whatever it took, she vowed to change his opinion and make him proud of her. Score said that it was in her room he'd decided to have her. Something must be in the air because standing there, she decided to give all of herself to him.

ELEVEN

WAITING WAS EXCRUCIATING.

Shyla had no idea what time Score was going to be home, so she jumped every time noise came from either the elevator shafts or the stairwells. Midnight came and went… She started to think maybe he wasn't coming at all. Something could've happened at the club, something which took precedence or maybe he'd just changed his mind.

Sitting on the couch, curled up with a book, her concentration was slipping. The terrifying idea that there may have been a horrific accident wouldn't go away. It was so intrusive that she almost didn't hear when the elevator did open. The thump of his heavy footsteps pulled her from her funk.

Tossing the book to the table, Shyla leaped from the couch and ran to the foyer to see him standing in the middle.

"Oh, baby, I was worried," she said, rushing forward, but he put a hand up to halt her. His scowl slunk down her body. She guessed he didn't like the silk maxi robe tied over her body. "I didn't want to take the risk that you wouldn't be alone."

Adrenaline pulsated through her. Her heart fluttered with palpitations that made her feel faint. Or maybe it was less about the palpitations and more about the man in front of her, waiting for her to loosen the tie of her robe.

Holding her breath, she gathered the edges at the center of her torso and let the delicate material flutter from her shoulders down her body to the floor.

Waiting for him to say something, she tried to stay still, but her hands drifted toward each other. His hand was still flat in the air between them. While his eyes enjoyed their journey over her figure, he curled his fingers until only his forefinger was left up.

"Put your hands on your ass."

Surprise caught her words in her throat. "Excuse me?"

"You heard me," he said. "Don't make me say it again."

The request was unusual, but she curved her arms around to her back and did as he said, resting a hand on each of her ass cheeks.

After what felt like a lifetime of him just examining her body, he turned his hand so the back was parallel to the floor and crooked his finger at her.

Shyla hoped his beckoning would lead to touching. If he didn't sate her desire, she couldn't wager how much longer she'd last.

"Phoenix," she whispered, tiptoeing nearer.

Just when she was ready to reach for him, he held up his hand to stop her again.

"Shh," he said, touching a fingertip to her shoulder.

The light touch parted her lips and closed her eyes. As it began to slide down her arm, her breathing quickened.

Curling his fingers around her elbow, he drew it up, allowing her hand to leave her ass under his direction. To see what he was doing, she let her lashes flutter apart just as he guided her fingertips to his lips in the most delicate caress.

Lost in the need and anticipation, she was so mesmerized that, at first, she didn't notice he'd lowered her hand to the zipper of his jacket. The cool metallic tab took a second to register under her touch. Soon she realized what he wanted and drew the zipper down.

Loosening his jacket, Shyla opened her hands on his tee-shirt beneath. Peeking up and half expecting him to tell her she wasn't allowed to touch him, she waited a second before trailing her hands down and up. He didn't say anything or stop her, so catching her lip in her teeth, Shyla satisfied some of her intrigue. The hard planes of his body beneath the warm cotton of his tee-shirt aroused her desire. Letting her hands ascend to his shoulders, she pushed his jacket back.

With his help shrugging it off, the jacket fell to his hand, he caught it by the collar.

"Can I do your boots?" she asked, though with her hands flat on his chest, she was sort of loathed to tear them away.

He nodded. Her hands skimmed down his form. Bending her knees, she descended to unlace his boots and he toed them off. Undressing him in this quiet, dim space was beyond hot. The intimacy of it heated her. The acts themselves might not seem sensual, but they felt that way.

Last night he'd asked her to loosen his belt too, so Shyla shifted to her knees and took the liberty of unfastening his belt, her eyes rising to his as she did. Once it was open, she undid the top button of his jeans. Because her fingers were beneath the edge of his tee-shirt anyway, she extended them to stroke the flesh of his lower abdomen.

He dropped his jacket. "Easy, baby," he said, dipping down to capture her wrists.

Hauled onto her feet in a rush, her next inhale was sharp. She almost fell against him, but he kept her wrists tight in his grip and thrust them high, extending her body to her tiptoes.

Wishing for his kiss, Shyla couldn't take her gaze from his mouth. "Please," she whispered.

Though she hadn't meant to beg, she didn't feel ashamed for doing it.

His grip stayed where it was, but he lowered his head. "I don't trust myself to stop after one kiss."

"Who said you had to?"

Clenching his jaw, he tried, like a man on the edge, to hold onto his restraint. "You and me got things to clear up before we think about getting physical."

Hoping that confirmed they were building toward sating their lust, she was taken by surprise when he jerked her hands down. In the same move, he spun her around and locked both of her wrists in one of his hands at her lower back. He used that point of contact to propel her forward.

Steering her across the room, he thrust her down onto the floor in front of the couch where he sat. Shyla was still trying to get her hair out of her face when he grabbed her chin to tug her face up close to his.

"You want to kick me in the balls, baby, you look me in the eye when you do it," he hissed.

Lost, she could sense his anger. "I… I don't understand."

"Say it again," he growled. "Say to me what you said right before Beeks and Fish walked in here." Mouthing into the ether, no sound came from her lips. "Come on, don't feed me the shit that you forgot. Fucking say it, Shy."

"You're ashamed to be attracted to me," she murmured, locked onto the ire in his eyes.

Yanking her closer, he hunched until her mouth was just a breath from his. "You better be careful what you wish for, Little Lamb, because after I claim you, there won't be any going back."

"Phoenix," she whispered and tried to slide a hand onto his thigh.

But he tossed her face away with such force that she lost her balance and had to catch herself on her elbows.

He sank back on the couch, slouching deeper into it, slapping his hands to his face. "What the fuck am I doing? I'm a McDade. McDade's don't get with women like you."

"Hey," she said, climbing up onto the couch on her knees facing him. "Look at me, baby… We're going to make this work, okay? We're going to…"

His hands left his face so his arms could lay along the back of the couch. The moment he did look at her, she couldn't remember any words.

"You don't know anything about my family, do you?" he said, a sort of resigned sigh in his voice.

Shuffling herself forward, her knees came up against the outside of his thigh. She rose up to slide a hand onto his opposite cheek to keep him facing her direction.

Shyla rested her forehead on his. "I don't want to be with your family," she whispered, stroking his face. "I want to be with you. You're the only McDade I care about."

"Don't think anyone's ever said that shit before."

Letting her lips curl, she eased back enough to find his eyes. "I don't want to be just anyone."

Taking his furthest arm from the back of the couch, he tucked a loose strand of hair away from her face. His lips stayed shut, though his throat moved as if he'd intended to say something.

After another few moments he let himself speak. "I've never had to be soft with a woman."

The prospect of that provoked her anxiety. But right then wasn't about her, he needed her reassurance.

"You can be hard with me," she said though she doubted her own ability to respond in the right way.

"I'm hard with you every fucking minute," he said, touching her hair again.

His hand drifted through her hair and returned to her face; he brushed his thumb across her lips.

In her naivety, Shyla hadn't even thought to look south of his belt when they were having these encounters.

"I… I can help with that," she said, ignoring her trepidation. "If you tell me how."

"No, baby," he said with a single shake of his head. "Sit round for me, properly with your feet on the floor." Twisting around, she did as he said, aware of his arm against her neck where it lay along the back of the couch. "You have a good day, baby?" She nodded, smoothing her hands down the front of her thighs. "Remember what I said about everything. I want the truth. The details."

He had said that; their trust would only come if she let herself be open. Picking up her feet, Shyla tucked her heels on the front edge of the couch and hugged her legs.

"I was happy this morning, looking forward to you waking up. I wanted to see you." Her head fell back to rest on his arm, she tipped her focus to his that was looming over her. "But when you came through and wouldn't look at me, I thought maybe you changed your mind or I dreamed the whole thing."

"You didn't," he said. "I want us to be secure before we let the outside in. After I've been inside you, that's when we'll let the world know."

After he'd been inside her. He said those words like it was no big deal, like it was inevitable. Shyla wanted it to be, but joining their bodies wouldn't be just a quick slip. The only way he'd know that was if she said the words aloud.

"I…"

"Do you like your present?"

Dropping her focus to her cleavage, she slipped her feet down to the floor to arch and show off the lingerie. "I love it. Thank you."

With her head on his arm and his face so close above hers, she began to drift on a warm sea deeper into the embrace of what was building between them.

"Did you think of me today?" she asked, less nervous about speaking to him that night than she'd been the previous one.

"Every minute was building to this," he said, examining her features from her hairline to her brows and eyes all the way to her chin and her breasts.

She smiled. "I didn't think you were the romantic sort… but that was pretty romantic."

"It's not my specialty."

"What is?" she asked, trying to wriggle closer.

"Fucking," he said and she stopped moving. "Is what it is, Shy."

The way he was twisted toward her meant he had a hand on his lap. Venturing to pick it up, Shyla was encouraged when he didn't resist her guiding it onto her body.

Pressing her hand over his, she flattened it just beneath her throat. "I want you to touch me, Phoenix."

"There isn't another soul who's used my first name. Never gave it a thought 'til I heard it on those lips."

Pushing her shoulders into the couch, she arched up,

easing her body closer to his and forcing his hand lower. Whether he was aware of it or not, she couldn't tell, but his hand slid onto her breast. With her eyes locked on his, she slowed her breathing when he began to squeeze. Through every second of his fondling, she read his desire growing heavier in his eyes. He squeezed her harder; the urgency of his touch rose.

"Yes," she breathed.

Her eyes closed and her legs moved up and down, rubbing together. Rocking with the rhythm of his fondling, Shyla couldn't remember ever feeling that good. His hand glided across both breasts, giving her the attention she craved.

All of a sudden, he curled his fingers into a fist that hovered just an inch above her cleavage. "Damn," he grumbled.

"What's wrong?" she asked, easing a hand up between them to cup his face.

He grabbed it away and planted it on her abdomen. Her heart was beating so hard, he could probably feel it. Reaching for her confidence, Shyla pushed up to try kissing him, but he recoiled.

"Relax," he said. "Just relax."

Confused about his resistance, she didn't know what to try next. Whatever he commanded, she'd do. Her lack of success so far proved just how much his direction was needed. Her complicity only began to waver when he skimmed her hand down her stomach, past her navel to the line of her panties.

With his palm still pressing her hand into her flesh, he used the tip of his finger to raise the elastic. Holding her breath in anticipation of what could come next, she waited for him to touch her. But her hand was the only one he guided beneath the fabric, his stayed above, cupping her hand from the outside.

"Phoenix—"

"Play for me, Shy," he said, leaning down to brush his lips on her brow. "Fulfil my fantasy."

Watching her play with herself was his fantasy? His hand left her crotch to scoop under her thigh. He hooked her leg over his and pushed the other away, spreading her legs wide, forcing her to slouch further.

"What do you like, baby, huh?" he asked. "Want me to talk to you? Tell you how wet I'm gonna get you before I slide my thick cock into your sweet, tight, little cunt?"

So transfixed by him, she didn't think about what her fingers were doing until a zip of pleasure quaked right from her sweet spot.

"Mm," she whimpered.

"I'm gonna fuck you good, Shy," he murmured, his lips moving on her brow. "I'm gonna lash those delicate wrists of yours to my bed and force you to submit … I'll put a blindfold over those big, innocent emeralds. You won't know when it's coming or how I'll take you…"

The growled words seemed linked to her fingers that were already coated by her juices. She slid them up and through and round, imagining what it would be like under his command.

"Yes," she exhaled.

"I'll tie your ankles to the corners so you won't be able to resist me. Your legs will stay wide open for me every minute of the day. Any second I think you deserve it, I'll feed my spunk into that hungry pussy of yours. You won't say no to me. It won't be allowed. You'll run my house. Do my chores and submit to me any time I command you to heel."

Squirming deeper into the couch, she opened her mouth in a yelp as her fingers quickened. "Would you like that, Little Lamb," he hissed against her. "To be my compliant little sex slave? Used to satisfy my cock any time I want to get off? You give me a pass and it will be morning and night. You'll be at my beck and call. I'll want your mouth, your cunt, your ass, all of you will belong to my cock."

"Yes," she said, digging her nails into the seat of the couch next to her. "Yes, sir. Yes."

"And it won't be gentle. I won't be tender. You'll take it hard, every hour. Any time I demand you strip and submit, you'll bow until I'm ready to let you suck my dick. And you'll thank me for the fucking honor."

"Yes," she said, bucking up at the impact of orgasm

that hit her belly so hard she gasped for oxygen. "Yes!"

Panting, she was lost to everything except her awareness of Score next to her. He was probably giving her a chance to return to Earth. As she did, the realization of what she'd just done hit her hard.

Yanking her hand from her underwear, Shyla didn't know whether to stay statue still or bolt for the hills. But her ass was falling off the couch, so she had to sit up and that meant grabbing for what was closest: Score's thigh.

Shyla pushed up just a fraction before it hit her that she'd wiped her hand on him. "Oh, I'm sorry," she cried.

The arm he had on the back of the couch was crooked so his fist could support his head. Shyla was still in the shadow of his body, but was on the cusp of bolting when he took her wrist.

"I'm gonna have that sweet nectar all over me soon enough," he said, guiding her hand to his mouth so he could kiss the fingertips she'd just used to pleasure herself.

With her mouth open, Shyla froze when he parted his lips and sucked her fingers, squashing them between his tongue and the roof of his mouth.

"Oh my God," she whispered.

Drawing the fingers out, he licked between them. "I will be. Soon."

Her God? He was already and she couldn't believe he didn't know it. "I'm afraid," she confessed.

His relaxed expression suddenly became a scowl. He lowered her hand. "Of me?"

Either she'd offended him or disappointed him. Her free hand leaped to his chest, forcing her to twist all the way toward him.

"No," she said, knowing that was his fear. "I'm afraid I'll disappoint you. I'm afraid of me."

"Don't think about that," he said, tightening his grip on her hand again. "We're doing this right."

Building the trust before rushing into anything. That's what he meant; they were taking it slow. Though doing that might be the end of her. Worried that she'd already conveyed herself as a selfish lover, Shyla hadn't done anything for him, and wanted to right that… somehow.

Dropping her hand from his chest to his thigh, she slid it upward. "Would you like me to…"

Taking the hand he had in his grip to the one that was moving, he captured them both. "No." Just no. "You have to take the pill for seven days before we're clear." And he'd already said that he didn't trust himself to stop. She trusted he would if she asked him to, but Shyla doubted stopping would be on her mind once they started. "Have you been tested?"

That question diverted her thoughts. "Have I been…"

"Tested. I meant what I said about there being nothing between our bodies. I want to be free to take you any way I want. I've been tested and cleared, I'm good."

"I… well, yes, I suppose so. The doctor did a bunch of tests when I registered. I don't know if all the results are back, but I can—"

"Good. Call them tomorrow." Releasing her hands, he eased back. "Go pour two glasses of scotch."

Straightening up, she put her hands to the edge of the couch and began to slide forward. Before rising, she narrowed an eye and twisted to look over her shoulder.

"Phoenix, I…"

The confession had lodged in her throat a couple of times, but she'd promised herself to be honest with him. There were only so many times the moment could go by before she was just plain lying to him.

"What is it?"

Sinking against the back of the couch, she was pleased when he straightened his arm along the backrest again.

"I have to tell you something… about me and I… I'm nervous to tell you."

"Why? I told you, I want to know everything. I won't judge. I can take it."

Peeking up at him, she rested her head on his arm. "You will?" He nodded once, but she could already see the concern on his face. "Even if it's about sex… about my sexual history?"

He moved away just a little to get a better look at her,

but his arm stayed behind her head. "What about it? Shyla, if someone hurt you—"

"No, it's nothing like that," she said, flipping onto her side and touching a ripple in his tee-shirt.

"If you had to sell it—"

"I've never done it," she said before he went through every depravity and desperation he could think of. She kept toying with the ripple between two of her fingers. "I... I fooled around with a boyfriend in high school, but I wasn't ready then. I thought I'd lose it in college, but with my grandfather and then Stan..."

His arm withdrew as he sat up straight and shifted to the edge of the couch, rubbing a hand over his mouth. She didn't like that he'd left her there, looking at his back, but appreciated that he needed a minute to process.

"I know it seems ridiculous and it wasn't through lack of trying. I did try to go on dates, but there was never anyone to be there for Bernard and Stan. I couldn't just leave them. I lived in an old people neighborhood, there was no one my age around and I... It just didn't happen for me."

He got up and strode to the bar. Shyla stayed on the couch, waiting while he poured and gulped down the scotch she maybe should have got for him before confessing the truth.

He drank another generous measure. A minute passed. Then there were another two. The longer the silence went on, the more she shrank.

"I'm sorry," she whispered.

"You're a virgin," he said, dropping the glass to the bar without turning around.

"I don't like that word, but... yes, I am."

Whipping around, he came stalking in her direction. "Then why the fuck did you say you wanted to have sex with me?"

"Because I do!" she called, leaping to her feet, not that it made much difference because he was so much taller than her. To give herself more height, she jumped onto the couch. "I wasn't saving myself for my wedding night. It wasn't noble. I just... I never got the chance."

His eyes widened and his head bobbed. "And I'm it, I'm your chance? Well, fuck, baby, ain't that swell for me."

Leaving her, he marched toward the elevators.

Shyla leaped off the couch to chase him. "Where are you going?" she asked. "What does this mean?"

"It means we're through," he said, sticking his feet in his boots and swiping his jacket up from the floor.

"But you said I was pristine," she said. "You wanted me to be uncorrupted."

"Uncorrupted, not untouched," he said, pressing the elevator call button.

"Phoenix, this is nuts! It doesn't change anything! It doesn't mean anything!"

"Spoken like a true virgin," he said, stepping back to see which of the two elevators would open.

"So, what? You only want me if I have special skills?" she asked. "Now you know I don't know how to give you head or ride you raw, you're not interested? Thanks, I guess I know what kind of guy you really are."

The elevator doors opened and he stepped inside to press a button. When he moved back, he looked her in the eye. "You better be damn grateful you never found out, Little Lamb."

The doors slid shut. She was left alone, aroused and angry and confused. Surprise was what she'd expected, it hadn't even occurred to her that he'd break things off.

Shyla didn't know why it mattered to him, but if it did, there was only one remedy to the problem… She had to have sex, and fast, or she'd lose her chance with Score for good.

TWELVE

THE NEXT DAY, Score was up and out an hour earlier than usual. From the laundry room, Shyla heard the elevator and assumed Beeks and Fish were arriving. They didn't arrive. No one did. Left with a full pot of coffee and no one to feed, Shyla sought out Score only to find his bedroom empty.

If he couldn't be in the same room as her, she wondered what her role would be going forward.

All was not yet lost. The decision she'd made the previous night gave her cause to be optimistic rather than downhearted. Up until the moment of her confession, their night had been going the right way.

Score had one problem with her, her lack of experience, and that was something she could remedy.

Later that day, Shyla sat in the pool lounge in her bikini top and sarong considering how she might go about gaining some experience. Gavin took care of that for her.

She'd seen him around before. Whenever they passed each other, he said hello. Until that day, she'd never been more than polite. But that day, when she spotted him staring, she held eye contact and smiled.

A man, who seemed to be interested in her, right there on her doorstep. It was a coup. Going to bars and clubs, trawling for a date, was her idea of a nightmare. The memory of her first night out still hung heavy over her. Those kinds of places might not be so fun if she wasn't throwing herself into the drinking they encouraged.

That was why when Gavin left his stool and came over to speak with her, she straightened up and welcomed his request to sit beside her. They talked for a while. He explained he was a freelance journalist, staying with his brother in one of the lower level apartments. His being in the building meant she didn't have to stray far to gain the experience Score required of her.

Gavin didn't push, which was nice. Their conversation was relaxed, easy. When he invited her to have a drink with him in the bar the following night, she tried not to be too eager. Dating could lead to intimacy, Score should be impressed by how quickly she'd fixed the problem.

Her duties still included cooking, as far as she knew. After leaving Gavin, she'd returned upstairs to make dinner. The table was set and she'd just put the food down when the three men came out of the elevator.

None of them said anything about her joining them, so she left them alone. Still excited, she went to her bedroom to pick out an outfit for the following night.

The trio were gone by the time she came back to the kitchen.

Shyla waited up. Stupid as it was, some part of her still hoped Score would come to her. By two am, she'd given up that hope and gone to bed. As per Score's instructions, she slept in the nude with her door open, just in case he changed his mind. Since he'd learned her truth, Score's bedroom door had been closed. The gesture wasn't subtle. He didn't want her to have access to him.

Fish and Beeks were there for breakfast the next day. Their demeanor was the same, which she guessed meant Score hadn't filled them in. Their secret wouldn't keep for long if Score kept shutting her out. Although he joined them for breakfast, he wouldn't so much as breathe in her direction. All Shyla could do was leave him alone to his brooding.

The next few days repeated the same. Each night she

met Gavin in the bar, sticking to the non-alcoholic drinks to ensure she wouldn't make a fool of herself.

On Tuesday, Beeks messaged her to say the three men were going out for dinner, meaning she wouldn't have to cook. The opportunity was too perfect to ignore. Before she could think about it too much, she texted Gavin to bring their usual meeting time forward.

Wearing a bikini top under a plunging kaftan shift dress that was shaped and short enough to show most of her thighs, Shyla put a condom in her clutch next to her phone. While waiting for the elevator, she took one last look at herself in the mirror. This was it. The day she was going to lose the burden she'd been dragging since her teenage years.

"You can do this," she whispered to her reflection and nodded once before blending into the elevator when it opened.

Gavin was waiting on a stool by the bar and got up to kiss her cheek when she joined him. "Wow, you look incredible.

"This old thing," she joked and hopped onto the stool beside him.

Her bikini was white. The dress was a shade of pale olive. Dressing casual took the pressure off, but it was an important night, so she'd made the effort to weave some skinny white ribbon through her loose, messy braid.

Shyla had worried her hair might not be sleek or sophisticated enough. Although she'd had it tidied up at the salon, she hadn't taken the plunge to get it cut short.

Gavin ordered their usual drinks and then second guessed himself. "Would you like something different tonight? Maybe something stronger?"

"The next one," she said, some Dutch courage might not be amiss.

Seduction wasn't in her repertoire of skills. Sitting there almost overcome by nerves, she began to see Score's point. Why would he want someone who didn't even know how to initiate intimacy?

Hoping Gavin understood why alcohol was on the cards, she took his smile as a positive sign. If he took the lead, there would be less pressure on her. They could both just accept where the evening was headed and get the deed out of the way.

As Gavin talked about his day, all Shyla could think about was Score. Doing something so amoral wasn't like her. Her plan involved being intimate with Gavin, not because she wanted to be with him, but because the man she wanted to be with needed her to be.

Score seemed to think that sex was a big deal to her when that wasn't the case. Her lack of experience was just something that had happened. She'd often cursed it, especially in recent years.

As a teen and in her early twenties while adjusting to looking after two elderly men, she'd assumed there would be time. But with no one else available to look after Bernard and Stan, there hadn't been the respite for her to go out into the world. Nightclubs were foreign to her and she'd missed the college experience.

Sometimes it bugged her. Most of the time, she just pushed it to the back of her agenda. Monday became Tuesday, January became December, and before she knew it years had passed.

She'd wanted to have sex. To have normal, modern relationships. It didn't matter that there were scores of articles written about how common it was for people to be virgins in their thirties, forties, and beyond. Shyla wanted to know what it was to be touched by a man.

That being said, she wasn't a floozy interested in grabbing any old stranger in an alley for the sake of getting it on.

Gavin was still talking. It wasn't like him to go off on a tangent. Anxiety crept in, she wondered if he was nervous. It would be hilarious if he too had little experience. If he was hoping she'd take the lead, he'd get a surprise.

Her clutch buzzed under her hand, so she interrupted him with a finger.

"Excuse me. I'm sorry," she said and popped open her clutch. "I'm sort of on call."

"Oh," Gavin said. "No problem. I'll order more

drinks? Would you like a cocktail?"

"Sure, just anything," she said, slipping her phone out of her clutch to read the text message she'd received. "*Upstairs. Now.*" That was all it read, but it was more than she'd got from Score all week.

Shyla hadn't expected him back, so she bounced off her stool assuming he needed a shirt or a tie or something.

"Everything okay?"

"Yes," she said, tucking her phone away and grabbing her purse. "Can I abandon you for just a minute? I have to run upstairs." She held up a finger and began to back away. "Just for a minute. Don't go anywhere."

Although he appeared flummoxed, he nodded. "Sure. No problem."

Having a bar in the building worked out for her again. Rushing to the elevator, she went inside and used her fingerprint to select the right floor.

It took less than a minute to get to the apartment. When the doors opened, she was loose and eager to get back downstairs. That optimism lasted until she was faced with a fuming Score.

"What is it? What's wrong?" she asked, having never seen him so tense. "Is it Beeks? Or Fish?"

Peeking past him, she saw no sign of anyone else. Either of their friends could be ill or injured.

Her attention was still on the body of the apartment when he stole her purse and yanked it open. Upturning it, he sent her gloss and phone clattering to the floor, the condom fluttered down too.

"What do you think you're doing?" she exclaimed and began to duck with intentions of checking her phone wasn't broken, but he seized her upper arm and hauled her up. "Score!"

"Just any damn cock will do, is that it?" he asked, kicking the condom across the floor. "You didn't miss a fucking beat, you jumped straight onto the next guy. No one makes a fool of a McDade."

The snarl of his angry words was intense, but she held her nerve. "You don't know anything."

"A fuck is what you wanted. When I didn't give it to you fast enough, you went sniffing for a guy who would. You got one at the bar, huh? Bet he's primed and ready… Why bother with a drink if you're that desperate, honey? Just tell him your pussy's hungry, he'll fill you up. I guarantee it."

Her arm ached in the tight grip of his hand. Shyla ignored the vibration of her anxious atoms and shook her hair from her shoulders. "You wouldn't… Are you saying he's more of a man than you?"

Sneering, showing his clenched teeth, he growled at her. "I don't fuck hos… And I don't care if you're lily white, a girl as desperate for cock as you hits that mark. Planning to ride and run? Sew those oats? I can't believe I thought you were different."

Releasing her arm, he shoved her away and flipped around to stalk a few paces away.

"I am different."

"No, you're fucking not. You don't give a crap who the cock is attached to. You just want your happy ending. You're a good time gal. I've had too many of those."

"I do give a crap. I… I give a huge crap," she said to his back and ran a finger across her face to swipe her hair from her lip. "I'm only trying to be what you want." His chin tipped toward his shoulder, but he didn't turn. Her adrenaline skyrocketed. Asserting herself with such vehemence wasn't habit. "You won't be with me because I don't have the skills to please you. You don't want a virgin. So, I don't want to be a virgin anymore… You know what, you're right…" Anxiety dried her raspy throat. "I don't care who the cock is attached to tonight. If that makes me a ho then that's what I am. And if I have to ride another and another to get the chance that maybe you'll notice me again then that's what I'll do… I'll ride a hundred cocks and need all those tests you asked about because if you need me to be dirty and broken and unclean, then I'll—"

Spinning around, he rushed forward, grabbing her up to drop her on the table beneath the mirror, sending one of the decorative statues tumbling to the floor.

"You will never let another man touch you," he

barked. "No other man will touch you. Not ever. You are mine. All mine. Only mine. Do you fucking understand me?"

Clinging to the surface beneath her, slouched against the wall, trying not to slide down on the slippery glossed surface, Shyla's heart hammered at top speed. "I…I understand."

"Goddamnit," he growled a second before scooping a hand around the side of her head to yank her higher.

Their mouths clashed in a manic kiss that was tongues and teeth and need and fury.

Ferocity erupted within her. Clinging to him, clawing at him, her desperation to hold him and possess him consumed her. She wanted to own him as he claimed to own her. It was madness, hysterical mania that forced them to devour each other like lunatics seeking the high of oblivion.

His fingers curled into the neckline of her dress. He tugged it down hard and the fabric tore, but she didn't care. Shyla arched when he bent to squeeze her breast into his hungry mouth. His tongue circled her nipple. He sucked her hard, forcing her shoulders deeper into the wall.

"Yes," she whimpered, her head rolling, her eyes closed, her body alive, fueled by his passion.

Shyla was still riding that wave when his mouth left her breast. All of a sudden he was turning away, the second statue in hand, though not for long. He launched the figurine against the opposite wall, smashing it to smithereens.

"Goddamnit!" he hollered so loud that she jumped.

The volume scared her, not the man.

Through her own confusion and the befuddling arousal that was making it hard for her to focus, Shyla reached for him.

One of her hands stayed hooked to the front of the cabinet, if she let go, she'd slide right off.

"Phoenix," she murmured, her fingertips just making contact with his back.

"Don't," he snapped, holding up a hand and stepping further away, out of her reach. "Just don't, Shy. Just don't speak. Don't say anything."

She wouldn't speak if he didn't want her to.

Something was going on; she'd never heard him so ragged and it worried her.

The contents of her purse were scattered through the remnants of the smashed ceramics. Into the silence, her phone began to buzz and skitter across the floor.

She wasn't sure what to do. Her shoes had fallen from her feet when Score picked her up. She didn't want to get cut, but if Gavin was the caller, it was only right that she tell him their date was over.

Without looking at her, Score sidestepped to pick up the phone. The statue shards crunched under his feet. He didn't acknowledge her before answering the call.

"Lose this number," he said, his voice little more than a primal snarl. "You think about her again and I'll find where you sleep. I'll put a knife through your eye and let you listen as I slaughter every person you ever cared about. I'll make you drink their blood and fuck their corpses and just when you think you're ready to die, I'll drag your balls out through your eye socket with a fish hook. Needs a very specific skill set that I fucking have… You fucked with the wrong guy's girl, asshole. You breathe wrong and I'll take you down. Think about that."

Hanging up the phone without waiting for a response, Score thought nothing of letting the device fall to the floor again when his hand descended to his side.

That was horrific and disgusting… and hot as hell.

Score turned in a slow arc to pin her under his stare. He immobilized her there, draped on the wall, clinging to the wood beneath her ass, one breast exposed, panting for more.

"I want to go to bed, Phoenix," she purred. "Please take me to bed."

For a second or two, he did nothing. When he did move, he came to stand in front of her. Much to her torment, he didn't touch her or speak.

Shyla pushed herself up onto her knees so she had a more solid base and height enough to tangle her arms around his neck. Using him as her anchor, she pulled herself to him for another kiss, a softer and shorter kiss than the last.

"Will you be mine too?" she asked, her mouth resting

on his. "All mine. Only mine?"

"I've been with other women, Shy," he muttered almost under his breath.

"I know that," she said, kissing him again then letting her arms straighten so she could slide back but leave them on his shoulders. "But from here. Will you?"

He nodded once. "We'll make this work. I don't have a goddamn clue how I'll do it yet. But if it's what you want."

"I want all of you," she said, preparing to slide forward for another kiss.

Before her mouth reached his, he hooked a solid arm around her. Locking it beneath her ribs, he slid her off the table and carried her away from her perch. Shyla coiled her legs around him, but was disappointed that they bypassed his bedroom.

"If I take you to my bed, I'll never let you leave," he said, as if sensing her reaction.

Opening her bedroom door, he took her inside and laid her on the bed. Excitement fizzed within when he kneeled between her legs and grabbed the edges of her dress at her shoulders to drag the already torn material from her body.

He cast it aside and bent over to loosen the strings of her bikini at the back of her neck. His large hand splayed the full span of her back when he scooped her upper body up like she weighed no more than a feather. He untied the back of her top to free her from the fabric.

With only her briefs left on, Shyla was laid out beneath him topless, exposed, vulnerable. The allure of it made her wriggle. Watching how he absorbed his new view of her was a turn on too.

When he bowed over her again, she anticipated a kiss. Instead, he looped the bikini top around her wrists. Shyla was still trying to figure out what he was doing when he extended her arms over her head and pulled the strings hard, tightening them around her wrists.

Her hands were locked in place, tied to one of the padded bars of her headboard. "Phoenix…".

One of his hands moved to her neck as a feral smile curled his lips. Her struggle seemed to please him. Running his hand through her cleavage and down her stomach, he slid it to her hip to loosen the strings on one side then the other. For a second, he left the fabric in place.

Anticipating what he was going to do to her, she stopped struggling. Her desire was immense. Their eyes met and he read it in her, she could tell he did. Still he said nothing, did nothing, he just appreciated the picture of her.

"I want it," she said, considering that maybe he was having second thoughts or needed her to be explicit.

"I know you do, baby. That's why your hands are tied. You're not allowed to touch."

Which was infuriating and frustrating, but also intriguing and arousing. Shyla was completely at his mercy.

THIRTEEN

"I'VE DONE NOTHING in my life to deserve you," Score said.

Shyla didn't agree. He'd served time in prison after being betrayed by those closest to him. No one deserved to face the horrors he'd endured, and death row couldn't have been a picnic. If she could offer him any solace, even for a while, she would.

Arguing wouldn't change his opinion, so she went a different route. "I care about today. I care about tomorrow and the next day and the future we can have. I don't care what you were. I care about what comes next, not the past."

Touching her cleavage again, he drew a fingertip down the center of her torso. This time when he reached the fabric of her bikini briefs, he whipped them away from her body.

Before she got to exhale her inhale of aroused surprise, he ducked down. Scooping her legs over his shoulders, Score's head disappeared between her thighs. Details became hazy as he spoiled her clit, flickering it with his tongue and sucking it between his lips to tickle and torment it.

The pleasure was overwhelming and not at all like the

times she used her fingers on herself. The sensation of his breath on her flesh as he licked and teased her triggered her body to writhe and her moans of ecstasy grow.

If sex was anything like what he was doing with his mouth, kissing and pleasuring her most intimate crevice, then she'd been missing a hell of a ride.

His arms curled all the way around her thighs, pulling them further apart and giving himself more space to work. He slipped his fingers between her folds, learning her contours and creases and worshipping each one.

"Phoenix," she whimpered when his tongue circled her opening, but he didn't push it into her or even use his fingers inside her.

Running his tongue through her juices, he lapped her up and hummed his own enjoyment through her clit. His skill sent skitters of vibrations to the well of pressure inflating inside of her. With his next flicker the balloon of her climax burst, hurling a surge of powerful endorphins to every corner of her whole being.

Her arched body was tense and still braced when he slid up her body to lie beside her. It wasn't until he laid a hand on her diaphragm that she even thought about opening her eyes.

Rolling her head in his direction, Shyla was pleased to have him lying beside her, looming over her. She was too breathless and weak to think about words.

"Just let yourself breathe," he murmured, pointing his middle finger more than the others to draw lines and circles across her abdomen, through her cleavage and over her breasts, enjoying her in his own way.

Under his caress, she tried to regain her equilibrium.

A minute or maybe five went by. With each second, Shyla became more and more aware of his fingertips grazing her flesh, sending heat through her, compelling each hair on her body to attention. She was ready to be commanded by him, all the way.

"Untie me, Phoenix," she breathed. "Please, baby."

"Not a chance," he said, drawing around her areola then leaning over to open his wet lips around her so he could breathe her in.

His act on one incited both to comply with his want. She squirmed beneath him, a smile forming on her mouth as she whined for him.

"Is that your favorite?" she asked, wriggling against the tip of his tongue when he let it tease the apex of her nipple.

"Hmm?"

"That's twice you've played with that one and you've never played with the other… you're playing favorites, sir."

She hadn't thought through what would happen when he stretched over her body to kiss and suckle on her other breast, but Shyla couldn't say she was sorry.

The cotton of his tee-shirt brushed her already sensitive skin. She tried to arch, pressing the small part of her body that was making contact with his deeper against him, eager to know what it would be like to have all of him lying above her.

"Phoenix. Oh, God, Phoenix, please… I want you inside me."

He planted a hand on her stomach, holding her down flat, and ripped his mouth away. "That's enough," he said, vaulting up off the bed.

Panic zipped over her. "What? No! Please, I'll be good. I'll be quiet. I'll be whatever you need. If you untie me there must be something I can do for you. Something. Anything." Frustration clenched her teeth. "God, I'm an idiot."

"Hey!" he barked, whipping around to show the glare on his face. "Don't talk shit about my girl."

Surprised by his vehemence, she blinked a couple of times. Clarity hit hard, yet it curved her lips. "Oh wow… I'm your girl now."

Some of his frown receded after he got back on the bed to lay the length of her. "Yes, you are," he said, nuzzling her mouth. "I will own you, Shyla Bellamy. I don't care what it takes."

Grabbing for his kiss, she wished she could do more than raise her head to respond to what his mouth offered. She was about to beg for her hands again when he stole his mouth away to turn his head.

The frown on his face suggested he wasn't as intoxicated as her.

"What?" she whispered, surprised by her shortness of breath. "Baby, what—"

"Shh," he said, touching her lips with his fingertips for a brief moment before replacing them with his lips.

His kiss was short; she was left wanting more when he pounced off the bed without making a sound. Putting a finger to his lips as an indication that she should be quiet, he crept out of the room, leaving her alone, tied to the bed.

Naked and exposed, Shyla was completely at the mercy of whoever walked in. For some reason, Score's instruction to stay silent translated into her staying still too, so she didn't move a muscle.

Just a moment ago, she'd been languishing in the kiss of her could-be lover. In a quick turnaround from that ecstasy, her priority was not descending into a full-blown panic attack. If something happened out there, she wouldn't be able to help Score.

"Hey, boss!" Fish's happy exclamation reverberated down the hallway. Shyla blew out a breath of relief. But he wasn't as happy the next time he spoke. "What happened here?"

Oh no! They'd left a helluva mess on the floor outside the elevators.

"You see nothing. You say nothing," Score's voice was so low that she only just heard his words.

"Sure. Sure thing," Fish said, always eager to please. "But uh… you coming to the club, boss?"

"Later," he said. "You get things started."

"For real?" The exuberance in Fish's voice made her smile. He was such a sweetheart. "I won't let you down, boss. I won't!"

The sound of the elevator carried to her. She could only guess that he'd left until Score came sauntering into the room. Standing at the foot of the bed, he didn't say anything, he just studied her in silence, his brow tense.

The power of his concentration made her forget

about her almost panic and slide into that cozy cloud he'd taken her to before.

"You know, a picture would last longer," she said, meaning to tease. Shyla didn't expect him to retrieve his phone from his back pocket or for him to hold it up to take a shot of her strewn across the bed. "Oh my God!"

Twisting her arms across each other, she managed to get onto her chest, and tugged her knees up under her. With her wrists still bound, there was nowhere else for her to go. The ribbon from her hair had given up long ago, her locks were a mass of tangles and kinks falling into her face.

"Want to give me any more angles?"

Spitting her hair from her mouth, her shoulders were burning, but she was helpless. "Phoenix!"

"Relax," he said and appeared on the bed again, lying at her side.

She peeked at him under her arm as he pushed her loose hair up out of her field of vision. "What if someone sees those?"

He let her hair fall. "No one steals from me, Shy. What's mine is mine. You trust that I wouldn't share you."

After what he'd said to Gavin in the lobby, yeah, she could trust that he wasn't the type to flash her around. Sliding her knees out from under her, she sank down on her stomach, her arms still stretched over her head.

Shyla couldn't even see through her hair, but she smiled anyway. "If you seal your promise with a kiss, I will," she said, hoping he understood her request was more about her need for his mouth than any lack of faith.

With a heavy hand, he pushed her hair away, once and twice until he could find her mouth to give her what she'd asked for. "I have to go to work."

"Fish has got it," she said, trying to lift her shoulder to his. She couldn't rise that far and ended up rolling onto her side instead, which took some of the pressure off her shoulders. "This has got to be more fun than work." She let her eyes bob down. "Look, naked woman."

"I noticed," he said and pressured her shoulder to put her on her back again. But as he admired her, the heat of his regard grew. Having that effect on him made her squirm. As she moved, he sighed, peaking her nipples under the cascade of his breath. "I have to go."

"I'll let you do anything to me, Phoenix… Anything."

"That's *why* I have to leave."

All this time, she'd been completely naked while he was fully clothed. It was only as he slipped off the bed again that she regretted not having a chance to see him as he'd seen her. He went over to her closet to explore inside.

"What if I said you *have* to have sex with me," she said, recognizing her urgency.

But he didn't sound worried. "And if I don't, you'll what? Murder my entire family? Good luck. You'd be doing me a favor. Take Razer out first or he'll take you down."

"I meant, I won't let you do anything to me except have sex with me."

"You're in such a hurry, Little Lamb," he said, pulling clothes and underwear from her closet to dump them on top of the dresser. "This is what you wear tomorrow."

"Tomorrow?" she asked. "What about tonight?"

"Tonight you won't need clothes. I'll lock down the elevator before I leave so you'll only be able to get out, in case there's a fire. I'll be the only one allowed in." Getting back on the bed, he drew a line from her throat to her cleavage, down the middle of her body until he sank his finger between her folds to begin massaging her clit. "Or I could just leave you right here."

Her hips moved in time with the bliss of his stimulating finger. "Tied to the bed?" she asked. "What if I have to pee?"

"Then you'll make a mess," he said, pressing her harder.

A whine of desire warmed her lips. "Make love to me, Phoenix."

But he shook his head and kissed her again. "No time."

"If we only had time for one thing, why did you choose… what you did instead of going all the way with me?"

"Do you like this?" he asked, his mouth resting on

hers. In reply, she opened her legs further until she slid a foot over his leg to nestle it between his. Just for good measure, she nodded. "It feel good when I ate your pussy?" She nodded again. "That felt good. What you're asking for won't feel good."

When he eased back, stealing his mouth from hers, she clamped her legs tight together, twisting them around his hand to trap it in place. She didn't want him to stop, she just wanted to pause for a second, and didn't want him to escape.

"I dream about having you inside me, Phoenix. I want to—"

"I'm a big guy, baby, and you're virgin territory," he said. "It will hurt and I'm not ready to do that to you yet."

She'd heard that the first time could be uncomfortable. He was over a foot taller than her, so it wasn't a leap that his body would be in proportion. Hearing him say he wasn't ready altered her perception. It wasn't only about her, he had to be ready too.

"Okay," she said. "We'll wait until you're mad at me or something."

"I was mad tonight," he said. "Did I hurt you?"

The last thing she'd meant to imply was that he'd take his anger out on her. "No, but you'll have to one day if the first time is going to hurt…" He'd been generous with her and once again, he got nothing from the deal. "Is there something I can do?"

His hand came out from between her thighs, shattering her illusion. She'd thought her hold on him was secure, turned out he was just being polite.

"Another guy is never the answer," he said, grabbing her chin to snatch her attention up. "I don't give a damn what we're fighting about. That thought ever comes in your head again, you scrub it out of there, or I'll do it for you… Never underestimate what I'll do to any man who thinks about coming anywhere near you."

After their phone encounter, Gavin would never even look her way again.

She shivered. "I thought I was doing a good thing," she said. "Solving a problem. Until you found out I hadn't had sex, we were great. I wanted us to be great again. I thought having sex would be the way to do that. I wasn't attracted to Gavin."

Not like she was to Score, but such potent attraction couldn't be common. Her need for him was so consuming that it overwhelmed in the most incredible way. Her dream would be to lose herself in it forever.

"Which is the only reason he's still breathing," he said, narrowing his eyes in a way that made her think he couldn't quite figure her out. "You're with a McDade now, Shyla. Do you understand what that means? You can't play games with people. Every interaction you have has the potential to get someone killed."

"Killed?" she asked, leaning away. "What are—"

"Sure I've cut ties with the family, but I'm still one of them. I'll always be one of them… which means if this works out, you're one of them too. Insulting or upsetting a McDade woman can get a guy killed… Seducing you, even thinking about seducing you… baby, there are veteran intelligence agents who'd wilt at word we're coming for them."

Shyla hadn't thought about how the wider world would react to the news they were together. With him illuminating reality, she had a better understanding of his need for discretion.

"I wouldn't ever ask—"

"You don't have to ask," he said. "Some guy shouts at you for stealing his cab and a wannabe whoever overhears, he'll bring me the guy's corpse just to impress me. People want in. Biz and me might not be tight, but Burl listens to me… Even when I don't want him to."

"What about Doran?"

He shrugged. "Did most of his growing up while I was inside. But he's smart. Knows to stay off Biz's radar. Likes the world to think he's a punk, but he knows what he's doing… Knows more than I did at his age." He sat up. "Never let a bitch set him up for murder."

Trying to tug her hands free to sit up at his side to comfort him was futile. No matter how she twisted and pulled, Shyla couldn't free herself. Score must have heard her efforts because he turned to look over his shoulder.

He watched until she gave up and sagged into the bed. "Help me," she said. "Please."

Flipping over, he reached up to loosen her bonds. "I've been tying people up since before I could walk," he said. "You won't get out of my knots."

The minute the string slackened, she pulled her hands down and looped her arms around his neck. "Kiss me again."

"Not a chance," he said, raising the circle of her arms to duck out from beneath them. "Get yourself something to eat. Clean up in the foyer."

He left the bed, tugging down his tee-shirt and running a hand through his hair.

She rose onto her elbows. "Will you come home to me early?"

"Not tonight," he said and must have read her disappointment. "We want to keep this quiet, Shy."

"I understand," she said on a sigh and sat up, crossing her legs. "Should I call Gavin?"

His scowl snapped into place. "The fucker from tonight? No, never talk to him again. Never, Shy. I don't give a damn if he approaches you, you walk away and call me immediately."

"What would you do to him?"

A moment of nothing passed and then his jaw shifted as clarity crossed his expression. "You want me to pound on guys to turn you on, I'll do it," he said. "You wouldn't be the first woman turned on by seeing others in pain."

Scrambling up to her feet, she ran to the corner of the bed and launched her upper body forward, catching her hands on his shoulders. "I don't care about their pain. I care about your want," she said, trying to pull him closer. "Seeing them hurt wouldn't mean anything to me. But just the idea that you could want me so much to protect me like that—"

Grabbing her thighs, he pulled them out from under her, sending her onto her back with a thud. Before she could breathe in, he was on top of her, dragging her leg up, curling it around his hip.

"Possessing you is all that matters to me," he growled

and crushed his mouth onto hers.

Wrapping her arms around his neck and her legs around his body, she was enamored by the weight of him pinning her down, but cursed their height difference. It limited her to grinding herself against his torso.

His kiss deepened. She ran a hand down his back to gather his tee-shirt in her fist. The draft on his lower back must have alerted him to what she was doing because he broke their kiss.

"You're a masochist," she breathed when he forced her limbs away from his body to free himself.

He stood up again, leaving her there, undone and desperate, but too boneless to fight him.

"No, baby," he said, rubbing a hand over his groin like he was in discomfort. "You're not my pain, you're my pleasure... No playing tonight. That sweet spot of yours is mine to touch, no one else's."

"Not even mine?" she asked, managing to drop the back of her hand to her forehead.

"Not unless you're under orders... I'm in charge of your pleasure."

"And my pain," she whined, pressing her legs together and drawing up her knees. "It's torture."

He might have been amused; Shyla's vision was too hazy to tell. "It's worth it."

"It's not fair. I've been waiting twenty-nine years to be filled by you... You had sex last week..." In a slow blink, she frowned at herself. "So to speak, I... I don't think you were having sex last week." Though he had technically ended whatever they'd started. From the way Fish talked of the club, they didn't specialize in jazz. Pushing her weight to her elbows, she tipped her head up to look at him. "All mine? Only mine?"

Coming to the corner of the bed, he leaned over her to lay a hand on her head. "All. Only."

She smiled. Whatever had come before, she wanted him as only hers from then on.

Sliding her foot forward, she was about to touch the denim of his jeans with her toe when he turned and left the room. It took her a minute to realize that his next stop would be the club.

Shyla got with it and leaped off the bed to hurry after him, slowing at the sight of the mess of the foyer. Keeping her distance, she relaxed against the corner between foyer and hallway.

"You know," she said, drawing his attention around from where he was waiting for the elevator. "If I'm going to be a McDade woman, you'll need to teach me how to protect you from other women."

"Fighting?" he said, sauntering over and planting a forearm on the angle of the corner high above her. "Baby, you'll never have to."

"All. Only."

The elevator opened and he ducked to kiss her hairline. "Behave yourself 'til I get back," he said and headed into the elevator.

"Implying I can be naughty when you return," she called out just as the elevator doors started to close.

He winked and then was gone.

Breathing out, Shyla scanned the mess on the floor. She had her work cut out, but the evidence of their passion didn't make her sorry. Every second she spent cleaning up after them would be a reminder of what they'd done. With a grin on her face, she pushed off the wall. It was going to be a night well spent.

FOURTEEN

SCORE'S BEDROOM DOOR was open the following morning. Walking past it without going in was torture. The temptation alone warmed her, which gave her a better appreciation of his rules.

Wondering about how she'd ever get any work done after they did have sex, Shyla came up with question after question. How would they tell Beeks and Fish? Would they share a bedroom or keep their separate spaces?

Two of three of her men were present. Fish's waffles were cooking; she figured he'd want juice too. She poured some for him and took it to where he was seated at the kitchen island.

"Do you have any tattoos?" he asked her, taking the glass.

"No."

Twisting around in his stool, he looked to Beeks who was, as always for that time of day, working on the dining table. "You got any Beeks?"

"Yeah, a big shiny one that says 'Kiss My Ass', want to see it?"

"Yeah, I do," Fish said, leaping off his stool.

Shyla laid a hand on his arm while Beeks glared over

the top of his glasses. "I think he was kidding, honey."

"Oh," Fish said, sinking back onto his stool and then shrugging off his disappointment to show her his forearm tattoo. "You like mine?"

"It's beautiful, honey. I've seen it before."

"Got it in prison, but I want another one." She returned to her waffles and was just opening the press when Score came around the end of the hallway wall. "Hey, boss!"

Score crossed to his stool, the one nearest the window, ignoring Fish who turned his stool in time with his boss's progress. Shyla went to the coffee machine to pour coffee for Score as she did every day. Just like any other day, nothing different, any other day, boring, normal day. Though she repeated the statements to herself, her hormones weren't paying much attention.

"I've got some stuff for you to read, Score," Beeks said. "Let me find it."

Retrieving his phone from his pocket, he hunched over it as he did every morning.

"Hey, boss," Fish said. "Don't the McDade's have like a symbol or something? What's their symbol?"

"The stag," Score mumbled.

"Yeah! That's it," Fish exclaimed, slapping the edge of the island. "Is that the tattoo on your back?"

Shyla carried Score's coffee around to him. "No, that's a phoenix," she said and put the cup down. She straightened up again only to note that all of the men were looking at her. "What?"

"How do you know what's on Score's back?" Fish asked.

While her friend's question was innocent, Score's interest was more probing. "Yeah, Miss Bellamy, how do you know that?"

"I… I don't know. We live together, I guess I saw it in passing."

Fish laughed and leaned over to hit the counter by Score. "Maybe she's perving on you in the shower, boss."

If instinct was in charge, she'd press her palms to her warm face and ask if they could turn up the AC. Hearing Fish guffaw was easier than feeling Score watching her. Now he probably felt violated and assumed she crept into his room to slobber on him while he slept.

"How did you see it?" she asked, going around to put the waffles on the plate. "You perving on him too?"

Fish's smile dropped. "No. No, Shy. I saw it in the gym, man, I never, I wouldn't…"

The panic in his voice made her wary. Fish always seemed so easy and relaxed around Score, and he hadn't minded implicating her. Maybe implying a male would violate a McDade was different to one being admired by a female.

"Quit your jabbering," Beeks said. "He doesn't give a shit about either of you gawking."

Beeks wasn't even looking, but seemed to be right. Score was done paying attention and was reading his phone again. Fish sort of relaxed and didn't even comment when she started round the island to serve his waffles to Score.

"Does every McDade have a stag tattoo?" she asked without really caring who answered.

"Those who swear lifetime allegiance," Fish said. "That's what I heard."

"Where is yours, Score?" she asked, licking cream from her fingers. "What does it look like?"

Pulling down the neck of his tee-shirt, he showed her the black ink just beneath his collarbone on the left side of his chest. The silhouette of a stag's head faced forward with the antlers slightly separate from the head.

"Here, read this," Beeks said.

Score twisted away. Shyla got even closer, inspecting the ink on his skin. Fish bounced off his stool to go get whatever Beeks was waving around. Insanity seized her. That was the only explanation for what she did next. Leaning in, she touched the stag with the tip of her tongue.

The contact made Score turn fast and she leaped back; no one else seemed to notice the sudden movement. His gaze zeroed in on her. Despite his judgement, she clasped her hands at her back, and sucked on her lip while shrugging. She hadn't meant to lick him, it just happened… Maybe she was losing her mind.

"Can I have waffles, Shyla?" Fish asked like it was the first time.

Either he was too polite to point out that she'd given his food to someone else, or he'd forgotten the last plate was meant to be for him.

"Sure, honey," she said, dragging her eyes away from Score to return to the other side of the island to whip up another batch.

When they were cooking, Fish returned to his previous point. "You wanna come get a tattoo with me, Shyla?" he asked. "We could get the same as Score's. Be like McDades."

"No," Score barked before she could respond. In an unusual move, he looked both of them square in the eye, one after the other. "I don't want either of you taking the mark of the family."

It might be irrational, but she was a little insulted by his vehemence.

"You can get it removed," Fish said, taking Score's assertion in a different way. "If you're really pissed at them."

"I'd go to war for my family, if I was called in," Score said, using the side of his fork to cut into the waffle. "Even if I fucking hated them all, that's what this mark means. Once it's on, it doesn't go away."

He was still part of the brethren, even if he didn't want any ties to them.

"Maybe we could come up with our own mark," Fish said. "All of us get something the same. Start our own posse…" Twisting around, he left just one elbow on the counter. "Beeks, you wanna get a tattoo with us? Boss, you'd get another one, right?"

"Shyla isn't getting a tattoo," Score said, reading his phone and eating at the same time. "Her skin stays the way it is."

Virgin, like the rest of her. She assumed that's what he meant.

"I don't mind needles," she said, cutting up some fruit to add to Fish's waffles. "But I don't think I could sit still long enough to be tattooed… doesn't it take a long time?"

"Depends where you get it and how big."

"Does it hurt?" she asked, building his plate and taking it to him.

Fish touched the inside of his wrist. "Hurts here and like your fingers and stuff... Shoulder doesn't hurt... Butt wouldn't hurt."

"I wouldn't get it somewhere I couldn't see it," she said, scooping some cream from the edge of his plate. "The artist could tattoo whatever he wanted, and I would never know what it was."

"We'd all get them at the same time," Fish said. "We'd be there to make sure no one tattooed any dicks on you or anything."

"Oh, well that's nice, thank you," she said, sucking her finger clean and then going to her station to clean up. "Do you really think that would be a comfortable experience for me? The three of you lined up behind some tattoo artist while I lift up my skirt? No, thank you. I think I'll agree with Score, no tattoos for me."

Fish made a sound of disappointment. Her gaze drifted to Score. For a brief flash, she caught him looking at her. Whether she would be interested in wearing a mark for him or not, she was coming to learn that following his orders, and they were orders, paid dividends in other areas.

"Aww, but how will we know you're in the gang?" Fish asked.

Shyla didn't want him to be disappointed. It was nice that he included her when really, she wasn't part of their gang outside the apartment.

"Why don't you buy me a nice piece of jewelry? I'll wear it every day and you'll know it means I'm part of your gang."

"But we're the only ones who'll know."

"True," she said, putting food items away. "But to be honest, I don't really want to be out on the street myself, or in a store somewhere oblivious and have someone come over and start beating on me because my gang upset them... I've never thrown a punch in my life. I'd be useless in a fight."

"I'll teach you to fight," Fish said.

"No, you won't," Score said, pushing his plate away.

Fish finished his food. Score stood up to return whatever Beeks had given him. They exchanged a few whispers while she finished with her cleaning up. Shyla was about to ask if they wanted more coffee when Beeks got up. Score backed away, giving him space to go to Fish.

"Time to get some work done, boy, come on," Beeks said, smacking Fish's shoulder, urging him towards the elevator.

She expected Score to follow. Instead, he brought his coffee cup around to her side of the island and slid it onto the counter next to the sink. At that side of the island, the hallway partition blocked them from the view of those at the elevators.

"No tattoos," he murmured, moving closer and scooping a hand under her skirt to grip her ass.

"I know," she whispered in response, letting him crowd her against the sink. "I heard you."

Opening her hands on his torso, she rose as high as she could on her tiptoes. Bending his knees, Score's hand left her ass to slide around to her waist. Like the previous day, he locked his forearm under her ribs and raised her off her feet. Her legs dangled toward the floor when he straightened up.

"Perving on me in the shower, huh?" he asked, boosting her higher to line up their mouths.

She smiled and had to work to restrain her laugh. "It wasn't like that. It was an accident."

"Tell me later," he said.

Her hope was automatic. "You'll be home?"

"Not for dinner, we have auditions, but tonight."

She nodded and mouthed, "Okay."

He kissed her quick. Just as she thought he might come back for more, Fish called out. "Boss, elevator's here… Hey, where's he at?"

"Behave," Score said, brushing his nose across hers before putting her on her feet and striding away.

Somehow, he always left her breathless and damn if she wasn't grateful for that every second.

FIFTEEN

SHYLA WAS OUT later that day when her phone buzzed. The alert that showed up stopped her dead in the street.

She'd been so busy losing herself in her new life that the old one was becoming a sporadic memory. It was coming back for her just when she'd begun to relax.

The news left her with another problem. For once, fortune put her in an advantageous position, geographically anyway. Shyla fired off a text to Beeks and adjusted her route.

Score wanted her to share everything with him and that was just fine, but the new predicament wasn't a part of her life with him. It came from her past. Dragging him into it when he had his own issues to deal with wouldn't be right. The last thing she needed to do to their young relationship was strain it by begging emotional support.

Score, the club, wasn't that far away. Fish talked about the club like the three men were always there. Even though going was convenient because she was out and about, Shyla would be lying if she denied her desire to see what the place was like inside. It wouldn't be open to the public that early in the day. Score couldn't be upset at her if the only thing she saw were nude, or almost nude, women. She had the same anatomy they did.

That was her reasoning until she walked in. Naivety smacked her hard. The dozens of women seated around the place didn't have figures she'd recognize in her own. A poster outside declared auditions were open. Hence, she supposed, why all the females were there.

The club itself was impressive. With seating at the top of the room and a bar to the right, the long room had a stage at the end. A mezzanine with its own podiums overlooked the main dance area.

A big guy in a black shirt came over to her carrying a clipboard. Shyla was still gaping at the sequins and nipple tassels and the sheer volume of svelte yet ample flesh on each of the gorgeous females.

"What's your name, sweetheart?" the guy asked.

He was poised to write on the clipboard. It took her a minute to figure out that he thought she was there to audition too.

The assumption made her grin. Shyla wondered what kind of woman showed up to an audition in denim cutoffs and a kaftan. There wasn't a sequin or a string anywhere on her outfit. On top of that, she was carrying a paper grocery bag and had her hippie bag slung across her body.

"Oh no," she said. "I'm not here to audition." She laughed. "I'm a C cup and only five foot two inches tall, I'm not…"

Her words trailed off when she realized he was scanning down the form and filling in what she was saying.

He gave her the once over. "You got long hair that's hot, could be your thing." She touched the end of the long high ponytail that hung over her shoulder. Knowing that Score liked it, she was learning to leave her hair looser. "The girls here will give you their surgeon's details. Look around, you see a pair you like, go to their guy. The boss might keep you a spot if he likes what you've got."

The boss… Score. He'd told her not to consider cosmetic surgery. He probably wouldn't appreciate this guy telling her to peruse the breasts in the room and pick a pair like she was choosing drapes for the living room.

"Here he comes."

The guy tucked his clipboard under his arm. She glanced over her shoulder. Score, Beeks, and Fish were coming through the door at the head of the club.

Turning her back on them, Shyla tried to hide herself. Maybe showing up without invitation wasn't such a great idea after all.

"Yo, boss," the guy in front of her said. "What size you want the cans on this one? She says she'll get 'em done if we hold her a spot."

Shyla didn't even want to turn and look, so could only guess that the trio were heading their way. The sense of anticipation from all the women sitting around bubbled up.

In contrast to the other females' interest, Shyla cringed when she was forced to look up at the three men who'd joined them.

Score's expression hardened in a heartbeat.

He didn't say a word to her, he just switched his attention to the clipboard guy and calm as anything said, "You're fired." While the guy blanched and his jaw sank, Score turned to Beeks. "Take care of this."

Snatching her hand, Score pulled her away from the stuttering clipboard guy. Dragging her down the length of the room, past the curious dancers and the stage, he towed her into an office secreted in the back. Well, it wasn't exactly secreted. There were black blinds over the window, which made it hard to make out. The door was there, she just hadn't seen it.

Score pulled her forward, swinging her into the office while he slammed the door at his back. "What happened?" he demanded.

Shyla tossed her hair from her face and put the groceries on the desk. "Nothing happened."

"Why the fuck is he talking about your tits?"

Had he reserved his rage for her? That was probably better than him unloading on the guy who'd just lost his job.

"It was a misunderstanding," she said, setting a hand on her hip.

He lunged toward her, his mouth open, but stopped within a breath of her. Controlling himself, he sealed his lips to silently seethe.

He didn't speak again, she guessed, until he trusted himself not to overreact. "A… how the fuck are your tits a misunderstanding?"

Not sure quite how to take his anger, Shyla touched his tee-shirt. "Are you really mad at me?"

Some of his anger ebbed. "I'm mad he talked about you like that."

Tipping her head back, she licked her lips. "Will kissing me calm you down?"

"No, kissing you never calms me down," he said and walked away from her finger to go around the desk. "Is that why you came?"

"For kisses? No, I came to talk to Beeks." Turning toward the wall, she couldn't see into the club because the blinds were down. "There are a lot of girls out there."

"Auditions."

"I got that," she said, creeping around the desk. "I think you should call your next club Shy's."

"Do you?"

She propped herself against the desk at his side. What she really wanted to do was sink into his lap, but she didn't have the courage for that yet.

"Mm hmm," she said, nodding.

"Let's see how this one does before you start auditioning guys to get their shit off for you."

"I don't want male strippers," she said, leaning back.

Although she hadn't really been looking, he turned over the paper on his desk to hide it from her. Until he'd done that, she hadn't cared about his paperwork.

"This isn't a strip joint. They're dancers." Who dance wearing very little, she got that. "You prefer I work with women?"

"Yes," she said. "Those women out there are professionals, here to earn a wage. If there are semi-naked male dancers, that means drunk, panting female customers. And let's be honest, you put every other guy on the planet to shame. Every night, you'd have different women pawing at you, seducing you… I don't want them treating you like a piece of meat." She grinned and ducked down. "That's my job."

He didn't smile. "Why are you here, Lamb?"

She was sure she'd already answered that. "To talk to Beeks."

"I'm here. Talk to me."

Peeking over her shoulder, she checked that the door was still closed and ventured to be daring. "The door's closed…"

"If this is what you're like before sex, I'll need to put you on a sedative after," he said.

Score didn't make jokes, not in any direct way, but she smiled anyway. "I'm sorry. I'm sure if we just did it I'd calm down."

One of his brows rose at a deliberate, slow pace. "You think after we have sex, you won't want sex?"

She shrugged. "Won't I?"

Score pulled his chair closer to the desk and opened a laptop. "Got a lot to learn, Lamb."

On a sigh, she gripped the edge of the desk to slide her butt onto it. "I wish I knew how."

"You'll do what I tell you."

That much was obvious. Shyla was eager to receive his orders; Score wasn't as impatient.

"I didn't mean that," she said, slithering off the desk to sink down on her knees at his side. "I wish I knew how to make you feel like I feel when we're together… I wish I knew how to seduce you."

Without turning the chair, Score pushed back to look down at her. On an exhale, he reached for her face. When his fingers caressed her jaw, she closed her eyes and moved to appreciate his touch.

"Why do you need Beeks?"

He'd said he wanted all of her and was proving he wouldn't forget his purpose.

"I got an alert, Stan's funeral is the day after tomorrow. I need the day off."

"You came to ask Beeks?"

"I was in the neighborhood."

"Are you sure you want to be there?"

Shyla hadn't considered not going. "He was my family, the last of my family."

"Your brother is alive," he said. "You shouldn't go—"

"I won't let Mick drive me away," Shyla said, wearing a frown. "I'm amazed that you'd be scared of—"

His fingertips met her lips. "You shouldn't go alone."

Oops, she'd jumped in early. "If I'm not working, you shouldn't have to give up Fish too."

"I'm coming with you."

Stunned, she hadn't expected he'd want to join her. "But you don't want anyone to know we're together. How will you—"

"We'll go together."

That was his decision; she wouldn't question it. In truth, having him at her side would be an honor. The idea of being anywhere *with* him excited her. The more she thought about it, the more overwhelmed she became. Mick sure wouldn't try any of his shit with Score in her vicinity.

"Sometimes I can't get over how incredible you are," she said, sliding her hand beneath the arm of his chair onto his thigh.

"That's a minority opinion," he said, taking his hand from her face to type something into the laptop.

Shyla couldn't drag her focus from him for long enough to check out the screen. "Do you talk to them?"

"Who?" he asked, preoccupied with the laptop.

"Your family."

His fingers stopped. "You don't need to think about my family. The further away you can stay from them, the better."

"I'd like to meet them one day. What would they think about me? About us?"

"I don't need my family's permission for squat."

The tension in his voice was growing with each new word. Pushing him on the subject wasn't a good idea, but Shyla wanted to know him like he wanted to know her.

"They'd hate me, wouldn't they?"

She wasn't offended. Shyla would be the first to admit she wasn't suited to the gangster lifestyle. Calling herself a liability was an understatement.

"They don't all think one way," he said, a harsh edge to his words. "The family line is set by Burl, and we wouldn't get his blessing."

So although the McDades didn't all think the same way, no one in the family would voice their disagreement outside their ranks. Burl was Score's father, the McDade patriarch. He told the world the McDades position and no one would contradict him.

"Does that bother you?" she asked.

Learning that someone wouldn't like her wasn't fun, but it didn't surprise her. It would only be a problem for them if it was a problem for Score.

He exhaled and leaned back in his chair to look down at her again. "We don't give a damn about them."

"You said Burl listens to you, so you must still talk to him. And if Biz doesn't like that—"

"If Biz doesn't like that, he can go fuck himself."

The office door opened just in time for whoever came in to hear those last few words. Boosting higher on her knees, she looked over the top of the desk. Beeks and Fish were standing in the doorway, probably not sure if they should retreat.

"My fault," Shyla said, brushing her hands down her thighs as she stood up. "Stan's funeral is the day after tomorrow."

"I got your text," Beeks said, distracted intrigue in his tone. "You want the day off."

"You worried about the dick from the house," Fish asked, squeezing around the frowning Beeks to head for the couch under the blinds.

"Not anymore," she said, shifting the angle of her purse. "Score says he'll come with me."

Fish blinked in surprise. Shyla didn't dare look at Beeks, but heard the door close, so she guessed he was coming inside to join them.

Once he'd had a few seconds to process, Fish smiled.

"Just like I told the guy, Score takes care of problems."

"Yeah, he does," she said, smiling when Beeks crossed between her and Fish to sit on the couch with him. "It probably won't be a big deal."

"Just in case, it's good to have someone with you," Beeks said. Whatever his frown had been for, he obviously got over it. "What time is the service?"

"Eleven," she said.

"Next couple of nights are on you two," Score said, laying his forearms on the desk.

"We'll take care of everything," Beeks said. "Want to delay the auditions?"

"No," Score said, closing the laptop and standing up.

Dwarfed by his form, Shyla didn't want to move, though she probably should. Beeks was already thinking something. Even though she didn't know exactly what it was, his curiosity was obvious.

Score didn't help diminish his lawyer's assumptions when he tucked his hand under her hair to grip the back of her neck. "Staying for it?"

The crazy question took her focus from Beeks' suspicions. "Am I staying to watch a bunch of women shake their tail feathers?"

Though the offer was sweet, she couldn't imagine much would be more uncomfortable.

Fish bounced to the edge of the couch. "You should stay… You should hang out here more."

"I have things to do," she said, reaching over the desk to snag her grocery bag.

Her hip pressed into Score's thigh. That contact gave her a flash of what else they might do if they were alone and she bent over his desk.

"Auditions will run late," Beeks said. "We'll probably order food here."

"Sure," she said, neglecting to tell him that Score had already said they wouldn't be back for dinner that night.

Loathed as she was to tear herself away, there was no reason for her to stay. Walking toward the door, she glanced at all of them. Thinking of them as family was premature, but she did have a habit of getting too attached.

Death had taken the last person she'd gotten too attached to. Soon she'd have to say goodbye to him. If she lost any of the trio around her, it wouldn't be such a final end, but it would be just as painful.

SIXTEEN

BEING SO USED to routine probably wasn't a good thing. That was what Shyla decided later that night. Her trio usually came back for dinner and then went to the club again. With the auditions preventing them from returning for dinner, she didn't have any distractions to keep her busy. The when kept her pacing; first in front of the fireplace and then out on the terrace.

The night air didn't calm her down. She couldn't tell which was making her edgier, not knowing when Score would come back or Stan's funeral. The alert she'd gotten came from the funeral directors. Mick hadn't let her know, but she couldn't blame him for that. He'd asked for a way to get in touch with her and she hadn't provided one.

Shyla seriously doubted he'd have been kind enough to extend an invitation even if he did have her details. In spite of his animosity, she wouldn't let him make her feel unwelcome. Everything was all over the place. She didn't know what to think. Feeling adrift, with no one to lean on, gave her a much greater appreciation for what she'd had with Bernard and Stan.

In her days with them, there wasn't much to be stressed about. But if she ever was, the two men didn't care if she went off on a rant about whatever it was.

The apartment she'd grown to love wasn't offering her much comfort. It had never felt so big or so empty. She didn't have a tub in her bathroom, so she settled for a long shower instead. The heat of the soothing water did help for a while, it worked as a distraction. No distraction could last.

Still wrapped in just her towel, Shyla went onto her terrace to breathe in the evening air. Evening may not be the right word, last she'd looked at the clock, it was approaching midnight.

Closing her eyes, she held the rail and inhaled. Score would be with her. Whatever Mick threw at them, Score would take care of it. Focusing on that idea, she came to realize that it wasn't Mick she was worried about. Score was the one making her anxious. In such an emotional setting, surrounded by memories of Stan, she was likely to lose control. He'd see her crazy and that could be enough to put him off.

Shyla tried to tell herself that it wouldn't happen. That he wouldn't break ties with her if she got emotional, but she just didn't know.

To the side of where she stood, light burst onto the terrace. The neat rectangle could only have come from one place: Score's room.

She went to the window just in time to see him pull his tee-shirt off over his head. When he was free of it, he spotted her, so she lifted her hand in a static wave.

He came over to slide the door open. "What you doing out there like that?"

"I wanted to breathe for a minute," she said, aware of how close they were. Though while on opposing sides of the doorway, there was a clear line they shouldn't cross. "Did you get the women you needed?"

He nodded. "I'm gonna take a shower, get some sleep."

That could've been either a statement of his intent or an order for her to follow. "Don't mind me," she said in an attempt at a joke.

"You need your rest too. It's after midnight."

Shyla didn't have the energy to seduce him and probably wouldn't be worth much to him if he tried to close the deal.

"Okay," she said, thinking about all the things she wanted to say.

That was her limit. Saying just one thing was beyond her ability. If she opened the floodgates, everything would come flowing out. Even the things definitely better kept to herself.

She retreated one step and then another. The way he was looking into her suggested he recognized something was on her mind. Already he was learning her moods and tells, yet she still felt completely at sea when it came to figuring him out.

***

GOING TO BED with Score in the room next to her wasn't easy, especially knowing his door was open. One thought kept cropping up. Someday, if they lasted, he'd have to see her worked up in more than just a sexual way.

That was why when she eventually glanced at her clock and read it was two thirty, Shyla sat up and tossed her covers away. Somewhere along the way, she'd stopped worrying about Mick and started to worry about how long her relationship with Score could last if she hid parts of herself. He said he wanted to learn all of her and anxiety was a part of her. Not one of the most alluring parts, sure, but it existed.

Getting out of bed, she stalked out her bedroom, across the hallway and straight into Score's room. Shyla didn't even think about the rules or that it might anger him; she had something to say and she had to say it.

A lot of her agitation faded when confronting the sight of him in bed, sleeping on his front, the covers at his hips, just like on her first day there. Seeing him calmed her. She could've stayed there all night, just watching him sleep. She didn't know how long she did stand there. It could've been a minute or an hour. One of his exhales was louder than the others; the sound snapped her out of her trance.

Climbing onto the bed on her feet and sinking down to sit at his side, she ran her fingers through his hair. Being close to him warmed her heart. She slid down onto her side and admired him while still combing her fingers through his hair.

He grumbled something, which made her smile. It didn't make sense as words, but she found herself wondering if he talked in his sleep or if he snored. More questions swirled in her mind. Did he always sleep in the middle of the bed or did he have a preferred side? Understanding what he meant about intimacy that wasn't sexual, she wriggled closer.

"Phoenix," she whispered and subdued a laugh when he frowned. Even in his sleep he could be severe. "Baby?"

His breathing changed and his eyelids ascended a fraction, not much, just enough to check who was disturbing him.

"Lamb," he groaned. "Go back to bed."

"I want to talk to you," she said, enjoying the sensation of his hair between her fingers.

"You hurt?"

Although she didn't have any physical injuries, she glanced down at herself. "No."

"In danger?"

So those were the only two acceptable reasons for her to intrude? He probably didn't think she'd wake him for anything less.

"No. I'm worried about us."

"We're fine," he mumbled, his eyes shut again.

"Yeah, but I'm worried about seeing Mick at Stan's thing. I was obsessing about it, then I was obsessing about us because I didn't want you to see me panicked. But you said you wanted to know everything about me. If we're going to last, you'll have to know that sometimes, I obsess about things." She stopped talking in anticipation of a response. When one didn't come, she edged closer. "Phoenix?"

"You're obsessing… 'bout what?"

"Mick is mean, and what if he's mean to—"

"I'm meaner."

"Yes, you are," she said. "But I don't want to get

upset in front of him… or in front of you. Saying goodbye to Stan is going to be hard and if I fall apart—" His arm rose to flop over her, so she stopped talking. "Phoenix?"

Instead of responding, he dragged her closer and rolled to his side. Coming to his bed wasn't meant to force him into sleeping with her. Though Shyla wouldn't complain, being in his bed was bliss.

Her fantasy changed fast when he came back toward her, looming over to join their mouths. Kissing Score changed the hue of her tension. Worry and anxiety became heat and arousal. Moving beneath him, she got as close to him as possible and relished having her hands free. Sliding them down his arms from his shoulders, she stretched her arms up to coil them around his neck.

His tongue retreated from her mouth. She tried to tempt it back, but he broke the kiss. Shyla sighed, disappointed that she'd lost his attention. Her sorrow froze when he reached across to brace himself over her. Raising hopeful brows, she expected him to take things up a notch. Instead, he climbed over to flop down on the bed at her other side. Confused about why he'd gone from the furthest side of the bed to the one closer to the door, Shyla guessed she'd got her answer about his preferred side.

As he lay down on his side, he pulled the sheet up to his waist and tucked it around himself. That made her smile. Protecting his modesty was for her benefit, but drawing her attention to it made her curious.

"Baby…" she murmured, reaching for him.

His stag tattoo was calling to her. That was the only spot on his body, below his neck, that her mouth had tasted.

"No," he said before she thought about asking a salacious question.

All her worries were gone. Just being near to him had done that.

Relaxed, Shyla breathed out and walked her fingers down his chest. "I like having my hands," she whispered. "Being able to touch you."

Closing his eyes, he punched the pillow under his head to bunch it up. "Hands to yourself, Lamb," he said, though he didn't go as far as pushing her hands away from him.

"Feels naughty, doesn't it?"

It did. Lying in the dark in his bedroom was the first time she'd shared a bed with a man who wasn't her relation. Even then, she could only remember going into Wyatt's room a couple of times as a kid afraid of her nightmares.

Score opened one eye. "Sleep, Lamb."

His eye closed, which left her to wonder what he meant. "Here?" she asked. "Here or…"

Again, he reached for her. Pulling her to him, he used his body to get her onto her side so he could tuck her against him as the little spoon. The heat of him was the first thing she noticed. As she wriggled to get comfortable and learn the new position, she became aware of something else. Something that was definitely aware of her.

"Quit moving."

Wearing a smile, Shyla took the liberty of pushing her ass into his groin. The sheet was between her skin and his, but there was no mistaking what she'd woken up.

"Phoenix—"

"No," he said. "Ignore it and sleep."

That was probably a command, but Shyla couldn't wipe the smile from her face. For the first time, she had a physical connection to his arousal. Curiosity wouldn't let her eyes close. She wanted to know more, wanted to touch him, wanted to pleasure him.

Keeping her breathing steady took effort. His arm was draped across her body, heavy and reassuring, holding her to him. Listening to both of them breathe, she tried to forget what was going on beneath the sheet. It wasn't easy. Shyla thought about it for so long that she supposed he'd fallen asleep again. Switching off wasn't as simple for her. She kept reminding herself that it wouldn't be right to satisfy her curiosity while he was asleep.

In spite of her own warning to herself, her arm wriggled its way free of his. Sliding her fingertips down her own body, she was careful about easing her hips away from his. Just as she was about to squeeze her hand between their bodies, he grabbed her arm.

Shocked by the sudden move, she gasped. "Phoenix!"

"Don't know when to quit, Lamb," he grumbled, rubbing his face in her hair. "I'm not in the mood to be patient or gentle."

Did that mean if she touched and aroused him, he take her hard and fast? Turning her lips into her mouth, Shyla tried to conceal a shiver of anticipation.

He freed her arm and clamped her close, pulling her so tight against him that she couldn't breathe right. With his elbow still holding her in place, his forearm moved to slide his hand up her body. A new release of bliss slithered through her when his hand curled around her breast. Even in sleep he could excite her.

Sliding his palm across to the other breast, he squeezed and stroked her until a sigh of arousal slipped from between her lips. An exhale of satisfaction left his mouth at the same time. He knew exactly what he was doing to her; he was proud of it.

Her whole body moved in the shield of his. He'd relaxed his arm enough to let her undulate against him, but still kept her trapped. Shyla whined in disappointment when he took his hand from her chest. She wasn't ready for it to be over, wasn't ready to lose the feeling of his ownership settling around her, holding her in his cocoon of safety.

"Phoenix," she whispered.

She wanted to scream, wanted to beg him to keep touching her. Turned out that there wasn't any need. He had a plan of his own. Skimming his hand down her body, Score straightened his arm and slid his fingers between her thighs. Lifting one, he pulled it back over his, opening her legs for his hand to find its home.

His fingers started slow, teasing her with his restraint. Score wasn't in any hurry, while she was a contradiction. Desperate to have him arouse her to climax and just as eager for him to indulge her forever, there was no middle ground. The sooner she came, the sooner his attention would ebb.

Whispering his name again, Shyla pushed her hips against his stimulating fingers. At that languorous pace, they could lie there together all night. It was difficult to think straight when he was toying with her.

He was hard, very hard, it couldn't be easy for him to ignore his own need. Aware of how little she did for him, Shyla tried to wrangle her arm free. Score clamped his down hard to stall it, which made his fingers stop.

"I want to touch you," she said, twisting as far around as she could in his embrace. "I need to learn how to turn you on."

"You do," he said, burying his mouth in her hair. "You move with me, feel what I give you."

"I do."

"I control this," he growled, circling her clit with a fingertip. "This sweet little pussy is mine to please anytime I want."

"Yes," she said.

"Tell me."

"Yours," she managed to say the word as his fingers pressed harder. "Oh, God…"

The burden of climax was weighing down on her. Shyla wanted to hold back, tried to hold on, but he was so hot there behind her. His body did own hers. She *wanted* him to take her for anything he wanted.

"You broke the rules, Miss Bellamy." Did she? Shyla couldn't remember what color the sky was let alone think about rules. "You came to my bed without permission."

"I needed you," she said, her hips in a rhythm with his hand, rocking against his body, imagining what it could be like to have him inside her.

"You needed this," he said, slipping his finger down through her wetness. "You wanted me to fuck you."

That wasn't why she'd come through, but it was what she wanted. "Yes… Please… Please, Phoenix."

"You gotta learn to take orders, Lamb… You don't make the rules."

"You make the rules," she said on a yelp and pushed hard against him. "Oh, God, baby…"

She gasped on the cusp of orgasm. Just as it was about to slam into her, his fingers disappeared. The orgasm drifted away. Still so stimulated that she could almost feel it there on her periphery, Shyla needed to finish.

Without even thinking about it, she tried to put her own hand between her legs. Score caught it and pinned it against her stomach, firm in his fist.

"You're mine," he said, using his chin to pull her head back to growl in her ear. "What are you thinking about?"

Her arousal, her need, her desperation to finish what he started. "You," she whispered and moistened her lips. "I want you… I'm thinking about how bad I want you and how bad I want to feel like this forever."

He rocked further over her, snagging the top of her ear in his teeth through her hair. "All you have to worry about is this… Is when I'll give you satisfaction… I'll take care of everything else. I'll take care of you."

Sex. What an incredible offer. A life without worry or anxiety. A life where the most stressful thing she'd ever have to think about was him withholding her orgasm.

"I want you inside me," she pleaded, trying to twist further around to find his mouth with hers.

But he was higher up than her and she couldn't reach him while he held her hand tight against her body.

"You trust me to look after you, baby? Do you?"

"Yes."

"No one will hurt you. No one would fucking dare. You need to obsess? Obsess about this…" He thrust his hips against her ass, grinding his erection into her through the thin layers of sheet between them. "You're gonna get it, baby, and you're gonna take it good. You're gonna learn exactly how to beg for what you want from me… But I make the rules, you take it when I give it."

She would, for as long as he would let her. Shyla was ready to be his girl. "I need you, Phoenix."

"You have me," he said, tightening his hold until her fingers began to go numb. "All. Only."

"All. Only," she said, reassured by his promise in those words.

When he let her go, she fell backwards, finding out at the same time that he'd moved. But he hadn't gone far. While she tried to figure out what was happening, he opened her legs and flicked his tongue over her. More pleasure, Shyla wasn't sure she could handle it, but she wouldn't refuse.

Phoenix was what she needed. He'd made such a difference to who she was already, so much that he was a part of her… Shyla wasn't sure she'd ever be able to repay the favor.

SEVENTEEN

THE HEAT OF THE DAY warmed her. Waking up in such a cozy glow was unusual. Given that a smile curved Shyla's lips before her eyes even opened, she doubted her contentment was all about the temperature. The rhythmic sound of water accompanied her drift out of slumber.

Stirring, she stretched her back and tried to do the same with the rest of her body, except… Her eyes opened at the same time she tugged on her arms. They wouldn't move, they were…

Tipping her head all the way back, she discovered her wrists were tied to the bedpost. The water sound stopped. Still confused, Shyla scanned the room and was reminded of the previous night. Phoenix. She was in Score's room. She'd come to Score's bed.

Obviously, he was the one who'd done his thing with knots again. The heat made more sense too. Her alarm was in her own bedroom, she didn't know exactly what time it was. Usually she was up and out before the midday sun had time to warm her sheets. If Beeks and Fish came in expecting breakfast—

"You awake?"

The shower door closed and she turned to address

him. "Yeah, I—"

Her panic vanished around the same time she looked at him. All of him. In all of his full incredibleness. Shyla hadn't closed her mouth and wasn't sure she'd ever be able to again.

Score didn't seem to notice or care that he was naked as he dried his hair with a towel. Damn. Shyla's desire to be introduced to his intimate anatomy didn't seem to know what to feel. The muscles across his abs and his solid thighs were drool-worthy, but his… his dick was… She didn't have any frame of reference of what a lover would feel like moving inside her, but still… As eager as she was to be with him all the way, she suddenly got a better understanding of what he'd meant when he said having sex wouldn't feel good.

Her anatomy was designed to yield to all shapes and sizes. Hell, she was supposed to be able to birth a child. It wasn't like—

"You have to learn." Shyla heard his words, but still couldn't quite make her mouth move to respond. "You didn't have permission to come to my bed last night, did you?"

No, she didn't. But given her current view, Shyla wasn't sorry she'd broken the barrier. Score turned around to walk across to the other side of the room. That gave her a view of his ass she hadn't enjoyed before.

Beyond how pleasing he was to admire, her appreciation for his high level of fitness grew. Sleeping with him could be an athletic experience. So while making a mental note to spend more time in the gym, her mouth finally relaxed enough to smile.

Score wasn't as happy. He wasn't a big smiler, but the stern judgement he wore when he turned back suggested he was less than impressed.

"Phoenix—"

"You had no right to come to my bed."

The last thing she wanted was to make him angry. If he felt violated or taken advantage of, he had every right to chastise her. Suddenly, nothing about the morning was worth smiling about.

"I'm sorry," she said. "I was worked up and I—"

"You made a mistake."

That wasn't the way she saw it. In truth, it hurt that he was so vehement.

"I'm sorry," she said again. "There's no excuse for what I did. I wasn't thinking and… you're right. I should have waited until I had permission to be here. I didn't mean to take advantage of you."

What she should do was leave his private space immediately. Except with her wrists tied to his bed, she couldn't go anywhere.

Score crossed to the side of the bed and crouched to nearer her eye level. With his scowl still intense, he took a section of her hair between two fingers to move it away from her face.

"I warned you; you didn't listen. You have to learn that I mean what I say."

"I know that," she said, without a clue what warning he was referring to. "I wasn't thinking. If you untie me, I—"

"No," he said. "You've shown that you don't understand the rules. You don't understand that you have to do what I say. Everything I say."

She would. She planned to. All Shyla could think was how stupid she'd been. "I can't leave if I'm tied up," Shyla said, wishing for freedom. "If you just loosen—"

"What did I say would happen if I brought you to my bed?"

Sorting through their experiences, it didn't take her long to hit on the answer. At the time, it had been a turn on. She wasn't sure what it was anymore.

"That you'd never let me leave."

"That's right," he said, reaching over her to check her bonds. "I don't say what I don't mean."

When he stood up to go to the closet area behind the headboard, she couldn't see him anymore. Her panic returned and she tugged at the bonds. He'd told her that she'd never break free of his knots. After using all of her strength to fight them, Shyla was sure he was right.

"Phoenix," she said, still tugging her hands. "I'm sorry. You don't have to leave me here. You can't leave me here! Beeks and Fish will be here soon and—"

"Beeks and Fish are picking up breakfast on the way to the club."

That meant he'd talked to them already. Set it up so he could leave her there? For how long?

"Why?" she asked. "Why did you tell them to do that? They won't understand why I can't make breakfast… Did you tell them about us?"

"Have we had sex?"

She stopped fighting the bonds. "No."

"They won't know until after we do."

Because he feared he'd lose interest in her or she would lose interest in him? If they weren't sexually compatible…

Score came around the corner of the bed to look down at her. She didn't say anything, just focused on his eyes hoping he was considering letting her loose.

Instead, he leaned down to throw the sheet from her hips, exposing her whole body. For a second, he went back to the closet. When he returned, he was holding his phone. Just like before, he took a picture.

"Phoenix," she pleaded.

"There's nothing to be afraid of," he said, hunkering down again. Bowing closer, he touched his lips to hers. "You're panicking… You didn't panic when I did this before."

Because he distracted her with his mouth. That had happened in the throes of passion. In the current moment, she was concerned he was mad.

"You're mad at me," she murmured, their lips still lingering on each other. "I want to show you I'm sorry."

Staying close, he began to stroke her body. "How would you do that?"

"Any way you want me to," she said.

His hand on her breast was loosening her up. The moment began to feel more like the one in her bedroom.

"If I want you to cook for me?"

"I'd do that," she said, trying to seek his lips again, but he held them just out of her reach. "I'd do anything for you."

"Anything. Except follow the rules."

"I didn't realize it was a strict rule. I thought you were just making a comment. If I'd known it was a rule—"

"What? You would have followed it?"

She nodded. "Yes. I will always follow your rules."

"You think we should let this indiscretion slide?"

"I think…" The torment of his thumb rubbing her nipple in slow circles made it difficult to concentrate. "I think you should decide."

"Decide if you deserve to be punished?"

Shyla didn't have a clue what punishment meant, but part of her was eager to find out. "How would you do that? How would you punish me?"

"Any way I want," he said. "I could leave you here, keep you tied up, so you don't have the choice to break my rules…" He kissed her. "Perhaps I should pick up something… something to make you climax over and over again until you lose your urge to defy me."

Over and over again? That didn't seem like such a punishment. Her body began to move, not only in response to his hand, but to his words too.

"What else?" she whispered, closing her eyes to picture his words.

On his next kiss, he didn't retreat and left his mouth on hers. "Maybe I force this mouth of yours to swallow my cock. Force you to give me head all day and all night. Maybe if my cock is your whole world, you'll learn you only have one thing to worry about. Your only worries should be how you'll please me and how you might tempt me to fuck you. That's it. Nothing else. You're so desperate for it, Lamb. So clueless. Once I have you, I won't stop pleasuring myself in your body. Your body will be open to me every minute of every day. Anything I want. Any rule I make, you'll be duty-bound to follow. No excuses. You do whatever it takes to keep my cock happy… That's your purpose. Your only purpose."

"Mmm," she purred, squeezing her legs together. "Yes, sir."

"Better."

At the same time his mouth disappeared, his hand did

too. Opening her eyes, Shyla couldn't see where he'd gone. Her body was alive. Alight with her arousal, ready to accept him, ready to be punished. But he'd vanished.

"Phoenix?"

No reply and no Phoenix.

The swirl of panic in her belly began to churn again. Something stopped it in its tracks. Before it became full-blown terrifying panic, she settled herself with one thought. Him. Phoenix. He'd put her there, left her there.   -

Whatever his reason, it didn't matter. Whether he meant it or not, it was a trust exercise. He wanted her to hand her existence over to him. He'd promised to take care of her. Told her that he'd take care of everything.

Instead of freaking out, she took a deep breath and let all of her muscles loosen. Some loosened easier than others. The heat he'd fired in her belly was still hot. Her legs moved, and she tried her best to pleasure herself. Without her hands, it wasn't easy. But imagining his words as reality kept her simmering.

If he hadn't still been naked, she might have thought that he'd already left. Gone. Out of the apartment, leaving her in his bed for whenever he might want to come home to her for pleasure.

Her whole existence up until she'd started working for Score was about responsibility. Shyla hadn't been able to rely on anyone to take care of problems for her. Sure, she had her grandfather and Stan, but caring for them meant being capable of everything. No matter what was going on or what had to be done, she was required to carry it out.

Score was offering the opposite. A life without responsibility. One where she could rely on him to take care of everything.

Her eyes were closed and her body moving. Her mind had been so busy that she wasn't even aware of his return until he skimmed both hands up the front of her legs. Opening her eyes, Shyla locked hers onto his. The stern look on his face was less angry, but that didn't make it any less intense.

As his fingertips slid higher, he kneeled on the bed and pushed her legs open. Terrified and thrilled in equal measure, Shyla held her breath thinking it could be the moment. His hands drifted from her hips and he rose higher, his fists dropping to the mattress on either side of her chest.

"Phoenix," she whispered, wishing she could touch him in return.

Bowing over her, he kissed each of her breasts. Taking a nipple into his mouth, he sucked it to a peak and flicked it with his tongue. A zing of delight shot through her; a gasp left her lips. He was taking his time. They were free. Beeks and Fish wouldn't interrupt. The day was still new, night was a long way off. Shyla was ready. Ready to be his. Ready to respond to him.

His mouth trailed down her abdomen. Kissing his way to the heat between her thighs, he wasted no time in sating the hunger he'd woken in her with his words.

"Yes," she said, her hips rising.

Words, actions, indulgence, Score gave her everything. He'd become her everything; she didn't ever want to lose that reliance. More than capable, stern and thorough, Score wasn't the type of man she'd pictured for herself. Yet, with such little experience of the opposite sex, picturing who she would end up with wasn't easy. Score knew. He knew how to give her what she needed. Even before she knew herself.

His slick mouth brought her to the cusp of orgasm and as she was about to drift into it, he pushed a finger into her to throw her over the edge. The sensation of his finger sliding free of her wrung all tension from her muscles. Being loose felt free. Yet, as cozy as she felt, she'd also never felt so powerful or alive.

Wearing a wide sated smile, she opened her eyes to tip her head toward the movement of the bed. Score was next to her, seated on the pillow, admiring her again.

"If that's what I get for being bad, I think I'll do it more often."

"I warned you," he said. "You disobey me again, I'll tie you up here permanently."

"I can think of worse places to be," she said, shifting onto her side, trying to twist her arm in the bounds so her shoulder wouldn't ache. "I want everything you said. I want to be yours and I want to pleasure you too."

His dick wasn't that far away and it wasn't as relaxed as her. The size of him was mesmerizing; even just the view of him intrigued her. Looking at something that could be the key to her pleasure was surreal. He was going to pop her cherry. One day she'd have rights to touch him any time she wanted.

If things worked out, they'd tell Beeks and Fish about their relationship. After that, they could be intimate any time they wanted, anywhere they wanted, without ever worrying about being caught or overheard.

The previous night, she'd thought joining him in bed was naughty. Once they broke the seal and started having sex, she could be much naughtier. Unless his rules required her to be good.

"You're tight," he said. "We're gonna have to take our time."

Shock jerked her head back. "Now? We're going to do it now?"

"No," he said, touching a finger to her forehead. "I have to get to the club early. Beeks will be there already... I'll be back early tonight."

Early was relative. Even though he'd come home after midnight the previous night, he probably considered himself early.

"Tonight," she said, raising her brows. "I mean... do you mean..."

He nodded and slid down in the bed to lie next to her. "Yes... If it's right."

"It will be right," she said, sure in how hard she nodded her head.

"Hasn't put you off?" he asked, curling a fist around himself.

Shyla had never been jealous of another person's hand until that moment. "I want it. I want you... I'm excited."

"We might not get there in one night. We'll have to—"

"Take our time, I know," she said, accepting his kiss when he moved closer.

His tongue tasted of her. The potent reminder of what he'd done drove her on to kiss him harder. The experience of losing her virginity might be a difficult one. But she'd do whatever it took to accept him. Yes, she trusted his experience and his rules; Shyla was ready to be his. All the way.

EIGHTEEN

AFTER MAKING OUT with her, Score clued her in on why he'd vanished. While she'd been in his bed, tied up, waiting for him to return, he'd gone to her closet to get her outfit for the day. Shyla asked if he'd untie her so she could put it on. He didn't. Instead he got dressed and ready to go out while she lay in his sheets, naked, watching him go about his business.

Score's instruction was to shower in his room, but she asked to use the bathtub and he hadn't objected.

With him gone, Beeks and Fish at the club, Shyla had little to do that day except pamper herself. The errands she needed to run were all close by the apartment. She got those out of the way and then focused on how to prepare for that night.

It could be the night. *The* night and she didn't want anything to ruin it.

Cooking dinner was more exciting than usual. Everything was more exciting than usual. Shyla wondered how it would be, how it would change her, how she might feel the following day once the deed was done.

The sense of exhilaration was new. During her dates with Gavin, she hadn't felt such an invigorated optimism coursing through her. He'd been a box that Shyla thought she had to check. Score was different. The passionate delight definitely felt more right. It was supposed to be Score, which made her all the more grateful he'd stepped in to stop her doing anything with Gavin.

When the elevator doors opened, she was in the kitchen, out of view. Tensing up, Shyla told herself not to give anything away in her expression or demeanor. Beeks and Fish wouldn't know why she was in such a state and it wouldn't be easy to explain if Score wasn't ready to reveal their relationship.

Thinking she should practice her poker face wasn't as straightforward as actually doing it. Fish was talking to Beeks, which Shyla only knew because Score came into view first. The moment her eyes met his, she smiled. Not just any smile, it was a smile that wanted to turn into an elated laugh. Score wasn't as impressed and found it much easier to remain impassive.

"I won't say it again, Lamb," Score said, a hand on the back of his chair at the table. "Three?"

"Sorry," she said, trying not to widen her smile.

He crooked a brow at her, which was probably a warning. Beeks and Fish were still engrossed in their conversation. The two were no doubt used to entertaining each other when Score wasn't chatty… Not that he was ever chatty.

Shyla mouthed "sorry" but wasn't sure he accepted her apology because his expression didn't flinch. Score turned his back on her to sit at the table. The other two did the same. She used the time to set her place and then take the food over.

Not setting her place was intended to be a reprieve rather than a defiance of Score. Sitting next to him, so close to him, could work her into a frenzy. Her mind was ablaze with the possibilities of what could happen later that night. She couldn't even focus on Beeks and Fish's conversation to work out what they were talking about. Score had her plate and was serving her food. Attentive and thorough, it always amazed her that he might belong to her.

The buzzing anticipation was so potent it almost had

mass. Her aura was heavy, but with the happy burden of expectation. When Score put her plate down and began to serve his own food, she watched him, taking in as much of him as she could. It was then Shyla realized her enthusiasm wasn't just about the sex. If they did it that night then as early as tomorrow, Score could be ready to go public.

That changed their situation from a private affair into a real tangible relationship. After they were out, Shyla would have rights over him in the same way he'd have rights over her. Even sitting at the dinner table, she'd be able to acknowledge him in a way she couldn't while their association was still clandestine.

"Shyla?"

Beeks voice stole her attention away from Score, who was already in his seat eating.

"What?" she asked, then noted the lawyer's frown. "Yes, sorry, I was a million miles away."

That wasn't entirely true, she hadn't been far from the table. She'd just been very focused on a particular person at the table and on what that particular person might do to her later.

"I asked if you were ready for tomorrow," Beeks said.

After reordering her thoughts, she figured out what he was talking about. "The funeral?"

"Yes," Beeks said, frowning at Score then at her. "What else do you have on tomorrow?"

"Nothing," she said, pushing aside a brief thought about possible morning sex. "Just the… Stan's thing."

Her emotions had been high and tight since waking up with Score. Grief had been the furthest thing from her mind. Guilt swamped her. How could she have forgotten that she would have to say goodbye to Stan? The funeral centered her. She stopped obsessing about Score and sex, and started to think about Mick and returning to what had once been her home.

"Have you heard from that asshole guy?" Fish asked.

"No," she said, shaking her head. "He doesn't have my number and we didn't give him an address, right?"

"He wanted your address?" Score asked.

She shrugged and started to eat. "It's a power play… or he thinks I'm a honed criminal."

"Not that far from one," Fish said on a snort, scooping up some food. "You sure you don't want me to come, boss? I can take that guy if you want me to."

"*I* can take that guy," Score said, calm, straightforward and completely composed.

"It won't come to that," she said, then second guessed herself. "I hope."

Mick liked to bluster, but from what she knew of him through Stan, he was also a chickenshit. She doubted he'd stand up to Score. Fish had intimidated him and the youngster was only a fraction as threatening as Score.

"If you need a protective order, I can arrange that for you," Beeks said. "We can go to the police station—"

"Really, I don't think Mick will cause trouble. He would if I was by myself, but I won't be by myself, will I?"

Her hand began to move toward Score's. Just in time, she stopped herself making contact. Touching him would remind her of her anticipation. Her mind went blank. For some reason, she couldn't remember how to act around him.

At a typical breakfast, there were tasks to keep her occupied. While working, she didn't have to think about whether or not to touch him. They were never near each other for more than a few seconds anyway.

That wasn't always true. She had licked him at breakfast once, but it was incidental… sort of, and no one had seen it.

Holding herself back, Shyla tried not to be too obvious about putting her hand back on the table. Somehow, she sensed people looking at her. The sensation wasn't the same as when Score looked through her. That was a warm kind of vibrating intensity, the current moment was the exact opposite. Beeks, at least, had to be wondering about the odd action. That wasn't the first time he'd been suspicious. Damn, she wanted to kick herself and hoped Score wasn't mad.

"How are things at the club?" she asked in an attempt to divert the conversation.

"You don't have to worry about that," Score said

before anyone else could think to offer anything.

Worrying was a strong word, she'd simply been trying to change the subject. Obsessing about the funeral would lead her in a loop. The previous night her loop was only broken by Score distracting her. At dinner, in front of their friends, she'd already drawn attention to them. Score wouldn't want to make them more suspicious.

"I want to know more," she said. "You guys spend a lot of time there. How were the auditions?"

That question was a guaranteed way to get Fish talking. Just the mention of it made him light up. With little prompting, he started to give her a rundown of each girl, what they'd done in their audition and who they'd hired. The names didn't mean much to her, but she got a better understanding of how Beeks got drawn into debates with him.

Beeks. At first, it started with Beeks offering little corrections. Eventually, Fish disagreed with one of the corrections. The men forgot about everyone else while they tried to figure out who was right.

Everyone's plates were clean and she had asked more than once if anyone wanted seconds. Beeks and Fish were too engrossed in their discussion to think about filling their mouths. Eating might interrupt their ability to interject and cut the other off.

Enjoying the feel of being with family, Shyla smiled at the two men at the opposite side of the table. Only when Score's knee brushed hers did she seek him out. Her head turning toward him was automatic. She shouldn't be so sensitive; sometimes the guy really did just make contact by accident. That time wasn't an accident though, he was looking right at her.

He stared right at her. Into her. Shyla wasn't sure what he was trying to tell her. If he was trying to tell her anything. There was a strong chance he simply wanted to unnerve her. No matter how hard she sucked on her lower lip and told her heartrate not to take his attention personally, her body didn't listen.

After half a minute, he got up and left the table. Beeks kind of glanced his way, but he already had enough to worry about with Fish's wild gesticulating.

Jumping from her seat, Shyla quickly gathered up the dirty plates and put the leftover food in the kitchen. Score had disappeared down the hallway. Doubting he went to the laundry room or into the stairwell, that corridor only led to one other place: their bedrooms.

Trembling in trepidation and excitement, she waited until Beeks and Fish weren't paying attention, and then slipped around the end of the wall into the hallway. Score wouldn't hesitate to tell her to return to the kitchen if he didn't want to be alone with her. But given the way he'd stared, Shyla was sure he had something to say.

Her imagination went mad with the possibilities. Each one flitted across her mind for a brief second before it was forced out by the next prospect. She didn't have to wonder where Score was, her bedroom door was closed and his was open. Shyla was out of the habit of closing her door; Score must have done it.

He'd been unhappy at her entering his space without permission. But he'd blocked the other option, so she guessed it was okay to go in.

When she turned into his bedroom, she didn't see him at first, the bathroom area was vacant. The bed was made and empty. The terrace door was open. Shyla guessed he might be somewhere outside. As she headed that way, his voice rose from behind, startling her.

"You're tense," he said.

Simple words, but they startled her into spinning around. He was in the closet area behind the headboard.

"Geez, Phoenix," she said, flattening a hand on her chest. "You scared me."

"Proving my point," he said. "What's wrong?"

"Wrong?"

"Are you worried about tomorrow? If you want me to take this guy out before—"

"No, I'm…" She took a step his way, but stopped when he came around the headboard to stand near the head of the bed. "I wasn't thinking about the funeral. I was thinking about us… then I felt guilty. I shouldn't be obsessing about us having sex when I have to say goodbye to Stan tomorrow."

He nodded once. "I thought you'd appreciate the distraction. We don't have to—"

"No," she said, holding up both hands. "Please don't... I do need it. I... I don't want to be sad about Stan and I'm worried Mick will open his big mouth, but..." Edging closer, she tried to take some of the gravity out of her tone. "We're the future. I don't have to shun my future to remember my past. I want to be with you... This is what I want."

Getting close enough to lay her hands on his torso, she wasn't positive she'd convinced him. With a frown on his face and the cogs in his mind working, Score contemplated her.

"We have to go back to the club," Score said.

Shyla guessed he meant him, Beeks, and Fish, not her. "Okay," she said. "You can talk to me about your work by the way. I don't worry about it, I know you have everything under control, but I would like to be involved in your life."

"You are," he said. "But I get your point."

Good, she was glad he did... though Shyla wasn't exactly sure what it was. "Do you want to talk about it?"

"Work? No," he said on a shake of his head. "We'll talk about that later."

Hopefully not in the time she'd rather be having sex with him. "Okay."

"After we're gone you have work to do."

"I do?" she asked, then inhaled. "I mean, yes, I do..." She frowned. "What work?"

He tucked her hair back from her face. "Everything that's in your room has to be moved in here."

Shit. Containing her enthusiasm for that task wasn't easy.

"Mm hmm," Shyla said, choosing to keep her lips tight together.

"I warned you about coming in here."

If he'd taken her agreement as unhappiness, she'd overshot with her restraint. "I don't have a problem with staying in your bedroom," she said. "But don't you think we should wait?"

"Until we've had sex?"

Yeah, that was what she was getting at. All of a sudden, her excitement chilled. "What if I don't satisfy you?"

Elevating her chin with a curled finger, he didn't blink as he spoke. "You already do."

He'd mentioned pleasuring himself in the shower, and he'd been in the shower that morning when she woke up. Her temperature began to ascend again. Being in the room with him while he… She smiled thinking how she could get used to being his muse.

"I'll bring everything through."

"Good," he said and began to turn away.

She grabbed for him. "When will you be back? Do you know what time you'll—"

"Relax, baby," he said, laying his hands on her shoulders. "You need to learn patience."

Maybe she did. Shyla had never been one for delays. But his statement niggled at her anticipation. "You're trying to drive me crazy, aren't you?"

He tipped up her chin again and bowed to join their mouths in a short kiss. "I wouldn't be doing my job right if I didn't." Score gave her a nudge toward the door. "Get back to work."

Back to work? Yes, there was still dessert and clean up to do. Transporting her things from her room to his would be a happy task, so she couldn't wait to do it. But before then, Shyla had to keep her head and not raise Beeks' suspicion again. Easier said than done.

NINETEEN

WITH HER MUSIC playing and her heart soaring, Shyla packed up her possessions. It seemed like she'd only just unpacked and there she was putting everything in neat piles and sorting through her clothes.

Although her time in that room had been short, she would miss it and her bed too. Though neither were good enough to tempt her out of sharing space with Score. Just living in the apartment with him was an adjustment. After that night, she'd have to learn how to cohabitate with a man in his own bedroom.

But it was Score.

She was excited.

So excited that she didn't know what to do with all her nervous energy. Swinging back and forth between elation and trepidation, Shyla finished moving and put on the lingerie he'd bought for her. Then all she could do was wait.

Every second seemed to drag as she waited for the elevator doors to open. Score would be home and as soon as he was…

The clock approached midnight. If something happened at the club, which would delay him, she doubted he would call. Surprising her, keeping her off-balance was one of his tricks. She couldn't blame him for it. As frustrating as it could be to not know exactly when he'd return, it was exciting too.

Like a kid anticipating Father Christmas, waiting for presents, hoping to catch the jolly man in the act, she shook with nervous excitement.

Sitting on the terrace, admiring the expanse of black ocean speckled with the occasional light of a ship, Shyla practiced her breathing. Calming herself, she thought of Stan, of her grandfather, of the life she'd left behind. Her future was with Score, that was what she believed, though they hadn't talked about what that might look like.

Although calmer than earlier, she was obviously still on edge because even from outside, the sound of the elevator doors snatched her attention. Leaping up from the patio chair, she went inside and smiled at Score who was standing in the foyer waiting.

She knew he was waiting because she knew what he wanted. Without saying a word, Shyla crossed the room to stop in front of him. After waiting just a breath, she took hold of his zipper and began to draw it down.

Every time she'd taken his jacket from him, it turned her on. This time was no exception. With his heavy eyes matched to hers, she listened to her heartbeat syncing with his breathing. Something she'd always wanted was right in front of her.

Despite not having any skills of seduction, she wasn't afraid. Score took all worry from her. He took her fears and insecurities. With just a simple look, he could erase them all.

The zipper reached its end and the edges of his jacket fell open. Instead of sliding her hands up his body to his shoulders as she'd done in the past, she went around to reach for the collar. Easing it from his broad shoulders, she absorbed his heat and tried to assuage her desire to touch him. When he wanted her to touch, he'd tell her.

The previous night she'd tried to touch him without permission and instead he'd taken control. Score was in control. Shyla eased the jacket from his arms and put it in the closet before returning to her spot in front of him. She expected that he'd want her to take off his boots too, but before she could descend, he spoke.

"Strip."

One word and it stopped her dead. Before leaving after dinner, he hadn't made any suggestions on what she should wear for him coming back. But, just as she expected from him, he wasn't shy about telling her what he wanted. On their first night of getting to know each other, he'd warned her he was bold.

Yet, in spite of that warning, every time he made a demand, a frisson of arousal bubbled up in her stomach.

Doing as he said, Shyla sought the straps of her dress and peeled them from her shoulders. Figuring they wouldn't want any delays, she'd gone for something that was easy to remove. After the cotton was bunched at her hips, she pushed it down to the floor and kicked it aside with her bare foot.

His attention was still fixed on her. As her blood pumped hard through her veins, Shyla bent her knees, intending to go to the floor.

Score caught her arm and held her up. "You're not done."

She wasn't... The lingerie was a gift, but apparently, he wasn't interested in getting his money's worth. A smile twitched at the edge of her lips. Enticed by his implication, she reached around to unhook the clasp of her bra. She'd been naked in front of him before, but not in the living room and not at his request.

Every time she'd been nude, they'd been in bed. As they grew closer and they crossed more lines, her boundary of experience was being pushed wider. After they were intimate, and they declared their relationship to the others, there wouldn't be anything to stop Score making any demand of her any time.

Hot and filled with butterflies, she tossed the bra aside and then slipped her thumbs beneath the fabric at her hips. Once she was naked, he could have her any way he wanted, any time he wanted.

Never one to refuse him, she was surprised not to feel any ounce of embarrassment or self-consciousness when she eased her panties down her legs. Score wanted her. He'd told her that he did. Shyla had to show him trust, had to show him that she was all his, every single part of her.

Naked. She stood there before him. He took a step backwards to widen his view of her body. He liked to look. Liked to take his time absorbing her features, enjoying her.

"Kneel," he said.

Without wasting a second, she sank to her knees. Honesty was her greatest ally. Although Shyla was concerned about missing something basic through inexperience, she didn't have to dwell on the possibility. Score knew the truth and wouldn't expect her to have any special expertise. Besides, she had a feeling he would enjoy talking her through every detail.

As much as she didn't want to tear her gaze from his, she had to do it to remove his boots. Putting them aside, Shyla rose higher on her knees. Everything about him seemed zeroed in on her. It didn't matter that she wasn't watching him as her trembling fingers slid onto his belt. The tension in her shoulders was all anticipation. They were there, alone, and about to leap the final hurdle.

Unbuckling his belt took a little longer than usual. Her fingertips were cool, but the rest of her scorched. In more ways than one.

She reached for the top button of his jeans but never made contact because Score took one clear step back. Wondering why he'd retreated, she questioned him with her gaze. As usual, his gave nothing away.

"Go pour two scotches."

Go? The last thing Shyla wanted was distance between them. "You don't want to…"

"Be patient, my love."

Though still uncertain about his intentions and how long they would delay, the last word spurred her into action. He'd never used that word in relation to her before. It jangled around in her mind bouncing off the inside of her skull until it settled itself deep in her brain.

He offered a hand to help her to her feet. Still speculating as to what would come next, she doubted the alcohol was meant for Dutch courage. He was experienced and didn't need any sort of liquid motivation. Perhaps he was thinking she'd enjoy having an excuse to loosen up. They couldn't drink too much. Score wouldn't want her to be inebriated before they got anywhere near his bed.

At the bar, she did as instructed. Retrieving glasses, she filled each with a generous measure and pondered whether technically, it was "their" room as all of her possessions were in there.

Before she'd turned all the way around, Shyla noticed he wasn't where she'd left him. He'd gone to sit next to the chess board as a matter of fact. Taking the scotch across to where he sat, she handed over a glass.

Score enjoyed a sip and then pointed a forefinger to the opposite side of the table. "Sit."

Shyla didn't want to sit, but it would be petulant of her to stamp her feet or whine at him. Not only was he more experienced than her, his mind was clearer, his thoughts more linear. On the first night they'd played chess, she'd promised to follow his command. That meant following it all the time, not just when it suited her.

Lowering to the floor, she put the other glass next to the chess board and examined the pieces. If she showed him her sullen look, he'd know that she wasn't happy about the delay.

Distracting her from her thoughts, he nodded at the glass she'd put aside. "Drink," he said.

Score was there and he'd told her she could enjoy alcohol without fear while he was present. So that was what she did. Picking up the glass, she poured all of the liquid into her mouth and swallowed hard. The burn in her throat tried to make her cough. Suppressing it, she put the glass on the table, and moved her pawn.

"Still impatient?"

That was one way to put it. Shyla exhaled all of her breath, clearing herself out before starting again. "No. I'm sorry, you're right."

In all her focusing on what was to come, she'd neglected to appreciate the moment. They would only do this for the first time once. Rushing into it while she had the courage wasn't necessarily the best route. Score wanted to take his time. She'd learned he knew how to turn her on with the simplest of gestures. There was nothing to worry about. They had time. The whole night. Savoring her moments with him was better than hurrying through them.

They played a few moves. Shyla hadn't expected them to sit in silence. Her anticipation was still live and she wanted to connect with him. If that couldn't happen physically, then mentally or emotionally was the next best thing.

"Everything okay at the club?"

"I'm not interested in shooting the shit," he said, pondering his move before taking it. "It's impossible for you to sit in silence."

She shrugged when he cast a semi-smile her way. "You could say that."

"Why?"

There was a question. Like many of her neuroses, Shyla didn't know the root cause of them. "I suppose when my mind is mixing things up and driving me crazy, I find it's useful to just open my mouth and fill the air."

"You don't have to."

"Are you testing me?" she asked, allowing a laugh to fall from her lips. "I'd fail miserably against you in a competition of who could be the most brooding."

"You don't have to measure yourself against anyone."

Seemed like a great idea in theory, not so much in practice. "I get myself wound up and then have no way to get rid of the energy. So I obsess or I ramble."

"I'll help you with that."

In her naivety, she was about to ask how he'd help. Just before her mouth opened, she caught sight of his sly gaze. Though his head was still tilted down to the board, his eyes were at the top of their sockets, fixed on her. He examined her, probably wondering if she understood the insinuation.

Shyla groaned. "You are doing this on purpose."

"What?"

"This," she said, waving both her hands back and forth between them. "You want to drive me crazy."

"You accused me of that earlier. If you're asking, do I want you turned on? Then yes, I do. We process anticipation differently. You want to rush through it. For me, it's half the fun."

Suddenly getting a flash of their future, she smiled. "So I'm going to be desperate, begging you to come to bed with me, and you're going to resist for as long as possible?"

"Not always," he said. "Have you had relationships with other men?"

He knew that she hadn't slept with anyone else, but that didn't mean she hadn't dated. "Nothing long-lasting. Like I told you, I had a boyfriend in high school. After that, there were a couple of years of adjusting to the way things were with Bernard, my grandfather."

"You missed out."

"Maybe," she said. "It didn't always seem that way at the time. I miss both of them. Yeah, there were times when it was just the three of us that I would look at my life and wonder how I'd ended up in that position. But looking back, I see it was a gift. I had the opportunity to cherish those relationships, to really get to know the men as individuals and together."

"You wouldn't trade it?"

"No," she said, finding an odd sort of peace within herself. "They helped mold me into who I am."

He nodded just once and they continued to play. Score was good at getting to know her. Not only did she offer a lot of information in her rambling, but he knew which questions to ask. His questions helped him learn more about her.

Shyla didn't want their relationship to be one sided. He'd already promised to take care of her, but she didn't want to only rely on him for the practical.

"What about you?" she asked before she could stop herself.

"Me?"

"Do you regret it?"

He took his next move and then sank back in the couch to lay his arms along the back. "Do I regret my upbringing? Do I regret trusting people I shouldn't have trusted? Do I regret meeting Siobhan? I don't know."

For a man who was always so certain in everything, Shyla wasn't sure that she'd heard him right. "Excuse me?"

"There wouldn't have been any other path. It's pointless to think about it."

"You could've walked away earlier."

He shook his head. "It doesn't work that way."

"What about your mother?"

"She's dead."

"I know, but maybe if she'd left your father while you were young…"

Score breathed out an almost laugh. "Women don't leave McDades. Sure don't leave Burl McDade." Shyla was confused. "It's not possible to explain to someone who's never been a part of it. It's… Anything I say will sound misogynistic and old-fashioned. It's about more than defending the family. The McDades have competitors, other families like the Dohertys and the Byrnes. If the McDades show weakness, that's an opening for them. You can't show weakness. You never show weakness."

"Weakness can get you killed," she said, having come to that conclusion on her own.

He shrugged. "Chances are you end up dead anyway," he said. "The Dohertys and Byrnes took a loss recently. There was a meet, the cops showed, and they ended up massacring each other."

Shocked, she couldn't imagine something that horrific. "Oh my God."

He sat up to snag his glass. "Yeah, Burl had a field day… McDades influence just went through the roof… There isn't a worse time to think about pissing off Burl. Christmas came early for him."

People dying made Burl happy. She couldn't wrap her head around it. Score was right that not living in that world made it hard to understand.

"I'm happy you're not a part of that world anymore," she said.

He shook his head and sank against the back of the

couch again. "It's not as simple as that. I can't escape it. I'll always be Phoenix McDade, which means there's always a chance someone could appear from nowhere to take a shot at ending me."

Someone could appear from nowhere to take him down. He'd already said there were those who might try to impress him through her. Saying it was complicated seemed like an understatement.

"But you've cut ties with your family."

"I still talk to Burl," he said. "I have to."

"Why?"

"Because he calls. I can't promise he won't call me back."

He didn't mean on the phone. "How could you ever trust him again?"

"I couldn't. Wouldn't. But making an enemy of him would be dangerous. Very dangerous, especially while he has my brothers leashes pulled tight. I don't worry about me, I can take whatever he dishes out, but you and Fish…"

"You don't want to be a part of that life. You don't have to answer the phone because of us."

"I have to protect you. Both of you. Beeks too. I don't have a network like I used to. I can't rely on connections from the old days."

"Because that's no longer a part of who you are. You're separated from that life."

"Am I?" he asked. "Am I separated from it?"

That was exactly his point. No matter how far away he got from where he came from, he'd always be one of them.

"Did Burl know what Biz was doing? Did he know it was a setup?"

"Not back then."

But, as far as Shyla was concerned, there was no excuse. At the very least, Burl knew the truth in the same way everyone did these days. Score was free, Siobhan wasn't dead.

That just increased her confusion. "I don't get it," she said. "You said Burl sets the family line, that acting without his approval would be insane."

He nodded at the board, reminding her it was her

turn. "Yeah, Biz took his life in his hands."

"How come Burl didn't hand him his head when he found out?"

She took her shot, but noted his shrug from the corner of her eye. "I don't know and don't care."

Shuffling closer to him, she ended up kneeling at the corner of the table, her frown set on him. "You must care. You have to. I care. I'm mad. I want to know what the hell—"

"Easy," he said, raising a calming hand. "You've gotta be careful talking like that." There was no one else in the room and she glanced around to prove it. "Shouldn't get in the habit of it."

"Someone should ask Burl for the answer."

"No one questions him, not on something like that."

It infuriated her. "You go to prison for six years, your own brother sets you up, and you're just meant to be okay with the fact your father did nothing about it?"

"We don't know what he did," Score said, moving one of his pieces.

Shyla couldn't even look at the board. "You didn't go back to them? After prison."

"Why would I? Nothing there for me."

"The guy who set you up is there."

"Yeah, and it wouldn't be easy to sit on my fucking hands like Burl would order me too. Why would I want to be around Biz, who's fucking cock of the walk up there now?"

"What about your other brothers? Were they in on it? Were they surprised? You must have talked about it."

"Doran enjoys the easy life."

Score spoke of Burl, Biz, and Doran; she'd noticed that he was less vocal about his other brother. "Your other brother is Razor, right?"

"Razer," he said, emphasizing the E. "Yeah."

"Why don't you mention him?"

"Zay and me were tight," he said.

"So it hurts you that he didn't believe you were innocent?"

"He did. But fuck all he could do about it when Burl

told him to stay away."

"He could've left. Stuck up for you."

"Then I'd be in prison and he'd be strung up. Never wanted anyone to go on a crusade for me. Yeah, I didn't kill Siobhan. But I'm not lily white. Can't say I didn't deserve to be where I was."

Whatever crimes he'd committed in the past, during his work for his family, he didn't deserve to be sent to death row by his brother or be abandoned by his blood. If Burl had believed in his innocence, wouldn't he have fought for his son's freedom? Shyla didn't know all the details and didn't want to force him to relive the dark times he must have gone through in prison.

"I don't understand why Burl just let it slide. Why Biz would be—"

"He's grooming Biz to take over. Razer doesn't have the patience and Play doesn't have the concentration."

"Is that why Biz did what he did? To get you out the way, so he could have top spot?"

"Biz is the oldest," he said. "It was always his. But yeah, maybe. I had a lot of respect on the streets. People feared Razer, still do. He'd put a bullet or a blade in a guy before he even knew he wasn't alone.… If Bosco was around, maybe he'd give a warning, maybe, but that's a big maybe."

"Bosco?"

"His best friend."

This whole other life had come before Score went to prison. Prison was like his second existence, and their lives together were like his third. Shyla wasn't sure she'd ever be able to learn all of him. The layers of a man who some might shrug off as nothing more than a criminal intrigued her. Score was more than that. He was more than one thing and she had no plans to give him up any time soon.

TWENTY

THEIR GAME LASTED a long time. Yet, Shyla hadn't looked at the clock and didn't care about the time. Score pondered each move. Maybe he hadn't been at the peak of his concentration the first time they played or maybe he'd just let her win to give her a boost. Whichever one it was, their current game was going only one way.

"Checkmate," he said and sat back on the couch. "Are you mad?"

Shyla just smiled and rose up on her knees to put their pieces back to their starting positions. "No," she said, tossing him a wily glance. "People who get mad about losing are insecure. Do I seem insecure?"

The question was only posed because Score had put it to her that way. Shyla hadn't really expected him to reply.

"You shouldn't be," he said. "You're beautiful, you're smart, and you're resourceful… You have nothing to be insecure about."

The compliment seeded itself inside her. Shyla wasn't sure how to respond. It wasn't like she'd spent her life accepting flattery from hot men like Score, or like anyone.

"Thank you," she said, finishing up her task then laying her hands on the table. "Do you want to play again?"

"If you want," he said, lifting his hand to turn his watch toward himself. "If that's how you want to spend our time."

Right. With the drinking and the talking and the game, Shyla hadn't only lost track of time, she'd lost track of their purpose. Suddenly nervous, she swallowed hard. For all her desperation earlier, facing the act was more difficult than she'd thought.

"No," she said, licking her lips. "No, I want to—"

"We don't have to. We can play—"

"Phoenix," she said, crawling around the table to kneel by his leg. "You won the game." Sliding her trembling fingers onto his thigh, she pushed them further while rising on her knees. "You can pick your prize."

"You're no prize, Lamb," he said, laying his hand on hers. "You're not a thing for any man to win."

"My virginity can be your prize," she said. "You can take anything you want."

Sitting up, he linked his fingers between hers and bowed over them until his mouth almost touched hers. "I plan to. You will be mine, Little Lamb. Tonight and every other night."

"Yes, sir," she said on a smile just a moment before their lips met.

Shyla's expectation of a deep, passionate kiss was turned on its head when he kept the joining brief. As his mouth left hers, he drew her arm up to hook it around his neck and then stood, scooping her from the floor.

On their walk from the living room to his bedroom, her atoms jumped and fizzed. Their bedroom. The door was already open, she'd left it that way. Nothing slowed them down and she was ready. In her stomach, a simmering need became blind determination. Shyla wanted this. Wanted him.

Phoenix put her on the bed, but didn't join her. While admiring her, he began to strip. When he'd asked her to strip at the start of the night, Shyla had complied, despite her nerves. Just that morning, she'd seen Score naked for the first time. She couldn't imagine a time when she might get used to it, when seeing his defined form would be pedestrian.

She shifted to the middle of the bed as he walked around it. When he got to the bottom, he stopped.

Waiting, watching, nothing happened so she rose onto her elbows.

"Shyla," he said, standing there shirtless and barefoot, his hands on the waistband of his jeans.

"I want to. I'm sure," she said, hearing his question without him having to voice it. "I'm ready. I know I am."

That was enough for him. Pushing down his jeans and underwear, he stood naked before her, a perfect sculpture of a man. She wanted to admire him all night but barely got a few seconds to drink him in. He dropped onto the bed, crawled over her, capturing her prone form beneath the cage of his.

"You're not ready," he said. "You have to trust me. Do you trust me?"

"Yes," she said, her gaze locked to his while her fingertips touched his solid arms.

"No touching," he said, confusing the hell out of her. "Do I need to tie your hands?"

"No," she said, shaking her head.

"Put them on the headboard."

Stretching her arms above her head, Shyla curled them around one of the bars. "Why can't I—"

"Shh," he said. "Trust me."

Of course she trusted him. If she didn't, she wouldn't be lying in such a vulnerable position beneath him. He kept his body above hers, but dipped close enough to kiss her. The long sweep of his sure tongue relaxed hers. It relaxed all of her; he relaxed all of her. Their kiss was long and slow, still not the deep frenzy of passion that she expected. The whole thing wasn't like she expected.

In her fantasies of him, of being with him, they were both in such a heightened state of need that their joining was fast and hard. Picturing it without knowing how it felt was always frustrating. Now she was getting a taste of the truth, of how it really was to be with him.

His mouth pressed hers once more then it drifted away to explore the rest of her body. The sensations of his lips on her neck as his hand searched her body were almost more than she could bear. Squeezing her fingers around the headboard, Shyla didn't even care about leaving nail marks behind. Keeping them away from him was driving her nuts.

"Phoenix," she whispered, wriggling and writhing beneath him, unable to stay still.

"Shh," he said, his teeth together against the nipple his mouth was spoiling.

"I can't," she panted, desperate to touch him, desperate to contribute and to play.

Heat suffused every crevice of her being. Inside and out, she was learning new ways to feel, new ways to experience him. Her mouth opened to take in a long breath. As she exhaled, a whine vibrated from her throat. He was more than skilled. His experience dwarfed hers, but if being with him was going to feel that way every time, she wouldn't be able to restrain herself.

"That's it," he said. "Just feel, baby… Feel yourself becoming mine… Every inch of you belongs to me now, Shy."

She managed another whimper. "Mm."

Everything about her wanted to be his and even if it took her a lifetime, she'd find a way to return this indulgence to him. On his knees, he ran his fingertips down her torso until his hands clutched at her hips.

Anticipating his dick slipping into her, she opened her eyes, seeking his. Before they did, he flipped her over, arranging her legs on either side of his again.

For the first time a whisper of trepidation crept in. Shyla didn't want him trying anywhere else before she'd had a chance to feel the real thing. She should've known better than to worry. He lay over her, still keeping his weight braced above her, and kissed the small of her back. That gentle kiss wasn't the only gift his mouth planned to give. The tip of his tongue ascended, skimming her spine with a feather touch until it reached the back of her neck.

Shivers of something she couldn't even call arousal shimmered through her. They met her heat with a tickle of desire unlike anything she'd ever felt. Her hands balled in the pillows, gripping them tight in her fists. Agitated by the deep reaches of his skill, Shyla almost came apart when he worked his way back down the same route.

Her mind was still flashing between dark and light. Her concentration was gone. Every nerve was raw, exposed to him, stimulated beyond her comprehension. Shyla didn't even realize he'd put her on her back again until he sucked her clit into his mouth.

"Oh God," she said, drawing her knees up as she sank her fingers into his hair. "Phoenix."

His order not to touch was completely forgotten. In her defense, his mouth reduced her whole existence to that place between her thighs. Nothing in the world could distract her from his talent.

Panting, aching with a profound craving to stay in that place forever, feeling that way forever, she moaned and clenched hard as an intense, almost violent orgasm ripped through her.

That orgasm didn't come and go, he continued to pleasure her from a different angle, faster than before, showering her with short, fierce aftershocks. Her mouth opened wide in a silent scream. Shyla didn't breathe, couldn't breathe.

When he pushed his tongue into her, another powerful orgasm slammed her. It hit with such unexpected force that she couldn't figure out how to process it. Many emotions rattled through her from so many different places. She couldn't focus on one thought, couldn't focus, couldn't breathe.

In no rush, Score's mouth drifted up her body again, dipping into her navel and circling each of her nipples as he passed. Her arms were loose on either side of her. While his mouth played and sampled her neck, she got herself together. Not all the way, but enough that she could run her hands into his hair again.

"Phoenix," she said, accepting his kiss when he gave it to her.

No doubt he was trying to silence her. His concentration was obviously important if he was determined to keep her mute.

"Relax," he said, resting one hand on her breast while the other braced his weight. "Take your time."

Take her time? Shyla hadn't done anything except experience what he gave her. "Phoenix," she said, leaving a pause because she half expected him to silence her. When he didn't, she panicked for a second having not decided how to articulate what she wanted to say. "I want to do something for you."

"Tonight's about you."

With a hand on his cheek, she smiled up at him. Their only illumination was light pollution from the city. They could see each other, but the mood was still intimate.

"I'm not going to be one of those girlfriends who's all take, take, take."

"No, you're going to be one of those girlfriends who does what she's told. You forget who you're dealing with? I'm not the selfless type. Tonight we take our time to maximize your pleasure and minimize your pain. Getting you through it isn't enough. You have to love sex, to want it, to not be afraid of it."

Her touch slithered down to his pec. "You're doing a good job so far."

He dipped to kiss her. "I know." Always confident, and with reason to be, Score didn't need to be reassured about his ability. "It won't always be like this. It won't always be about you. When I need you, when I want you, I'll take you any damn way I want. You won't always see it coming and it won't always be slow."

A new kind of excitement bubbled around, deep in her gut. "Tell me," she whispered.

One corner of his mouth rose just a tiny fraction before dropping again. She liked it when he talked; it got her off. Both of them knew it. That almost smile betrayed that she'd pleased him.

He kissed her again, and held his lips just a millimeter from hers. "My lily-white little virgin is gonna get a crash course in red-hot, raw, animal sex. You're gonna learn to fuck, to be fucked hard and quick. You're gonna take it anyway I want to give it. I won't be gentle. I won't be slow. You get me hard and I will use you to satisfy myself any fucking way I want. You strut around, turn me on, expect to be bent over and screwed.

"It'll be your fault if you make me want you. I'll punish you for flaunting yourself around me. Your pussy's gonna get so used to being filled by my cock, she'll be empty without it. You'll be empty. You'll want it. You're gonna be addicted to it. You'll wanna ride me hard day and night; you'll be desperate to please me, desperate for scraps, desperate for my attention. You'll get that sweet pussy ready for my dick. Always. Whatever I want, you'll give; I'll make you give it to me. You will do anything I tell you, everything because you're a slave to my cock, a slave to what I want. My cock will be your master, and whatever it takes, you will give all of yourself to it. Do you understand?"

Her mouth wasn't working, nothing worked except the intimate space he'd already tormented. "Phoenix," she whispered, trying to pull his body across hers.

Without a word, he changed his angle and pushed her legs further apart. Shyla wasn't nervous, she wasn't scared, not when her fierce and determined master was in control. He guided himself close to her. The pressure of his dick against her opened her mouth like before; she wanted to breathe, wanted to feel him. If he thought he was hurting her, he might stop, so she set her expression when he pushed deeper.

The pain was more like a burning, like tissues that hadn't been touched before were suddenly getting too much attention. He pulled back and she breathed out, then he pushed on again. It took time, too much time probably. Without a frame of reference, she didn't know if the pain was normal, and didn't know if he was going further than other, less well-endowed men would.

After another dozen pushes, he pulled out.

"Phoenix," she called and grabbed for his waist.

"Taking our time," he said as a reminder and came down to kiss her.

His hips were still between her legs, and she could feel the weight of his torso against her pelvis as he kissed her.

For the longest time, he stayed there, kissing her mouth, touching her body, awakening her to each new treat she never knew she'd missed out on.

He'd been playing with her breasts and hips for a while, so when his fingers danced their way across to her clit, Shyla moved her hips with the motion of his caress. They slid lower, dipping into her juices and returning to her clit. Another orgasm was just on the edge of her consciousness when his fingers moved again. That time, they didn't return, one of his fingers, broad and hard, slipped into her.

Surprised by his intrusion, she stopped kissing him. Tense and aroused by the new sensation, Shyla was focused on that when he found her gaze and pushed a second finger into her. For a minute, he pushed them in and out, parting them wider, teasing the path his dick hadn't been able to forge.

"Mm," she whimpered, pushing her hips up, begging him to go faster.

He did. Fucking her with his digits, they kept their attention on each other. She wanted to feel him and it seemed just by watching her reactions, he was feeling her.

Without asking permission, his fingers slid free of her body and he was shifting again to push himself into her. The slickness of her juices helped. The first couple of inches weren't as difficult as his first attempt. Retreating and advancing, he loosened up those first few inches without any urgency or speed. His body rocked over hers, teaching it how to take what he wanted to give. What he needed to give.

"Phoenix," she said, stroking his face.

Shyla couldn't convey how incredible he felt, couldn't tell him what he was doing to her was amazing. All she wanted to do was feel. Closing her eyes, she pushed her head into the pillow, arching up, moving her hips in acceptance of him.

A sudden pain shot up through her, which she realized was him forging deeper, being more forceful about taking what he wanted. The initial burn of pain subsided at the sight of his frown. He didn't want to hurt her, but his own need was growing. Want emanated from him, it flared out of him, lighting up his darkness. He'd been so adamant about taking their time, it seemed like his assertion was coming back to haunt him.

"More," she said, lifting her hips. It might hurt, it might wind her, but she'd endure it. Pain was momentary in comparison to the pleasure they'd have together for the rest of time. "Baby, please... I need more."

Gritting his teeth, he pushed hard. She didn't catch the yelp before it leaped from her mouth. Instantly, he pulled back, but she grabbed for him.

"No," she said. "Don't. I want all of you... Please."

He drove forward again, forcing his way into her. Catching the sound of pain before it fled, Shyla exhaled after he relaxed. He was inside her. Her man. The man she wanted to spend her life with had taken something precious, but she'd never been more grateful.

A minute passed and he didn't move. She appreciated him giving her the chance to learn what it felt like to be a woman complete. Testing the connection, she wriggled, and that was enough for him. Pulling out and pushing in, he forged ahead, conquering her most intimate space, energized by his own desire.

The discomfort of before vanished fast. Replaced by a sense of urgent demand, she wanted to give him some of what he'd given her. With the barrier broken between them, she was ready to go all out for him.

He surged in and then halted again. A noise of disappointment charged the air between them; her noise of disappointment.

"Gotta slow down, baby," he said, closing his eyes.

"No," she said. "No. No slowing down. Please... Phoenix."

Still inside her, he opened his eyes and set a discerning look on her. She was trying to figure it out when he took her hand from the bed and directed it down to where their bodies were joined.

"Play."

One single word. A command. Shyla had pleasured herself while he watched in the past. Her muscles were still learning what was expected of them, so she didn't feel the need. But it was what he wanted.

Rubbing her clit, Shyla made contact with his shaft for the first time. She blinked up at him, but he was still just watching. Parting her fingers, she pushed them down on either side of him, feeling how he filled her. Swollen, wet, and aching with need, her tissues responded to her touch. He began to move in and out of her again, slower, with more care.

As intent as he was, she had to smile. "You're driving me crazy," she murmured, accusing him for the third time.

"You'll always go first."

The deep promise in his voice united with the stimulation of her fingers and the torment of his dick. Just like that, her body fell into the abyss of orgasm again. Shyla didn't hold back her scream, didn't hold back her release of wonder and joy and love. Her body squeezed tight around him. It felt like she wanted to capture him and keep him inside her forever.

Score was stronger than her; he pulled himself free only to slam into her one final time. With a growl, he emptied himself inside of her and then slid out to flip onto his back.

Her mind was alight, her body invigorated, and she didn't have a clue what to do. Already, she felt different. Whether it was the sex or the man, Shyla didn't know. In that minute, she didn't care. Staring at the ceiling, she calmed herself, tried to order her thoughts, and did her best to remember what had come before.

TWENTY-ONE

"PHOENIX," she said without knowing how long they'd been lying there in silence. When he didn't respond, Shyla rolled onto her side, propping her head on her fist. "Are you mad?"

"Mad?" he asked, his attention snapping around to hers.

She laid a hand on his torso. "Happy? Sad? What do you feel?"

"What do *you* feel?"

His deflection was unexpected, though it shouldn't have been. More than once he'd told her that the night was about her. Still, his reluctance to answer didn't fill her with confidence. But, in truth, Shyla was too energized to feel negative about anything.

Despite the ache in her muscles, she leaped over to straddle him, flattening both hands on his chest. "I'm ecstatic!" He caught the curtain of her hair to sweep it back over her shoulder. "I don't know what you did to me, how you did it, but I feel so alive, so different, so amazing."

"Good."

"More than good! I feel incredible."

Adrenaline had a lot to answer for. Shyla didn't care

about the cause, she didn't question her euphoria and wanted it to go on forever. Lunging down, she forced her mouth over his and kissed some of her elation into him.

"Easy," he said, taking her upper arms to ease her away.

Shyla tilted her head. "You don't seem happy." She gasped. "Did I do something wrong?"

"I'm happy."

Score hadn't ever been the type to jump up and down. The guy barely smiled, so she shouldn't expect him to suddenly have a personality transplant. Not disappointed or upset, Shyla was concerned about him.

"Talk to me," she said, stroking his cheek. "Please baby. We share everything, remember?"

Drawing in a breath through his nose, he took his time about exhaling too. "I don't like being out of control," he said. "You make me feel out of control."

With a smile, she shifted her hands to the pillow on either side of him to get close. "You're not out of control. I give myself to you. Whatever you need, anytime, I follow your orders."

He shook his head. "That's not how I mean." She still didn't understand what he meant, but he swept her hair aside to cradle her cheek. "You are different, Shy."

That made her feel good. Pride warmed her. "Worth your time?"

"Yes."

Lying down on him, she tucked her head under his chin. "I feel different."

"You'll be sore tomorrow."

Stan's funeral. Without wanting to dwell on anything negative, Shyla appreciated what Score had said about the distraction. She did need it. They'd done the right thing.

"Thank you for coming with me tomorrow," she said. "It means a lot to me. I'll feel better with you there."

"Anything I should know about this Mick?"

"One thing," she said, rising to meet the concern in his gaze. "He doesn't belong in our bed." His concern ebbed. "He's a weed. No threat to you."

"Where you're concerned, no threat is too much for me to handle. You know I'll always stand between you and trouble."

She smiled again and kissed him quick. "What if I am the trouble?"

Moving fast, he put his arms around her and flipped her onto her back. No bracing his weight, no keeping his distance. Nothing stood between them. The physical obstacle had been obliterated. Score didn't have to worry about scaring her or making her uncomfortable, he'd been inside her. She'd had all of him.

"I'll discipline you," he said. "You disobey me, there will be consequences."

Shyla could hardly wait. "Phoenix," she said, squeezing her arm out from his grip to trace her fingertips from his jaw down his throat to his chest. "I want to be with you." Seemed like an odd thing to say given what they'd just done. "I mean... I want to be with you for more than just tonight, more than just a while. I want to be with you."

"You are with me," he said, though she didn't know if he understood just how much she felt for him. "But this is your first time."

So she couldn't trust her own feelings, was that what he meant? "I've known how I felt about you for a while."

"You remember what I said about women and McDades?"

"Women don't leave McDades," she said. "I wouldn't, but you—"

"Shh," he said, using his mouth to silence her.

If he wanted her to keep quiet about how she felt then she would. At least for one night. Making big decisions when she was fired full of hormones and emotions probably wasn't a good idea. But Shyla wasn't ashamed of Score or her feelings for him. Whatever it took to prove to him that she wasn't uncertain, she would do it.

But with his mouth reminding her of how good he could make her feel, Shyla couldn't hold onto definitive thoughts for long. They had forever, that was the way she saw it. He could silence her for a night, he couldn't silence her forever.

***

SHYLA PANICKED upon waking up alone. Score wasn't in the shower or the closet. So used to him binding her in bed, it took her a minute to figure out he hadn't tied her down the previous night. Grabbing up the sheet as she leaped off the bed, Shyla wrapped it around herself and hurried out of the room.

"It's not my call," Score's voice carried from the living room. "I'm not weighing in on this one… I get that, Burl, but…" Somehow, as she approached the end of the hallway, he sensed her. It was a helluva skill. He wasn't even facing her direction, yet he stopped talking and turned to set his focus on her as though she'd announced herself with a bullhorn. "Gotta go… Whatever."

Score hung up and started toward her, tossing his phone onto the dining table as he passed it.

"That was your dad?" she asked, tucking her hair back while still clutching her sheet in a fist at her cleavage. "You didn't have to hang up. I can give you privacy."

"Don't need it," he said, stroking her shoulders. "You hungry?"

"Starved, but do we have time to eat?" she asked. "I don't know what time it is."

"We have time."

Relaxing her weight into his hands on her shoulders, she flashed him a smile. "How much time?" she asked, sidelining the aches in her body. "Do we have time to—"

"Why do you think I left you in bed alone," he said, turning her around. "Go shower. I'll order something from downstairs."

The restaurant in their building usually needed residents to let them know in advance if they wanted breakfast. The rules probably didn't apply to Phoenix McDade.

"Is there a problem?" she asked over her shoulder as he marched her forward. "At home, with your family?"

"There's always a problem with my family," he said, stopping her at the bedroom door. "But this is my home."

Shyla stepped over the threshold into the bedroom, but about-faced to address him again. "And there's no problem here."

"None other than you," he said, nodding past her. "Shower."

"You could come with me," she said, trying to touch him.

Score stepped back, out of her reach. "You're not ready for shower sex."

"Make me ready," she said, hitching her chin. "Please."

"Stop it," he said, raising a finger. "You push me and you won't be ready for what happens next. Who makes the rules around here?"

She gave a mock salute. "You, sir."

"Right, so go—"

"Shower. Okay."

Playing with him, teasing him, it was all in fun. Shyla went to the closet to retrieve a towel and left it on the bathroom vanity before stripping the bed. Score was smart. He didn't only choose last night because it would distract her from saying goodbye to Stan. Though he hadn't said it, she suspected his second motive was as a distraction for them. If they only had to get up to do their jobs, he might have been tempted to keep her there all day… maybe all week.

The club was his. He could decide when he wanted to go there and could delegate any important tasks. Her job was to feed him and keep his home for him; she could do that and still pause for sex whenever he wanted to have her.

Coming to this apartment was supposed to keep her off the streets. Instead it had given her a new, wonderful life. One that she wanted to embrace in every way she could.

Carrying the linen to the laundry room, Shyla put the washer on and spun around, but gasped when she was confronted by someone in the doorway. Someone being Score.

"Stop sneaking up on me," she said, soothing her

rushing heart. "Geez."

"That was the quickest shower in history."

She smiled. "I had to put the laundry on or it won't be done for me to switch into the dryer before we go. I'm being efficient."

"And disobeying orders."

Moseying in closer, she picked up his hand to lay it on her breast. "Discipline me," she said. "Isn't that what you said would happen?"

"Don't have time."

So they had time to order food and eat, but not enough time for her to learn what his discipline would involve. Probably sensing her intrigue, he bowed to kiss her. Just once, a short kiss that reminded her of his possession.

"Phoenix," she breathed, moving in closer.

"Shower," he said, stepping aside to give her a push into the hallway.

Before she started moving, he swatted her ass. She'd never been spanked, but it got her to move. Shyla glanced back over her shoulder to see his arms were folded and he was leaning against the wall, much like he had been the first time she laid eyes on him.

Score had warned her there was a lot to learn. But if any of what was to come was half as good as what they'd shared already, she couldn't wait to bathe herself in all of it.

TWENTY-TWO

SCORE WAS ASTUTE, that was no newsflash. Despite knowing he paid attention, the black limo awaiting them on their departure had been a shock. Even though he probably hadn't made the call to reserve the vehicle himself, it still meant something that he'd thought ahead to ensure they had chauffeur driven transportation.

The service was more traditional than Shyla had expected. Stan, like Bernard, planned his own funeral several years ago. From what he'd said at the time of the planning, she'd anticipated something unusual. Instead, there was a sermon on top of the eulogy delivered by Mick, who did a great job at appearing the devastated son.

Shyla didn't want to be cynical about the broken words and long pauses, which apparently he needed to compose himself. He'd lost his father, it stood to reason that he'd be upset. Yet, she did wonder why Mick, if he truly did love his father so much, hadn't made more of an effort while Stan was still in the world with them.

Having Score at her side was more strength than she'd ever need. People glanced their way when they entered and sat down, hands linked, clearly together. Throughout, he'd let her take the lead. Odd that in their private life, he was the dominant partner, but in the sensitive situation, Phoenix let her pick where they should sit, and who they should talk to.

There wasn't much time to talk to anyone between the service and the graveside. The wake was taking place at Stan's house… now Mick's house. People were dispersing to their vehicles, arranging who was taking who on the drive back to Mick's.

While others had discussions in small groups, Score kept her right hand in his and laid his left on her back to guide her toward their car. The driver got out to open the door. Score funneled her into the back. She skootched across the long seat, expecting him to get in after her. Instead with a hand on the roof and the other on the top of the door, he bowed to look inside.

"Stay here," he said.

"Phoen—"

Before she got the word out, he slammed the door. The windows were tinted, but she dipped her head to watch him stalk away from the car. Mick was out there. Shyla didn't think Score planned to do anything to him. Others weren't so sure; several people kept an eye on Score's progress across the grass.

As unwelcome as any kind of scene at Stan's final farewell would be, Shyla wouldn't rush out to drag him back to the car. Whatever he did, he'd always have her support. He'd done an amazing job at supporting her; returning the favor was the least she could do.

Except as she watched, Score passed by all the groups without getting close to any of them. As he kept on going, those dotted around returned to their conversations. Wherever he was going, there was purpose to his stride. Being used to seeing him in the apartment, she didn't often get the chance to see professional Score.

The sight of him that morning when he'd come out of the bedroom in his black suit, black shirt, black tie, he looked devastating. In every definition of the word. Like some kind of lethal assassin, a cool, composed professional, and a man who could melt the panties right off every woman he came into contact with. Shyla had forgotten to breathe for at least half a minute.

Just the memory heated her up again. Despite watching him progress away from their car, she still felt connected to him. All of her was part of him. Shyla couldn't believe that he was her other half. Her partner. Her significant other. Nothing he did or said suggested he had any plans to abandon her any time soon. Yet, each time she told herself to get used to them being together, doubt niggled at her.

How could she be with a man like Score? They were so different, complete opposites in just about every single way. What would their future be? In her mind, the future involved home and family. But the more she thought about it, the more flexible her dreams became. People often thought they wanted what society and tradition expected without considering that it might not be for them.

Her thoughts were interrupted when Score stopped by the parallel road. A car pulled forward, just enough for her to see the hood and a little of the windshield's profile. Phoenix went to the passenger door, it opened and then it closed. Tilting her head, she peered closer. With the distance between them, it was impossible for her to see the driver. Her man was in that vehicle and she didn't have a clue why.

Something was going on.

Suddenly, the lack of answers about the club became more significant. Anytime she asked about his work, Score changed the subject. In each instance, Shyla hadn't wanted to pry or had quickly forgotten because he distracted her. Had she been naïve? As far as she was concerned, her comment about him being separated from his previous life was fact. Score hadn't been as definitive.

Those from Stan's congregation were drifting toward their rides. The gravesite was empty, abandoned, Stan was alone. Fixating on the flowers around the hole he'd been lowered into, Shyla considered the finality of the day. Her old life was over, the last of it would be buried with Stan. Score had numerous lives; he was used to adjusting, dealing with what was in front of him and sucking it up.

Shyla wasn't as adaptable.

Her thoughts wandered and so did her focus. She

didn't even notice Score was on his way back until the door opened, startling her. The second he closed the door, the car began to move.

Surprised by his return, she expected him to say something. He didn't. He sat there next to her, scowl on his face, staring straight ahead.

"What was that?" she asked.

"Nothing."

Most other men would probably try to offer an excuse. Not Score. He didn't apologize and didn't answer to anyone. Even her.

"Was it work?" she asked, persisting. "You got in a car… Who was there?"

Despite sounding like a jealous girlfriend, she didn't actually think he'd been talking with another woman. Maybe it was the heightened emotion of the day, but Shyla began to think more about the past of the man at her side. He was capable of anything. He'd suggested that although he hadn't killed Siobhan, he may have killed others.

That made the fact they'd just attended a funeral sort of ironic. Did he or his family think about the people they eliminated or did they see death as a business transaction?

"Did you know any of them?" she asked, fixating on him.

The random question got his attention. "At the funeral?"

"The massacre," she said. "You said the Dohertys and the Byrnes wiped each other out."

"Not completely," he said. "But yeah, they lost people."

"Did you know any of the people who died?"

"Yeah," he said, frowning at her. "You shouldn't be thinking about that now."

"Were they your friends?"

Touching her jaw with the back of his fingers, he peered into her. "McDades aren't friends with Dohertys or Byrnes. If a McDade meets a Byrne or a Doherty, it's kill or be killed."

"Even now? With all they've done to you… You're

still loyal to the McDades?"

"I am a McDade," he said, like that was an obvious and valid response to her question.

That meant something for their future. Her attention drifted to the opposite window. Being with Score may one day mean marriage, which would mean taking his name… Being part of the family who'd done everything in their power to ruin the man who would be her husband.

Their children would have his name too. Whether they literally had it or not, they'd be under the McDade umbrella. Burl would be their grandfather. Biz, who'd betrayed his brother in such a final way, would be their uncle. Holidays with the family wouldn't be picture perfect.

Judgement didn't feature in her pondering. Not judgement of Score anyway. She'd always known who he was, what he was. Saying goodbye to Stan brought it home that she was alone, with no family to support her. Her brother would get out of prison one day. Finding out she'd linked them to one of the most notorious crime families in the country wouldn't do much to encourage Wyatt onto a straight, crimeless path.

"Lamb."

The single word brought her focus around to him. Still peering at her, his scrutiny brought a smile to her face.

"I'm in love with you Phoenix," she said, putting it as plain as possible. "I don't know what that means to you. I don't know what it means for the future." He inhaled like he intended to speak, but she kept on going. "I know you're going to tell me this isn't the time. That after last night and given what today is… I don't know much. I can't understand your past. I can't understand what you don't tell me. All I do understand is what I feel for you… I love you."

"You can't trust what you feel today."

Because emotion was high, maybe he was right. Before she could experience offense or condescension, a sliver of comprehension crept into her.

"Were you in love with Siobhan?"

"What?" he asked. "No, I—"

"Phoenix," she said, taking his hand. "It's okay to feel

something for me. I'm nothing like her. I am loyal to you. Only you. I don't give a damn who tries to persuade me otherwise. You'll always be safe with me."

Might seem like a crazy thing to say because he was stronger and had promised to take care of her. But even if he consciously ignored his past, some part of him had to be wary of relaxing with anyone. His family set him up in conjunction with a woman he'd been intimate with. Trusting anyone after being betrayed by those closest to him had to be difficult.

His exhale was a mix of irritation and resignation. "I'm not afraid," he said, stating something he probably resented having to voice. Shyla had no time to reassure him. "Not for me. If I was still in the family business, we wouldn't have met." Truth. "Even if we had, I wouldn't have let you near me."

For her safety or because he wouldn't have noticed someone like her?

"Why not?"

"My point, Lamb, is this should never have happened."

It seemed topsy-turvy that his response to her reassurance was to speak like he intended to end their relationship.

"You don't have to love me, Phoenix. I know I'm not the kind of woman you pictured yourself with… But if you give me a chance—"

"If I love you, I'll marry you," he said. "If I marry you, I'll expect us to have children."

Score would be an incredible father. Maybe it would take him time to get used to little people crawling all over him, but he'd be protective and fierce in his love for them. Shyla was sure of his conviction so couldn't understand what was holding him back.

"You don't want me to be the mother of your children?"

"I'm not in a position to do either of those things. And you have to think long and hard about whether you want to birth McDades."

In their own life, in her mind's eye, they could be a

family. Fish and Beeks would be protective of their kids too. She trusted them to do their best not to corrupt the little ones. But could she say that about everyone?

"Would your father want to be in their lives?" she asked.

"My father would expect them to be under his jurisdiction."

Like they were property to control or pieces on the chess board to be maneuvered.

"They would be under our jurisdiction," she said. "I'm not going to give birth to soldiers for your father's war."

"And if they choose that life?" he asked. "Don't underestimate the appeal. They would be the first grandchildren. That means something to Burl. The eldest inherits."

That seemed to mean it didn't have to be the firstborn's first born who took over the reins. "I thought Biz was married."

"He is," Score said. "Hasn't happened for them."

"Does she want kids?"

"Nicole is the perfect daughter-in-law," Score said. "She's whatever Burl tells Biz she's to be."

Following Score's orders aroused Shyla. Taking Burl's orders wouldn't have the same effect.

"We live so far away," she said. "Maybe we could—"

He exhaled. "I've already told you I can't promise Burl won't call me back."

Yes, he'd told her that. Shyla hadn't factored that in to the future she wanted for them. "You would leave me, and our children, to go back to him?"

He pushed up her chin. "If Burl calls me back, he'll want you too, and our family."

Although she hadn't exactly thought the words, Score's hesitation to accept their future had offended her. Their conversation was giving her a new appreciation for why he held himself back.

"Phoen—"

"I don't want you exposed to that life."

Shyla considered the prospect of life in the bosom of

a crime family. By the time she snapped herself out of it, they were almost at Mick's, so she must have been sitting in a daze for a while.

"If we get married, I belong to your father as much as I belong to you," she said, laying it out to show she understood the dilemma. "If I belong to him and we go back there, you'll have to be who you were before."

"I'm still the same man," he said. "You've said it like that before, like I'm some sort of reformed figure." Curling his fingers around her throat, he pulled her closer. "I'm still the same man. I am a McDade."

She couldn't say what prison had done to him. It hadn't scared him straight; he wasn't the type of man to be afraid of anything. But he was trying to tell her something. Trying to make her see that the prospect of being involved with a crime family was much closer than Burl and his brothers.

"You're my McDade," she said, caressing his face. "I'm in love with you and I will follow your orders… If you tell me I have to submit to your father and your family, I will. But it's your command I follow, not theirs."

If he told her to move there and obey, she would. Shyla could give herself to him completely. Though children wouldn't be so easy to sacrifice.

Perhaps Score's sister-in-law, Nicole, was choosing not to have children. If she didn't have them, she wouldn't have to hand them over to Burl's tutelage. Shyla considered the same choice.

Being with Score meant being a McDade. Shyla was going into it with her eyes open. If she couldn't hand her children over to that life, which she doubted that she could, then she wouldn't have children.

Her Phoenix was worth that sacrifice. Few people had chosen him over all others. Shyla vowed to remain at his side. He didn't have to be afraid with her because she would never betray him. She'd give up anything for him, everything, so long as they could be together. His dilemma was hers too. She just had to prove that making a choice not to be together simply wasn't an option.

TWENTY-THREE

STAN USED TO HANG out on the porch with the other old-timers from the neighborhood. They'd sit and lament the old days, discuss current events, or play some dominoes.

Still, when Shyla walked into the house, the number of people present shocked her. In standing room only, she shuffled through the hall and into the living room. She'd intended to keep going to the kitchen or even out to the backyard. Not only did she need space, but she didn't think Score would be too fond of being crushed. The guy took up a lot of space on his best days and always carried an invisible beacon warning everyone to respect the perimeter of his personal space. In his case, that was a clear couple of feet from his body.

Unfortunately, Shyla didn't progress that far into the house. Once one person had stopped her, all of them did in their turn. Many people from their block had mobility issues, so they couldn't make it to the service. They hadn't seen her around either, which everyone reminded her about more than a few times.

Stuck in another conversation, Shyla glanced around for Score who was no longer at her side. Hoping he wasn't being quizzed, she intended to apologize for being waylaid. It was a surprise to find him on the other side of the room, just inside the doorway, observing her from afar. Peace permeated her. He was there, watching over her, giving her the room to do what she needed to do.

Rather than be concerned that Score wasn't at her side, she was encouraged by his distance. It showed how he wanted her to say goodbye to Stan, to say goodbye to her past. Not because he wanted her to be rid of it, but because it was best for her.

"I heard a rumor," Mrs. Francis said, bringing Shyla's attention back around to her. "A rumor that the man over there belongs to you."

The long answer would involve going into too much detail and throw her into a fit of overthinking, given what they'd discussed in the car.

Rather than go into that, Shyla just smiled. "Yes. I suppose he does."

A group of half a dozen ladies had gathered around her. They were the starlings of the neighborhood, always in a group, drafting and gliding with each other. As much as they could also be described as busybodies, their interest never offended Shyla. Living in a household with only two men for company, sometimes it was nice to have maternal figures fussing. Even if that did include answering awkward questions.

In the past, while she'd lived there, Shyla hadn't had a man to explain. The new position was comforting in its own way, especially claiming a man she could be so proud of like Score.

"Oh," Mrs. Evans squealed. "We're happy for you, honey."

"You deserve to be happy."

Mrs. Denver was more discerning in her scrutiny of Score. "Seems severe to me."

"He's a man who's a man," Mrs. Evans said. "Not one of these all about his feelings and whining. Doesn't look like a snowflake, that what you mean?"

Just considering that word in the same sentence as Score's name almost made Shyla laugh.

"He's a real man," Mrs. Francis said.

Expecting women so set in their ways to be more politically correct was expecting too much. Shyla doubted Score would mind the tag anyway, either being a "real man" or not being a snowflake.

"Where are you staying now? Do you live with him?" Mrs. Evans asked, on track to collect as much information as possible. "Are you getting married?"

"Oh, leave the girl be," Mrs. Francis said. "She's still adjusting."

"Adjusting is difficult," Mrs. Denver said. "I remember when my Bennie passed... The house is just empty."

"Empty, even though they have five sons," Mrs. Evans said, bobbing her head while making deliberate eye contact.

Mrs. Francis was quick to sigh. "Today's kids just don't understand their responsibilities. My mother would be turning in her grave."

Last Shyla heard, Mrs. Denver's boys were in their fifties welcoming grandchildren of their own. That didn't excuse them ignoring their mother or not checking in as often as they should, but it did put calling them "kids" in perspective.

"You know if you ever need anything, you can just give me a call," Shyla said.

Mrs. Francis took her hand. "You need to think about yourself now. You've missed out on so much, my dear."

"What you did for your grandfather," Mrs. Denver said, exuding awe and gratitude. "Not many people would've done that."

"And to stick around for Stan," Mrs. Evans said.

The women were all agreeing with each other, making sounds of praise that were difficult to accept. During the service, Shyla had teared up a few times. Clinging to Score helped to get her through. Having him near gave her strength.

With him all the way across the room, he wasn't close enough for her to hang on to. She could turn around and look at him. One look would be enough to convey that she needed him. But he wouldn't enjoy being fawned over by the starlings. Maybe he wouldn't dislike it, but they weren't the type of people he was used to handling.

Any illusion that the wake would be an easy affair vanished when someone grabbed her shoulder to jerk her back. Shyla had been so focused on the starlings that she hadn't been aware of who was nearby.

Mick forced his way into the group. "What are you ladies talking about?" he demanded. "This is my dad's day."

His dad's day, but he wasn't to be forgotten either. The first any of them knew of the ensuing intrusion was the rising level of hubbub in the room.

Before Shyla could even seek Score out or check what was going on, an arm appeared between her and Mick. With a sure grip, it grabbed Mick by the throat and yanked him around. That was when Shyla noticed Score. Maneuvering Mick with his straight arm and sure grip, Score marched the host backwards through the guests and out the living room door.

Her man took charge rather than moving anyone aside or introducing himself. The word "pussyfoot" wasn't in Score's dictionary.

Having just claimed the man, Shyla figured the starlings would have something to say. Before any of them got a chance, she spoke up. "Uh," she said, throwing a sheepish smile their way. "Excuse me a minute."

Everyone in the room was fixated on the door, rubbernecking in their attempts to see what was going on. No doubt plenty of judgements were being made about Score's actions. Though imagining Mick had charmed people with his usual lack of finesse, she hoped there was a chance of some support too. Mick had a special way of pissing people off, as he'd just proven.

Shyla hurried out of the living room, closing the door behind her, sealing them in the empty hall. Whatever was about to happen, it was probably best that the masses didn't bear witness. Though if Score took Mick outside, the picture window in the living room would become a movie screen for those inside.

So far, Score hadn't ventured out. He stood at the bottom of the stairs, Mick in front of him, pinned to the wall by the grip on his throat. Any time he tried to move, Score used just one hand to slam him back.

"How dare you! This is my—"

"You made a mistake," Score growled, pressing his fist into Mick's upper chest. "You're gonna admit that and apologize to the lady, or you and me are gonna take a ride."

Shyla didn't know exactly what that meant, but figured he wasn't just planning to show Mick the view. Standing with her back to the closed living room door, she wasn't sure what to do. Leave him to work or step in before Mick thought to press charges?

"Who are you—"

"The woman you put your hands on belongs to me," Score said, planting his hand on Mick's throat again to jerk him higher. "No one puts their hands on what's mine."

"Baby?" Shyla said without leaving her spot.

"I got this, Lamb," Score said without taking his focus from Mick who was beginning to sweat. "Go upstairs and get what's yours."

The only thing Shyla had mentioned being sorry to leave was the clock. It wasn't a major deal, but she didn't think that was the moment to tell him.

"This is my—"

Mick's words stopped when Score's grip tightened. "Anything that she wants, she gets. If that means erasing you, that's what'll happen."

His grip constricted. Mick grabbed for the hand cutting off his air supply, trying to loosen its hold. Not that he had a chance.

Shyla swallowed and took Mick's gasping and clawing as acquiesce. If she didn't do as told, then Score might not let go before Mick lost more than his dignity.

Ignoring Mick's gargled pleas for mercy and his wild eyes searching for hers, Shyla passed the men and ran up the stairs to take her clock from the wall. Pausing at the door on her way out, she glanced around the space that had been her sanctuary for years. Part of her wanted to take a tour, to wander around and breathe in as many memories as she could before leaving for what really would be the last time.

But knowing Mick's predicament, she sighed and retreated, closing the door behind her. Instead of showing haste and running down the stairs to offer Mick aid, Shyla took her time about descending. Score stayed fixated on the man under his rule, ignoring the desperate wheezing and futile grappling. Her love didn't flinch. Not a single hair moved, his glare remained intent on the man who'd put his hands on her without permission.

Shyla wasn't used to being in a romantic relationship. That was really her first outing as a girlfriend. But if it was like that every time, she was definitely going to enjoy it.

Stopping on the bottom stairs, she held the clock in one hand and smiled at Mick when he tried to crane his desperate eyes to hers.

"Want the house?" Score asked, his voice still a snarl. "The fucker will sell it to us for a good price."

"I think the fucker doesn't deserve our money," she said, switching the clock into her other hand. Cursing wasn't normal for her, but she did enjoy the panic it wrung from Mick. "I want to leave… I don't want to be anywhere near him ever again."

Other than being arrogant and pompous, Mick hadn't really committed a crime. Not against her anyway. Many would see the way he ignored his father as a moral crime; Shyla didn't think she'd ever forgive him for that.

Bernard loved having her near. As much as she was like a grandchild to Stan, there were times she found him looking through old photographs, a wistful look on his face. Those times reminded her that being abandoned by blood wasn't an easy insult to get over.

Score yanked Mick higher and bowed to get his face up close. "Think about her again and I'll come back. I'll finish you in one second, before you even know I'm there. I'll snap your neck and throw your body in the sea… No one will mourn you."

On a shove, he stepped back. With a curl of disgust, Score wiped his hand down the front of Mick's jacket and offered his other hand to her. As Shyla linked her fingers between his, Score drew his eyes away from Mick, and turned to stride out the open door.

They kept going down the path and out to the street. Score didn't even look before crossing over to get in the back of their limo. Being a residential street, it was quiet. But even if there had been traffic, Shyla got the feeling that Score's sheer will would make him impervious. Any driver who saw his purpose and determination would take their lives in their hands if they thought to keep driving or, god forbid, hit the horn.

Score guided her into the back and then got in. Without a word, the moment the door was closed, the car started to move. She didn't know much about what Score did in the daytime, but that couldn't be the first time he'd used the service given the responsiveness of their driver.

Question marks hung over them and their relationship. Yet, despite how immoral it was, she grabbed Score's lapel and dragged him to her as she twisted to plant her mouth on his.

Though there wasn't exactly surprise in his kiss, it was slow to respond to hers. Once he relaxed and took control of the union, he put a hand on hers to guide it down from his lapel. Shyla's excitement anticipated him directing it to an intimate place so they could continue down the carnal path she'd initiated. Instead, he flattened it on his thigh and broke the kiss.

"I think pounding on guys *would* turn you on," he said, curling his fingers around hers. "I meant what I said, no one is allowed to put their hands on you."

Because he was possessive or wanted to protect her, either way was a win as far as Shyla was concerned. "Thank you," she said, licking her lips. "No one has ever done anything like that for me."

"Better get used to it if we're gonna be out together in public."

Used to it? She wasn't sure how, but was willing to learn. "You're incredible. I can't even... If you hadn't been with me—"

"I'll always be with you, Shy," he said. "I meant what I said about the house too. You want it, I'll get it for you."

Sometimes she was just over-awed by him. He hadn't put word to his feelings for her and may never, but she could feel it in the way he looked at her, the way he was with her.

"I want you," she said. "All. Only… I want to go home. To our home. That's where I want to be."

Apart from anything else, living in the suburbs would put her further from Score's workplace, which would mean longer travelling time. Shyla didn't want to waste a single second of their life together with anything unnecessary.

TWENTY-FOUR

"I SHOULD MAKE something for dessert," Shyla said as the elevator doors opened.

While her mind and body were so fried, she couldn't really come up with anything quick and easy, or anything that appealed to her taste buds. She put her clock on the side table and started on a trajectory meant to take her to the kitchen. Before she got more than a few steps, Score snatched her hand and whipped her around to face him.

Off-balance, still trying to figure out what had happened, Shyla got dizzy. Score didn't leave her wondering about his motives for long. Lifting her hand to place it on the knot of his tie, he communicated what he wanted. His jacket was already gone, in a heap on the floor behind him. At least, that's what she figured the dark mound was; she was too focused on him to look any closer.

Loosening his tie, Shyla began to slide it free of his collar. Just as the end was about to fall, Score grabbed it in a snap, showcasing his incredible reflexes. The already charged moment became something much more intense when he took a step back and used the strip of fabric to tie her wrists.

Once her hands were bound together, he wrapped the free end around his knuckles and passed her to lead the way down the hall. Her love didn't explain himself and she didn't ask. Filling the moment with too many words would ruin it; Shyla simply trusted him and complied. Worked out for her because going with the flow got her into his bedroom. Hope and anticipation sparked and smoldered as she speculated about Score's intentions.

He took her right to the edge of the bed, standing at her side to pull her forward while he went around to her back. Because he still held the end of the tie in his grip, her connected hands were drawn to her hip. Waiting, the pulse thrumming through her sped up.

How could he arouse her so much with such little action? Shyla was eager and appreciative. Even without words, he was touching the deepest part of her. Heated speckles danced across her skin, pricking every hair, enlivening every pore. Score began to draw down the zipper of her dress, igniting the embers of her need. He pushed the straps down her arms to her tied wrists and took the clasp from her hair to toss it aside. Just the tickle of her own locks falling around her shoulders and down her back brought a whimper to her throat.

Although Shyla wasn't as naked as she'd like to be, what Score had done to free her from the conservative outfit gave her some relief. She wanted to be with him. Naked, alive, and beneath him. She needed him. More than anything in the world, she craved whatever he wanted to give and would always want more.

When his fingers curled around her throat to pull her head back against him, her ensuing moan of aroused surprise ratcheted the tension up another notch.

"You need something," Score muttered in her hair, forcing her chin higher. "Something to remind you why you're here."

Cooking up dessert in the kitchen would've reminded her why she was there. Except Score hadn't taken her to the kitchen. He didn't want to remind her of her job.

Her ideas of what he'd do to her would probably pale in comparison to the reality. Still, she would let him take the lead.

"Why am I here?" Shyla asked, licking her drying lips.

Before he did anything else, he unhooked her bra. Shaking her arms as best she could with his grip still tight on her leash, she got it to her wrists, where the straps of her dress rested.

Score was liberating her in ways he could never understand. Removing the clothes she'd said goodbye in felt like a real cleansing.

Bernard and Stan weren't in that house. Mick didn't own them. Her life with the two men she cherished had shaped her into the woman she was; the woman who wanted to go into the future with the man standing behind her, holding her up.

His leash hand swept up her torso to rouse each of her breasts before laying it flat on her stomach. "You were incredible today, Lamb," he said, tightening his hold on her just a fraction. "Beautiful and bold."

Shyla couldn't say she'd thought the same way that day, or on any day. Score's view of her was unique. The way he spoke to her, the way he acted, gave her a whole new perspective on herself. Score saw her as a woman, an arousing one who interested him. It didn't matter that she didn't get it, he did… and he wanted more.

Discovering how he'd been thinking of her inspired more than just her confidence. "Phoenix," Shyla breathed.

Though she wanted to touch him, he only gave her enough slack to make brief contact with the hand he had on her abdomen. After just a second, he yanked her hands to her side again.

In the same tug, he grabbed her hip to spin her around, then he bent low, coming closer to her level. "You belong here."

Drifting on her expectations, Shyla nodded. "I belong wherever you are."

Sticking to the contours of her body, his hand slid downwards from her throat. There was no way to know what was in his mind, yet she leaned in to his touch, just experiencing his entitlement. His eyes grew more discerning, suggesting he was trying to read what was inside her.

"Sit," he said, nudging her backwards.

The bed was so close that she could only do as told. Score came down over her, using his grip on her leash to yank her backwards. All the while, his mouth flirted with hers. She wanted him, wanted his kiss, but he withheld it, teasing and taunting her with the possibility. They stopped the ascent when he jerked her arms up and flattened his own hand on the tie against the headboard. She couldn't move, that anchor kept her where he wanted her.

Rather than any slow show of affection, he got rougher. Compared to his deliberate actions of the previous night, Score's jostling and jerking was much more tempestuous. His urgency felt wild and dirty, yet it was no less exciting. If anything, the desperation of his desire heated her faster.

While using his legs to force hers open, he rammed the skirt of her dress up, out of his way. With the skirt bunched at her hips, Shyla tried to wriggle lower, but Score wouldn't have it. Dragging her bound hands higher, he used the anchor point to brace his weight and with a few quick moves opened his pants. Pulled in many different directions, with her own bra obscuring her view, Shyla was shocked when Score reared up and began pushing into her.

He'd only shoved the crotch of her underwear aside and their clothes were still restricting them. There was no kissing or touching or building up to the apex. Score wanted her and had no plans to wait. The potency of his desire and the discomfort of their positions was new to her. Instead of focusing on what she didn't know, Shyla just let herself be overwhelmed.

All day they'd been buttoned up and presentable in a somber environment. Score was casting that from both of them, taking control of what they were. Being home, being alone demanded that they throw respectability aside to surrender themselves to the race for gratification. Their need was real. Score's need was real. They were together and when it came to their desire, nothing would get in their way.

Being unable to see him heightened other sensations. Although he slipped into her easier than he had the first time they'd been together, it wasn't as quick or as easy as Score would've liked. A growl betrayed his frustration. Shyla tried to relax, but it took time to get used to the new angle of their bodies.

His pillows pushed against her lower back, thrusting her hips toward him in a different way than before. Score pushed on, proving he wasn't going to let her body refuse him. He thrust hard, forcing a yelp from her throat. Pulling back to drive into her again, his next advance went right through her. The head of his cock hit somewhere new in her, some place she hadn't known was there. Her yelp of surprise was a mixture of pain and pleasure that even she didn't understand.

Score stalled, but Shyla gasped in. "No!" she begged. "Do that again. Oh my God, do that again."

A grin split her face and that time it was him who did as told.

Oh, she liked it. Whatever it was, whatever that secret corner of her body was, it liked his attention.

So much so that when, after another couple of thrusts, Score embedded himself inside her and stopped, she couldn't control the movement of her hips or the whispers of breathy desire slipping from between her lips.

"Phoenix," she murmured, her eyes almost closed.

He was moving too, stimulating her without ever losing contact with the heat that felt so good.

Her hunger shifted up a gear. Moving her hips faster, Shyla worked with him to bring herself right to the edge of climax. When it exploded deep down between her legs, her whole body experienced it all at once. Every part of her awoke to sing and scream in response to the new sensations her man showered her with.

While she was still trying to feel everything and everywhere, Score began to thrust again, speeding his way toward sating his thirst.

The need of his body penetrated hers. The weight of him reassured and excited every part of her. She was fizzing and simmering in the hormones of pure pleasure he'd released within her.

"Yes," she whispered, feeling his climb to climax as

his speed increased. "Yes, baby, please!"

He roared and drove himself hard into her, almost crushing her with the pressure of reaching his limit as he surrendered to the gratification he'd chased down.

From being occupied and cocooned by him, Shyla suddenly found herself freed. Score flipped over, letting go of the tie, releasing his claim of ownership. For that minute anyway.

She wriggled down to a more comfortable position. Score shifted his forearm for just long enough to loosen the binding from her wrist, then it dropped onto his forehead again. Freeing her hands gave her the opportunity to strip down.

Though she'd thought she was right at the peak of feeling amazing, being naked actually took her happiness up a notch. Once her clothes were somewhere in a heap by the bed, she clambered onto Score and began to unbutton his shirt.

"I should hang all that up," she said. The dry cleaning bags were in the closet, so close and yet not close enough. Score's only response was a sort of movement of his brow above his heavy eyes. "That was amazing." Opening his shirt, she laid both hands on his chest. "You are amazing."

"Finished yet?" he asked.

Shyla frowned. "Finished?"

"You said once we did it, you'd be over it."

A grin leaped to her lips as she swooped down to steal a quick kiss. "And you were right to mock me... I think we should do it some more. Do it in every corner of the apartment while we're alone."

"That's a lot of corners."

Okay, maybe that was a bit much to ask for in one day, but Shyla had never been so exhilarated. "I don't know why anyone ever does anything else," she said, slithering down to rest her head right in the middle of his chest.

"Doesn't always feel like this."

Tipping her chin up didn't mean she could see him, but it did bring his stag tattoo into view, so she traced it with a fingertip. "Because I'm new to it?"

Or because there were feelings involved with them?

Shyla didn't ask the last part figuring she'd asserted her feelings enough for one day.

"Partly that," he said, resting a palm on her hair. "And because we're not anonymous."

Wasn't quite an admission of love, but it was something. "I can't imagine having anonymous sex. Just picking any random guy and inviting him into my body…" She shivered. "Isn't it just awkward?"

"Can be. Close your eyes and get some rest."

The day had been fraught with a lot of emotion; she was more tired than usual. The endorphins of orgasm were beginning to wane, but she wasn't ready to disconnect from him yet.

"We're going to be okay, Phoenix… aren't we?"

He put a hand on hers to flatten it against his tattoo. "You'll be safe. Nothing will ever hurt you."

Except there were different kinds of hurt. Even though Score would never hurt her in anger, that didn't mean he'd never break her heart. If he walked away because he thought it was best for her or to return to his family, she'd be in all kinds of pain.

Turning her head, she kissed his chest and then closed her eyes. He'd asked her to trust him, told her he'd take care of her. Except, he'd given no declaration of love or assertion they'd always be together. Shyla wanted him to love her. But there were no guarantees, no promises on his lips. Trust was the only way forward. They'd have to let their relationship play out. No matter what, Shyla was ready to fight for what she wanted. She'd fight for Score and hope he'd do the same for her.

TWENTY-FIVE

SOMETHING WOKE SHYLA up. She didn't know what and didn't really care. The breeze from the open terrace doorway refreshed her contentment. With a smile on her face, she opened her still heavy eyes. The first thing she spotted was the cause of her happiness.

Standing on the terrace wearing only a pair of jeans, Score was on the phone. With one hand on the aluminum rail that topped the glass terrace barrier, he seemed tense. Shyla liked to think maybe the call was an inconvenience because he was eager to get back to their bed. *Their* bed.

Rolling onto her back, she pushed her arms out wide and arched to stretch her back. Her whole body ached in the most wonderful way. Score had been right when he'd said she would be sore. All morning tender twinges reminded her of what they'd done the previous night.

Given their afternoon session, she guessed those twinges wouldn't be going anywhere. That wouldn't stop her from trying to tempt him into something that night. Providing he stayed home with her. It was possible he'd go to the club.

Twisting in their sheets, she examined the tattoo on his back. One of the first intimacies she'd known about the man after walking in on him on her first day. Seemed like so long ago. The longer they were together, the more she could only remember him. Her future. Her certainty.

Though Shyla was tempted to call out to him, she kept her mouth shut. Score's phone calls weren't usually frivolous; he wasn't the type of guy to just shoot the shit with anyone.

What she should've done was get up and out of his bed the minute she opened her eyes. Unfortunately, that didn't even occur to her until movement drew her eye away from Score's incredible physique.

Someone was on the terrace, coming around the corner from the living room side. Not one someone, two someones: Beeks and Fish. Damnit. Shyla noticed them just a fraction of a second before Score did.

She froze. If she sat up or tried to slip out of bed, they'd be more likely to notice her. As it was, they were focused on Score who'd turned their way and held up a hand in acknowledgement, asking for a second. Shyla couldn't think. She didn't know what to do. Score might think she was still asleep, or he'd assumed she'd been on the ball enough to hear the men come out of the elevator. They'd only search the terrace if they were looking for someone. For Score. For her. More likely the former.

The duo wouldn't have been certain she and Score were back from the wake. They could've called Score to check. If they had, and he'd known they were coming over, he should've warned her. That way Shyla would've been up and respectable before they were…

Fish noticed her as he and Beeks stopped in front of Score who'd just ended the call. Her friend's mouth opened, only a tiny bit, but enough to show his shock. Beeks was talking to Score who kept his phone in his fist and folded his arms.

It wouldn't be fair to ask Fish to lie for them, but she couldn't understand why Score wasn't herding them back the way they'd come. He could get Beeks out of there before he noticed that she was—

Beeks head moved a fraction so he noticed Fish was fixated on something. Following the younger man's focus led him to… The moment his eyes landed on her, his lips stopped moving. Laying a hand on her chest to hold the sheet in place, Shyla lifted the other in a static wave.

Score didn't even turn around. But, she guessed, he didn't really need to; he knew who he'd left in his bed. He hadn't wanted Beeks and Fish to know until they'd had sex. They had been intimate, but their relationship was hardly assured. If anything, Score's comments in the back of the limo suggested he was having second thoughts about their future.

Her lover nodded, and said something, but Shyla couldn't make out more than a deep mumble. None of the words had been decipherable yet. Score began to walk forward, which forced Beeks to turn. Fish was still in stunned mode, so Beeks put a hand on his shoulder to turn him around. The three men walked around the corner, past the window that she'd first seen them in.

The moment they were out of sight, Shyla threw back the sheet and leaped out of bed. Putting on her own clothes would take too long, instead she snagged Score's shirt and tugged it on while heading out of the room.

She slowed to do up the buttons on her walk up the hall. The closer she got, the clearer the men's conversation became.

"…buried a man she loved today," Beeks said just before she appeared at the end of the hallway.

If she'd been thinking straight, Shyla might have noted the irony of her position. She stood in the same place Score had when she first saw him. Things had come quite a way since then. The three men stood near the chessboard, where she'd been sitting in that same moment.

"No one took advantage of me," she said, attracting the attention of the others. "I'm sorry you found out this way."

"Found out what?" Beeks asked, setting his frown on Score. "I knew she was besotted with you, Score, but she's a girl, a child. I thought better of—"

"What?" Score barked, his head snapping around so he could set a glare on Beeks. "You place your bets on the morality of a McDade, you're gonna lose, old man."

"That what this is?" Beeks asked. "Sport? Thought you'd corrupt the innocent—"

"I am not innocent," she said, striding further into the space to stop by the dining table. "And I am not a child. I knew what this was, what he was before I—"

"You think you know," Beeks said. "You don't have a damn clue, Shyla."

"Watch how you speak to her," Score growled.

But Beeks didn't shrink, his disapproval was written all over his face. "Does she know?"

With no other *"she"* present, Shyla couldn't mistake that the question referred to her.

"Does she know what?" Shyla asked.

She didn't start to get suspicious until no one spoke. Fish's silence was especially telling. Usually, he had something to say about everything. Even if he didn't know anything about the specific topic at hand, he always found a way to pivot to something that he did know about.

Since he'd seen her in Score's bed, she hadn't heard him say a single word. Was it just shock or was he concerned about the same thing as Beeks?

"I'll take that as a no," Beeks said. "Never mind."

"No, not never mind," she said, grabbing for the back of the nearest chair. "What don't I know?"

"She doesn't need to know," Score said, plain and straightforward in his sentiment.

Except he'd been the one to champion honesty. He wanted to know her. Everything about her. Yet, apparently, he had something going on, some secret, that she wasn't a part of.

The way Beeks had brought it up proved it wasn't anything positive like a party or a gift. Everyone would expect her to be ignorant to something like that. There were too many frowns and glares being tossed around for her to be optimistic about the secret.

Giving up on Beeks revealing the truth, Shyla fixed her attention on Fish. Score wouldn't break, and he wouldn't even feel bad about it. His meeting in the cemetery took on new significance. Whatever he was hiding might be business related. But that didn't mean it wouldn't affect their home life. It was seeping in already.

"Fish," she said. "What are they talking about?"

Both Score and Beeks looked at the younger man. Shyla didn't break her focus either. Fish's frown loosened to something nearing panic. "I… Shyla, I…"

"You keep your mouth shut," Score said. "I'm handling it."

"Handling it?" Beeks asked. "You have to end this or Burl will learn about it. If I had to put money on it, I'd say he already knows."

"Doesn't matter now."

"No, it doesn't matter now, but it will… It will and you know it."

Score didn't respond. Not with words. He turned his back on all of them to cross to the terrace door. He didn't go out, he just stood there looking toward the ocean.

"I am not afraid of Burl McDade," she said.

Beeks smiled and Fish made a sound like a disbelieving laugh.

"You are in so much danger you can't even comprehend it," Beeks said. "Fall in love with this McDade and I promise you another one will kill you. Maybe not today, but eventually. They'll do it themselves or order someone else to do it. Burl is strangely specific about his boys, about the rules they have to follow and the punishments they face if they step out of line."

"What about Biz, huh?" she asked, figuring if they were talking about it then they should damn well talk the truth. "What about what he did? He put Phoenix in prison!"

Either raising her voice or using his first name surprised Beeks and Fish, maybe both. As Fish stepped back, Beeks grew stronger.

"That's not what we're talking about here."

"No, because no one ever does! He gets away with sending his own brother to death row and everyone's just supposed to be okay with that."

"Lamb—"

"No!" she argued with the man at the window who

hadn't even bothered to turn around. For all his strength, it frustrated the hell out of her that he wouldn't fight for himself. "It's not right! They come in here and judge us, judge you, but no one ever takes Biz to task! No one demands he answer for what he did! Burl McDade couldn't even—"

"Enough," Score roared, spinning around to glare at them all. "No one talks shit about the McDades when I'm around." She blinked like his scowl actually slapped her when he turned it on her. "I warned you."

Warned her? The last time he'd told her to be careful of talking about the McDades in any negative way, specifically his father, they'd been alone. They weren't alone at that moment, but she'd believed his trust in Beeks at least was absolute. If the apartment wasn't a safe place for her to talk, if Beeks and Fish weren't trustworthy, hell, if her own lover wasn't confident about keeping her confidence, she didn't know what any of them were doing.

"You told me no one would hurt me. That you would take care of me. You meant no one except your own family; that you'd only take care of me until they asked you to sacrifice me."

"I told you to trust me, Shyla. That's what you're going to do."

She retreated a step. "Is it?"

Continuing backwards, she turned to go down the hall and into the laundry room. Grabbing a pair of her cutoffs from the pile of laundry waiting to be put away, she pulled them on and tied Score's shirt around her middle. Her hair ties were lying all over the place; she was grateful for the one on the shelf by the laundry detergent. It had probably been taken from a pocket before something went into the washer.

Her purse was in the closet by the elevators. Loitering around the men and their poisonous secrets wasn't an attractive prospect. Shyla needed to breathe. Leaving the laundry room, she didn't bother to look their way on her walk to the elevators or after retrieving her purse. She pressed the call button and waited with her back to the room.

"Shyla," Beeks said. "You shouldn't leave."

"Why? Because I might meet a McDade who wants

to kill me? According to you, that's going to happen no matter what I do. I knew they wouldn't like me. I had no idea they'd hate me so much they'd want me dead."

"It isn't about that. It doesn't matter if they like you. If I thought that was the only problem—"

"Then what?" she asked, whirling around to address the men. "If this isn't only about me not being good enough for the McDades, then what is it about?"

Although the tension in the air was still thick, there were fewer frowns exchanged when the three men glanced around at each other. Score was the one she settled on. Even from a distance away, she could read the warning in his expression.

Nobody was going to answer her. Score didn't want her to know and that was enough to keep Beeks and Fish quiet.

In the weeks she'd worked for Score, Shyla had believed that the three men cared about her, that they were becoming closer. But it was an illusion. McDades aside, the three men came from the same world. Different angles of it, sure, but the same world. Shyla wasn't from that world. No matter how much she thought the trio were welcoming her or she believed she was adjusting to her new life, it wasn't real. Nothing was real.

The elevator opened behind her. None of the men even looked at her as she went inside and selected her floor. She had no idea where she was going; she just couldn't be there any longer. Shyla had to make some decisions and she had to make them fast.

TWENTY-SIX

SHYLA DID CONSIDER going somewhere far from the building. But the alcohol of the in-house bar beckoned. Without any real thought, her finger hit the button for that floor. For a woman who hadn't ever been much of a drinker, the oblivion alcohol could offer would be a welcome break from reality.

The plan was to have a couple of drinks, just enough to loosen her up, then she'd go for a walk in the evening air to clear her head. Like that was possible. Shyla didn't know who to trust anymore. Score had been right when he said she couldn't trust her feelings.

Sleeping with Score, saying goodbye to Stan, then dealing with Mick being Mick, it all took its toll. Being in Score's bed had blinded her to reality. It hadn't been deliberate. She hadn't meant to be naive or fall into some ridiculous dream that everything was going to be perfect. Crashing back to Earth wasn't easy or painless. So, after gulping down her first drink, she ordered another.

The sound of the stool next to her moving almost made her groan. With an elbow on the bar, she turned intending to tell whoever was joining her to go away. But upon seeing Beeks, she curled her lips into her mouth, waiting to hear what he'd say.

At least one thing had become clear from the mess she'd created: filling a silence got in the way of others' confessions. Not that Score had ever planned to confess to her. In that moment, it wasn't clear if she knew him at all or if she ever had.

The bartender came over with a drink for her. Beeks paid for it and ordered one for himself.

Then the lawyer turned to her. "Shyla—"

"I was just leaving," she said, trying to slip off her stool, doubting that she was ready to hear what he might have to say.

He put a hand on the back to stall her. "You just ordered a drink… You didn't plan to drink it?"

Snatching the glass, she tossed the scotch into her throat and then slammed it down. Closing her eyes, Shyla braced against the heat burning in her throat. Scotch was a heavy introduction to pain-relief, but it was what she was used to drinking with Score.

Score… She should drink something that didn't remind her of being with him.

"Shyla, you didn't have to leave the apartment. We can—"

"What? Talk it out? No one wanted to talk to me. I gave you all the chance; no one wants to be honest. Let's face it, there's no point in bothering with the small talk. I fucked my boss, and I can't be with my boss, which pretty much means I'm out of a job."

Her outburst came before she'd really faced that reality. As the truth sank in, some of her anger ebbed.

"No one suggested you had to leave your job either."

Sighing, she sagged in her stool, slumping onto her tired arms. "I didn't think this through," she murmured.

Since starting her job there, any thoughts about the future featured Score. Featured her and him together. Now it was seeming that wasn't possible, the alternative wasn't a rosy picture.

Frustrated with herself, she should've taken Score's hints. From what he'd said, more than once, their chance of a future together was unlikely. The words all and only played on repeat in her mind. Those were the words that always reverberated whenever she had doubts.

Shyla had ignored the truth because she didn't want to face it. Wanting to be together wasn't the same as actually being together.

Score was complicated, she'd always known that. She just hadn't accepted how complicated a relationship with him would be. They were incompatible. He wanted honesty from her, but wouldn't give it. He wanted to know everything, but wouldn't reveal everything. Other women who got together with McDades probably understood from the gate that there would be a double standard. Score had told her that he would look after her; she'd been seduced by that. The abstract was so much easier to handle than the reality.

The reality of being with a McDade meant secrets. It was the only way he knew how to be. It wasn't his fault… But there she was making excuses for him again. Shyla had to start looking out for herself and stop making excuses for others.

Maybe she could live in a relationship where she didn't know everything. Where she had to trust her partner while always knowing their relationship wasn't equal.

Beeks' certainty that she would be killed by her potential in-laws wasn't something to be ignored either. Lies and secrets were one thing. Murder was another. Could she trust Score would step up and protect her from his father and brothers? Shyla didn't even have to think about that one for long. He'd already told her that he'd answer the call if Burl requested his return to the family base.

The years, the betrayal, it meant nothing. It diminished none of Score's loyalty. In his own way, he'd told her that. On more than one occasion, he'd asserted that he was a McDade. Being a McDade was a prominent part of his identity. Maybe he just didn't know who he was without that part of himself in place.

She and Beeks had been sitting in silence for at least a minute. Shyla would've stayed that way, lost in her own head, except he spoke up.

"You're a good person," Beeks said. "Kind and

generous. I think you're a wonderful human being. I thought you would be good for him. It's my fault that I wasn't more vigilant. I should've said something at my first inkling you were attracted to him."

Which would've been the minute she first laid eyes on him.

"It wouldn't have stopped me," she said, staring at her empty glass. "I need another drink."

"That wouldn't be smart." He was probably right, it didn't take much to push her over the edge. "I am sorry, Shyla."

"It wasn't just a one off," she said. "He didn't take advantage of me in a vulnerable moment. You can think he's some kind of evil playboy if you want, but it really wasn't like that."

"Score isn't a playboy, I know that. But he is more worldly and should've known better than to get involved—"

"With a child?" she asked, tipping her chin his way. "That was harsh. I might be sheltered and inexperienced when it comes to men, but I am a woman. All grown up."

Seemed silly to be so dogged about ownership of her decisions when she'd made so many wrong ones. Her first real relationship had lasted all of a day. She had a lot to learn. Being a fool had been easy. In her naivety, she'd believed her and Score were just beginning their life together, when in truth, they were already over. All those lessons others learned in their teens and early twenties would've flagged the relationship as temporary. Shyla had missed out on those lessons at the time, but was in the midst of a crash course.

"You are. I'm sorry. I didn't mean physically. It's just that you—"

"I know what's wrong with me," she snapped, not in the mood to have her faults listed.

Beeks put a hand on her arm. "I am sorry, Shyla. This isn't about you. It isn't about what's wrong with you. McDades are dangerous—"

"So people keep telling me," she said, twisting her stool to sit up straighter, removing her arm from Beeks' patronizing consolation. "I understand I'd be easy to kill. I don't know how to protect myself or even what to look for in an assassin. What I don't understand is why they'd hate me so much I'd drive them to murder. I don't think Burl has killed every girlfriend his boys ever had. Far as I know, he didn't order Siobhan dead and she caused Score's incarceration."

Even though it had been orchestrated by Biz, Shyla doubted Burl would care about that. If he wasn't going to punish one son, he could vent some of his frustrations on the woman who'd been instrumental in taking another away.

Beeks paused. His expression grew more serious as he licked his lips. "You are not in danger because of anything you have done."

That didn't clear anything up. "But I am in danger." He didn't confirm or deny that, but he didn't need to. He'd been explicit upstairs. "Why? What don't I understand?"

"Being involved with a McDade puts you in danger."

Hearing that was almost tiresome. On a loose nod, she raised her shoulders. "Yes, okay, I get that. Score told me that his enemies could hurt me. He knew that, he admitted that. That doesn't explain why Burl is a danger to me. What is it? Just because I'm not good enough to be a McDade?"

"It's more complicated than that."

"You know, the easiest way to stop thinking of me as some blind child is to stop treating me like one."

"I know," he said, talking over her last loud word. "You think it's simple, but it isn't. Score doesn't want you to know everything."

"How do you know that? How would you know that? You asked if I knew something. Why was that the first place you went?"

If Beeks hadn't known about their relationship, his first reactions were the most honest. Something had come into his head before anything else. She didn't know what it was, but whatever it was, Beeks' initial thoughts took him straight there.

"I can't tell you," he said. Once again, she tried to turn away, but he got hold of her. "Shyla, Score said he asked you to trust him. You have to trust that he's doing what's best for you by keeping you in the dark. He's protecting you."

"You didn't think so. You wanted to know if I knew this big secret. The one, I'm guessing, that would put me in danger with Burl."

"Not only with him," he said. Arching a brow, she wasn't impressed. Beeks exhaled. "Forget about everyone else, Shyla. Score is dangerous. On his own he's dangerous to be with."

She couldn't honestly believe that Beeks imagined Score would ever be violent with her. "If you think he'd ever hurt me, you don't know him at all."

"Hasn't he already?"

That brought his point home. She'd thought the lawyer's opinion was ridiculous at first. Except he was right. Score wouldn't physically hurt her, but he had hurt her heart and her pride.

"I thought he cared," she murmured, her attention drifting to the bar. "I really did."

"I don't doubt that he does. Caring doesn't change what he is. He's a dangerous man with dangerous links to dangerous people. You are not the type of woman who should be in a relationship with a criminal."

"He isn't a criminal," she said, jumping to his defense. "Not anymore."

Beeks wouldn't be talking about Score's spell in prison, his statement referred to his darker past with the McDades. When he didn't respond to her assertion, she glanced his way. The grave expression he wore prickled the hair on the back of her neck.

"Shyla—"

"Oh God," she whispered, in fathomless shock, twisting herself back to the bar. "This isn't about the past. It's nothing to do with the past…" She turned her head to look at Beeks. "You're talking about now, about the future. He's running something." Beeks didn't answer. "Tell me what it is. What is he into? What is he into that could hurt me? Something Burl wouldn't want him to be into."

After a score of silent seconds, Beeks inhaled. "He's a McDade. Score is a McDade."

Which meant? Damn, Shyla was frustrated. All she

wanted was a straight answer. No one seemed willing to provide it. Beeks was right about one thing, it wasn't simple. The deeper she went into the rabbit hole, the more messed up everything became.

"This isn't my life," she said, rubbing her forehead. "How am I supposed to make sense of this?"

"You trust him," Beeks said.

When he laid a hand on her arm, she spun around, throwing it away. "You think I'm an idiot. A child. He thinks it too, he has to, he wouldn't lie to me if he thought I could handle it."

Score knew that she couldn't take care of herself. Going from her grandfather's to Stan's then to Score's, Shyla had never stood on her own two feet. She had never lived. Her brother had. Wyatt went out into the world and learned hard lessons. For whatever reason, he'd turned to crime, and that landed him in prison.

Maybe it was in their blood. It could be that Shyla was supposed to be involved in the darker side of life too and had somehow missed the signals.

"I have to get out of here," she said, picking up her purse from the bar.

Beeks got up just a second after her. "Shyla, please… Come upstairs. Talk to Score."

"If he wanted to talk to me, he would've come down himself."

Not only that, but he would've told her the secret that was apparently keeping them apart. Going upstairs and looking into him would relax her; she'd breathe and convince herself to forget the red flags. Her naïve desire to be with the man would blind her to their reality all over again.

"Where are you going? When will you be back?" Beeks asked.

She turned, but didn't have an answer. A few seconds went by and then she sighed. "I don't know… I'll get in touch when I need my things."

Leaving it at that, Shyla departed the bar and the building. With so much unknown and many secrets, she couldn't decide whether or not to accept whatever Score was doing. If he was doing something illegal, setting up his own racket, it could bite either of them on the ass. It would also impact their future family.

In all Score said about his father, Shyla never got the impression that he wanted to emulate the man. That could be the future for any children they had. Score would become Burl and their babies would be groomed to inherit Score's empire.

Walking down the street, she began to understand why Burl would be unhappy about Score setting up on his own. That could take his business and would be an embarrassment. The man was used to ruling all McDades. Unless Score had his father's permission, it would be an affront to the family to separate himself.

An affront that could lead to retribution. That had to be why Beeks asserted Burl would kill her. She would be the price for Score's insubordination.

TWENTY-SEVEN

SOMETHING BROUGHT SHYLA to that place. She couldn't say exactly what it was. After leaving Beeks in the bar, and walking for a long time, she'd ended up crashing in a motel. The next morning, she woke up with a new sense of determination and a plan. Once the necessary calls were made and the paperwork filled out, Shyla waited for her authorization.

Eight days had gone by since she'd walked out of Score's building. He hadn't been in touch, no one had, but that was likely because she'd left her cellphone behind. Not on purpose, she'd taken it out before Stan's service and hadn't put it back. The radio silence kept her head clear. She needed that clarity to endure going to that place.

Shyla had never been to visit her brother in prison. Half of her didn't know why she was there and the other half knew that was the right place to be. Sometimes certainty didn't make sense.

The worst was over. After jumping through all the security hoops, she'd arrived in the vast visiting room. Wyatt had authorized her visit. There was no reason to believe that he wouldn't show up. Yet, her nerves wouldn't stay still.

Shyla, along with all the other visitors, sat waiting for

the inmates to be brought in. The whole experience was disorientating. Wyatt was practically at her table by the time she noticed him. His hesitation suggested he wasn't wholly sure it was her, and she knew where he was coming from.

Years had passed since they'd seen each other. The man peering at her was more weathered than her brother, harder, and his hair was longer. Still, when their eyes met and he smiled, she saw the kid from her childhood.

"Shit," he said, coming to the table.

Shyla leaped up and accepted his hug. Her brother had never been the tactile sort. But as they stood there hugging, she wondered how long it had been since he'd experienced any kind of affection. That was on her. The guilt hit hard.

He released her and they both sat down. An awkward kind of air settled between them. She couldn't look at him, so instead fixated on her fidgeting fingers.

Wyatt startled her by laying his hand on hers, stalling the fiddling. "What's up, sis?"

The concern in his tone was undeserved. Raising her attention to steal a look his way, Shyla found it written all over his face.

"Thank you," she said. Sitting there in silence until the guards kicked her out wouldn't do either of them any favors. "For agreeing to see me."

"Gotta say I was surprised," he said, his hand sliding away from hers as he leaned back on his stool. "Never expected to see you again."

Which was her fault. Score had offered a reminder of her brother when she declared herself without family. Needing a reminder that he existed was habit. A terrible habit. Overlooking Wyatt was her custom. She'd been neglecting him for too long. More guilt chewed at her.

"I'm sorry. I should've come to see you… I should've made the effort."

"Why?" he asked. "I made my choices. What I did put me here. This isn't the kind of place for someone like you."

"Someone like me," she murmured. "An innocent

child."

"Well, you're no child… Where you based now? You married with twenty kids already?"

Her grandfather had written to Wyatt, though Shyla didn't know how often she was a subject of those letters.

"You can't have much left of your sentence," she said, deflecting. "You've been in here a long time."

"Okay, you don't want to answer questions, I get that. Your life is your business. But you didn't come here to talk about prison. What do you need?"

"Advice," she said, making eye contact.

"'Bout?" When she hesitated, he straightened and sucked in a breath. "Drugs are bad, booze has a lot to answer for, and it's true, guys are only after one thing… I can keep going throwing the random shit out there. Be quicker if you just tell me what's going on? You didn't come to me for scrapbooking tips or Great Auntie Whoever's meatloaf recipe. I'm probably the last person you'd come to unless you were out of options… So, what do you need a brother or a con?"

The question highlighted her selfish behavior. Wyatt didn't put it in that way, but what he did say told her a lot about his belief in his worth to her.

"Both," she admitted. He raised his brows to prompt her. Her focus fell to her fingers linking and releasing. "There's this guy…"

"Murder isn't my gig, but I can hook you up."

Shock raised her chin. Shyla couldn't even tell if he was being serious or making a joke, which was probably deliberate on his part. A life of crime must have taught him to keep things ambiguous. In a court, he'd want to be able to deny wrongdoing or claim anything over the line was a joke.

Considering that he might suspect her of being duplicitous, Shyla figured the best way to reassure him was to lay out her own shady connections.

Leaning closer, she flattened both hands on the table. "You know the McDades?" she asked, lowering her volume.

He pushed out his lower lip and shook his head. "They from the old neighborhood? Don't exactly get back much. Oh, wait, were they the ones on the corner with that weird tree in their yard. That kid was into you."

Shyla didn't know who he was talking about, but it didn't matter.

She shook her head. "Not those McDades, *the* McDades. You heard of Score McDade on—"

"Death row in Texas," he said, bobbing his head. "What about him?"

"He's not on death row anymore."

"Yeah, I know the story. This is the kinda place news like that gets a lot of guys excited. So, what is it? You want to write a book or something? Stan will fucking love that."

"Stan's dead," she said, remembering the letter she'd written him after Bernard died.

"Shit," he said, sliding his hands toward each other. "When?"

"Month ago."

It had been longer than that, but specifics were irrelevant. Looking back at everything that had happened since then, it felt more like a year.

"Sorry, sis, I know you were close." Yeah, they were. To deny she'd ever missed that simpler life, especially over the last eight days, would be a lie. "What's that got to do with this McDade? I'm surprised you even know about the McDades."

Before going to work for Score, they hadn't been more than a name to her.

"I, uh… Phoenix and I…"

"Phoenix?" he said, wearing a frown.

"Score… Phoenix is his real name."

"Huh, don't know if I knew that."

With her forearms on the cold metal table, she pushed her fingers together again, raising them up. "We were a… thing."

When Wyatt didn't say anything, she peeked up. His frown was still there, but was more quizzical.

"You know the guy?" he asked. "I don't get what you… What do you mean a thing? What thing?"

Her inexperience with men correlated to an inexperience in talking about them. Maybe starting with her brother hadn't been the best idea.

"Like a together thing," she said. Arching her back a little, she squirmed. "Like a… physical thing?"

"You had sex with him?"

The booming declaration attracted the attention of a bunch of people.

Shyla lunged over to grab his hand. "Shh! Geez, Wy."

Bowing, he pulled her closer so they were both hunched over the table. "Are you seriously fucking telling me that you're screwing Score McDade?"

"I was," she said, her eyes and head tilting to the side. "I… don't know what we are now."

"You're whatever he says you are. Seriously, Shy, I don't even want to guess how it happened, but getting mixed up with a guy like that…Why'd he send you here? He on a recruitment drive or something?"

"He didn't send me. We were… well, whatever we were, we weren't exactly… public knowledge." She didn't blame him for appearing confused. "But we became public knowledge and—"

"Now there's a price on your head," he said. Sitting up, his shoulders fell. For a second, he seemed to be thinking then a snap of tension went through him. "He's not the married one… is he?"

She shook her head. "Biz is married, Parker McDade, to a woman called Nicole."

"You met her?"

"No, I haven't met the family. Score hasn't been back there since… you know."

"Where is he?"

"Home probably. He opened a club in Miami."

His brows went up. "What kind of club?" he asked then answered his own question. "Guess it doesn't matter if it's a front. He won't pedal his product through his own place; he might run it out the back door. A club is a great way to clean cash."

Shyla hadn't even asked a question about crime and Wyatt just got it. Her brother got it in seconds while she hadn't been able to figure it out at all. Everything people said about her was true. She was an innocent child. Score might not have been aware the truth was a secret. Maybe not talking about it wasn't the same as withholding. Chances were, he assumed she would know these things like Wyatt had known.

As soon as he said it, so much became clear. Demanding Beeks spell it out felt idiotic in light of Wyatt's declaration. Why would someone like Score open a risqué dance club? He didn't care about ogling semi-naked women. He was a McDade, he could snap his fingers and fear alone would bring women running to jump on his cock. He listened to soul and jazz; he sure wasn't the type of guy to bust a move or care about keeping up with the latest music trends.

The only reason a man like him opened a nightclub was to launder money. Beeks words came into jarring focus. *"He's a McDade. Score is a McDade."* Whether he was in the bosom of the family or not didn't matter. Given what he'd said about knots, he'd been coached in the family trade since before he could walk. That meant one thing.

Wyatt's fingertips touched the edge of her hand, reminding her that she wasn't in the best place to go into a trance.

"I thought he felt something… something for me."

Wyatt shrugged. "Maybe he does. He say otherwise?"

She shook her head. "I didn't get it… I don't get it."

"Get what?"

"He doesn't need to be doing anything like that anymore. Pedaling product, cleaning money, I thought that was in his past."

Surprise smacked Wyatt hard. "He told you he was on the straight and narrow?"

Fidgeting with her fingers again, Shyla admitted her own stupidity. "I sort of just… assumed."

His snort of disbelief wasn't appreciated. "Sorry, sis. Look, guys like that don't know how to be any other way. Don't take it personal. It's who he is."

Everyone just accepted that Score wasn't capable of anything else. The strong, determined, confident man she knew could be anything; he wasn't any one thing. Yet, everybody seemed eager to classify him as a bad guy no matter what.

"I can tell you one thing for sure," Wyatt said, inspiring her hope. "No woman ever changed a man who didn't want to change." He side-nodded back and forth. "Sometimes we say we'll change, but, you know… we don't always mean it."

Which looped back to his advice about men only wanting one thing.

"Score didn't tell me he was going to change."

"No, 'cause you thought he was on the righteous path." Even if he didn't mean to sound amused by her stupidity, she heard it in his tone. "You want my advice? Run fast and far. A woman like you—"

"What is that?" she asked. "A woman like me? I don't know if I can handle it. I know I have a lot to learn. But as sure as everyone is that Score is evil, they seem just as sure I'm a saint."

"Don't think you're a saint, but…" He paused to inhale, held the breath then released it in one long sigh. "You wouldn't be here if you didn't have a problem with it." Her offense must have been obvious because he raised a calming hand. "Don't worry about it, I get it. It's a dangerous life and what the fuck are you gonna do if he ends up inside while you're left out there to deal with the crazies alone? If he's out of reach, you take the heat on the street."

"I'm not worried about heat," she said, though that wasn't a hundred percent true. With all the other issues, Shyla hadn't gotten to thinking about random people yet. "Some people think…" Meaning Beeks. "They think the other McDades could cause trouble."

"For you? They could, but why would they? Just because Score's running his own racket down here doesn't mean it's unconnected to Burl's gig."

Her brother using the patriarch's first name really brought the reach of the family home.

"You think he's still working for Burl?"

Wyatt shrugged. "I don't know, I'm just saying, wouldn't be smart for him to set up on his own without the nod from his father. Maybe he gets that by agreeing to run money for him or act as a go-between for whatever… Alotta drugs come through this state. Won't be much the McDades aren't into." When he hunched over the table again, she copied, moving closer to him. "You've gotta be careful who you talk to about that family. Like who hears you talking. If you say anything negative—"

"Believe me," she said, sitting up straight again. "I got that."

Score had said it to her, more than once. What he, and apparently Wyatt, didn't understand was that she couldn't decide how to go forward without talking about the McDades. Whether she wanted them or not, they were going to be a key influence in her relationship with Score… if she had one.

"You think about marrying this guy or having kids with him, you've gotta know you won't get to decide much about their lives… Then when they're old enough, they'll be expected—"

"To do what Burl says."

Another thing she'd been told.

"If you know everything… what are you doing here?"

The truth was pathetic. "I didn't have anywhere else to go." Pity bled into his gaze. "You're all I have left."

"Shy," he said, leaning over to snag her hand. "Not used to being by yourself, are you?" She shook her head while resenting her eyes for warming. "Being alone is tough, but sometimes it's necessary, you know?" She nodded, keeping her focus on their joined hands. If she looked at him or spoke, Shyla feared tears might slip out; that was the last thing she wanted. "You want to be with this guy, be with him."

"He's lying to me," she said.

A desperate sob escaped before she managed to seal her lips again.

"Not because he wants to, because it's necessary."

That was his advice. If she couldn't handle an unconventional relationship with Score, then walking away and being alone was the only option. The alternative was staying with him. If Shyla chose that, she'd have to accept being low on his list of priorities. Their relationship would always come after his family and his work… whatever that may be.

Seeing Wyatt had been worth journeying from one end of the state to the other. Not only because he told her what Beeks and Score wouldn't, but because it reminded her that he wasn't such a terrible person.

"How long you got left?" she asked after composing herself.

"All going well, less than a year."

She smiled. "Will you call me? I mean, will you come see me?"

"Sure," he said and managed a brief laugh. "I always figured staying away would stop you getting involved in anything shady... Boy, sis, did you surprise the hell out of me?"

His wide smile gave her permission to relax and laugh. "He's not all bad," she said. "It's just how he was raised."

"Not an excuse I have is what you mean," he said, resting his weight on his forearms. "What do you do on a date with a guy like Score McDade? Can't quite picture him going to a movie or out dancing."

"Chess," she said. "We play chess."

"Wow," he said, honestly surprised. "You used to be good at that. You gotta let him win every time?"

"Men who get mad about losing are insecure," she said, fighting to subdue her smile for a second before letting it loose. "Phoenix isn't insecure."

"You light up when you talk about him... You're really in it."

In love. In lust. Infatuated. Inconsolable. Incompatible. Inspired. Inexperienced. Shyla was in it all. Wherever she chose to go, Score would always be a part of her psyche. He'd been her first. The first man to open her eyes to dedication in love beyond what it meant to care for family.

She loved him, but didn't know if she'd ever be able to handle being with him.

TWENTY-EIGHT

AFTER SPENDING AS MUCH of the day with Wyatt as was allowed, Shyla gave him her cell number. Although the phone was still at Score's apartment, she did intend to get it back eventually. Either way, she'd promised to write to her brother, something she probably should've been doing for years.

Catching up on basically their whole adult lives didn't take long, on her side anyway. Wyatt prettied his up and skimmed over a lot of details, so Shyla filled the time with stories of Bernard and Stan. Mending their relationship would take time, maybe a long time, but Score was right to remind her that Wyatt was her family.

Back in her motel room, the intention was to eat and get some sleep before making any decisions on what to do next. Around midnight, still staring at the ceiling, Shyla's questions wouldn't let her sleep. That was why she rolled onto her side and picked up the phone to call Information.

Even in the nights she'd paced in anticipation of Score coming home, Shyla had never called to hurry him or ask for an ETA. Yet, there she was, listening to the ring in her ear, waiting, terrified and exhilarated at the same time.

For a week, she'd had no contact with anyone

connected to Score. It kept ringing. Her eyes closed as her head questioned the virtue of a call. She had no idea what was in Score's mind. If he was done with her then a call would just erase any last shred of dignity she might have left.

Just when Shyla was about to take the phone from her ear to hang up, the ringing stopped. At first, there was no voice on the other end, though she could hear a bass line and the murmur of music in the background.

Her mouth dried. Had someone answered? What if it was someone else? What if Score wasn't there and—

"Yeah?"

That was him. Without a doubt, the curt word came from his mouth, the same mouth that had feasted on her not so long ago. Typical that all it took was one word from him and her mind went straight to that intimate place.

The strength that she'd wanted to exude abandoned her. Calling him was a sign of weakness. All week, while she held a purpose, Shyla had stayed strong. His power over her hadn't diminished. Her world might be topsy-turvy and her future uncertain, but her heart knew who it belonged to.

"Lamb?"

Sitting bolt upright, Shyla opened her mouth, shocked that he'd identified her without her uttering a syllable. "How did you know it was me?" she asked in a rush of breath.

"Think I get a lot of prank calls?"

She smiled. His tone was no less severe, but his point was valid. Few people would take the risk of screwing around with a McDade just for sport.

"No, I guess not."

"Are you safe?"

"Physically," she said, pushing up the bed to lean against the headboard.

"Where are you?"

Maybe she should've thought about what to tell him before picking up the phone. "I visited Wyatt."

Their relationship had gone to pot when she discovered he was withholding information. Lying to him would just be spite. There was no reason not to tell him. Playing games wasn't going to make anything about their situation better.

Neither of them said anything, but neither hung up either. She'd called him for a specific reason. Her courage was beginning to falter. All she wanted to do was talk, to gush about all the things Wyatt had said, to share her guilt, to get his acceptance and reassurance. That was something a girlfriend would do with a boyfriend. Given the way she'd walked out, it wasn't clear if that's what they were or not.

"He helped me figure a few things out."

"Things?"

The edge in his voice narrowed her eyes. Wyatt could be in danger if Score thought he'd said anything out of turn. Except Shyla couldn't imagine that he would ever hurt her brother. But he was a McDade capable of hurting anyone, wasn't that the point? Score didn't have to do it himself, someone else could do it for him. Especially in prison where fights happened all the time and inmates didn't get the highest level of healthcare.

"I was naïve and ridiculous," she said, admitting her starkest conclusion. "It didn't even occur to me that you could still be involved in—"

"I don't know if this line is secure."

Again. She'd done it again. Being with a man like Score meant being constantly vigilant. Law enforcement had screwed up with him once. The embarrassment of convicting a man of murder when the victim was still alive wasn't something that would just go away when the man was released.

Score was the double whammy too. Agencies wouldn't give up on the idea of getting him for committing a verifiable crime. In addition, his connection to Burl meant surveillance could lead to more than just one conviction.

"I want to see them," she said.

If Shyla went back to him, they could discuss Wyatt's revelations and her own shortcomings in person. That would assuage the worry of forcing him to confess anything while others could be listening in.

"See who?"

Shyla bolstered her courage and swallowed hard.

"Your father. Your family." Silence reigned on the other end of the line. Yet, she could almost feel his muscles tightening. "Do you want to be with me, Score?"

"No." The reply was so unexpected that its impact was equivalent to a gut punch. Winded, she opened her mouth in silent surprise. "Not if it means you're gonna kill yourself. You go anywhere near a McDade and—"

"What should I be afraid of? Them… or you? Far as I know, they don't know who I am. But sometimes when your family come up, you say things that… That make me wonder where your loyalty lies."

Telling the truth was a dangerous proposition. Thus far in their relationship, she'd been all about following his orders and desire had been a big part of their interactions. Moving beyond that meant talking about the difficult subjects.

"My loyalty lies with my family," he said, more sure than she'd ever heard him. Piercing her heart with his words, he confirmed she'd been chasing the unattainable. "You are my family, Shyla Bellamy."

Was she? The dejection that had lowered her chin slipped away as her head rose again. "I want to be your family, Score. I am trying, I am really trying to understand—"

"You have to trust me."

"I do," she said because regardless of what he was involved in, he had never endangered her.

As Beeks had said, not telling her everything was his way of protecting her. She understood that. If she knew the details and the feds did descend on Score, she'd be their next collar.

"Then get in a cab and come home."

"It's almost four hundred miles."

"I don't care. I'll pay it," he said. "You're in a dangerous place without enough protection."

"I don't need protection."

"My girl always needs protection," he said. "Think no one saw you with Wyatt? He's got enemies too. Burl has eyes everywhere. I can't tell you who will come for you, but I will tell you that it won't be pretty. Four hundred miles is too far. You don't travel that far without me again."

"I plan to go further," she said. "I need to see him."

"Shy," he warned. "It's crazy. No one walks up to Burl McDade. No one."

"Then I'll talk to Razer or Play. Someone must be able to get a message to him."

"No," he said. "That's it. You don't need his permission."

"To be with you? Maybe not. But I need it to…"

She needed it to live. That seemed like the relevant thing to say. If Shyla planned for their relationship to go longer than a month, it was up to her to prove her lack of fear. One way to do that was to show up and declare she had no intention of causing trouble for the McDade family.

"This your big plan? You walk away without a word and think you can stir up the hornets' nest then just waltz on back."

"I don't know what else to do," she said. At the end of the day, the McDade family were his. If going to them would end their relationship then it was doomed either way. "I don't want to be weak. If we're living in fear of them all the time, all I am is a liability. We can't be together like that."

"No matter what, you will always be a liability."

Nice. Her optimism faded again. "Then I shouldn't come back. This should be goodbye."

Though even thinking about where to go or what to do without him was beyond her. The prospect of him gave her strength and purpose. Even with the uncertainty of how it would play out, Shyla realized in that moment that her aim had always been to return to him. Women didn't leave McDades, not because they were dangerous, though they were, but because they had their own gravitational pull.

"You're coming home," he said.

"If I'm a liability, you should want rid of me. You should cut ties and get—"

"You're a liability because I love you," he snapped. "That's never gonna change. Doesn't matter if you're here or on the other side of the planet. Doesn't matter if I train you to fight or arm you with weapons, I will always do whatever it takes to keep you safe. Whatever it takes."

On picking up the phone, and listening to the ring, she'd feared talking to him would be a mistake. His last words erased those doubts. Shyla couldn't have predicted such a revelation.

Walking away wouldn't make a difference to his feelings. It hadn't made a difference to hers. They were tethered to each other, whether they wanted to be or not.

"I missed you this week," she whispered. "I'm so lost."

"Come home," he said. "You can pack up, walk out of that motel room, and get your ass back down here, or you can stay exactly where you are and I'll be there before the sun rises. But you are coming home, Shyla Bellamy."

All the things that she wanted to say and wanted to ask tangled together to form a ball of trepidation deep in her gut.

"Nothing will be different if I come back now," she said. "If I'm a liability, if they'll want to hurt me—"

"We can't talk about that on the phone," he said. "Come home and we'll talk."

Would they? Maybe. Maybe not. Shyla had promised to follow his commands and he was giving her one. If she was honest, she didn't want to face the McDades alone. If for no other reason than she'd embarrass Score. Proving her naivety and ineptitude wouldn't impress Burl McDade. It could actually make their situation worse.

"I need answers," she said. "I can't just wait for the axe to fall."

"I promised to take care of you, didn't I?"

"It shouldn't all be on you. If I am the one causing the problem—"

"You're causing it now," he said, both impatient and tense. "Get yourself back here and that problem goes away. Seeing your brother opened you up to more enemies, now they know what you look like."

"I don't think Wyatt has enemies like that."

"Not his enemies, mine," he said. "Anyone who knows we're together, knows who your brother is, you just gave them a face to go with the name."

Shyla shook her head. "No one knows we're together, not anyone in the prison. Wyatt didn't even know it."

"Maybe they didn't before you filed your paperwork. What you wrote on that page put you on a whole bunch of radars."

"I wrote that I was unemployed," she said. "I didn't want to assume that…" She had wandered off and left him without someone to take care of the day to day things that were usually her duties. "I didn't put your name on it, I swear."

"You put our address on it."

Because she'd had no other choice. She didn't think they'd accept a motel as a fixed abode. "No one would know that was your address. How would anyone know that? How would the McDades know to monitor—"

"You think I don't have eyes everywhere? You think I haven't known exactly where you are all week? You really think I'd let you walk into a prison, any prison without greasing the guards? Anything goes down, you've gotta be a priority. I've had people watching your brother for weeks."

Shyla didn't know what to say. Early in the call, he'd asked for her location like he didn't know it. "Phoenix…"

"I kept my distance," he said. "Didn't crowd you, let you breathe. But, baby, if you go to Burl now, I'll be right behind you and we won't ever get out. No one can defend you against him except me. I wouldn't trust anyone else to do what needed to be done."

Yet, Score always spoke as though his father's orders were gospel. That implied he wouldn't hurt his father… But even in her state of confusion, Shyla couldn't be sure what Score would do if it came down to a flat choice, her life or Burl's.

"I'll come home."

"First bus leaves Gainesville at six forty. I can get you a flight—"

"The bus is fine," she said. "It'll give me the time to get my head clear."

All being well, she'd be home not long after Score was usually out of bed. Nothing was certain yet and she still wanted to speak to Burl. But Score knew the players better than her; he had more experience. He wanted trust. In so many ways, that was easy to give. In others, she didn't know what the hell to think.

TWENTY-NINE

AFTER SPENDING HOURS on a bus, Shyla was grateful to be upright, stretching out her idle muscles. Her mind was the opposite of idle. For days, all she'd done was think. Her head needed to rest. Once she saw Score and got an idea of his mood, then she'd let her brain off the hook for a while.

Being optimistic was easy right up until the moment she reached his building. Their building. Whatever it was, she wasn't sure.

Beeks and Fish could be inside. Some part of her craved the normalcy of cooking for them and being back in her old position. The other part was terrified that everyone would act like nothing was different. If that happened, she would never get any answers.

The last time she'd been nervous going up in the elevator was the day she'd first arrived to apply for the job. No one could've foreseen where they would end up. That she'd fall for her boss, who also happened to be a member of one of the most notorious crime families in the country. Oh, and he'd spent over half a decade in prison. For a crime he didn't commit, granted, but those years hardened him even more than his family in his childhood.

There couldn't be a man more opposite to her.

Shyla's only experience with criminality was through her brother. Even then, he'd kept it away from the family and hadn't exposed them to his misdeeds.

Running away and starting afresh was probably the smartest course of action. Yet, love carried her into the elevator despite her nerves. Whether it worked out or not, Shyla had to be able to tell herself that she'd tried everything. Hearing Score out was the least she could do.

Leaving in the way she had didn't give him any chance to answer her questions. He probably didn't want to, but she needed to give him an opportunity to make a different choice. After all he had done for her, Shyla couldn't just turn her back and give up.

That being the case, her trip wasn't one of mercy, not for Score. Shyla missed him too and hated how she'd walked away. They deserved one last chance to lay it all out. After that, they'd have to see if there was any glimmer of hope that they might win. That was it. Either they both won and kept each other, or they both lost, cornered by their own undoing. Checkmate.

As the elevator doors opened, Shyla held her breath. So much was different, different to how it had been when she first arrived full of optimism.

The vast blue ocean was a comfort that brought a smile to her face. Absorbing its beauty, she speculated about what she might do differently if they could start all over again.

Nothing. There was nothing that she could change. Adjusting anything from the way it originally happened could alter the outcome. Maybe she wouldn't have gotten close to Score. No matter how it turned out, Shyla wouldn't give up their history for anything.

Holding her head high, she strode out of the elevator doing her best to convince herself that her confidence was real.

That didn't last long when a tall, gorgeous Latina woman appeared from the kitchen.

"Hello," she said, drying her hands as she came closer. "I am Maria. You are Shyla, yes?"

Was she? At that moment, Shyla was suffering what

felt like an out of body experience. Someone else was in her place. Another woman was doing her duties.

"Maria." Repeating the name took so much effort that it came out in a single burst. Startling the woman wasn't the best first impression. That demonstrated how at least one thing about her hadn't changed since her first arrival at the apartment. "What are you doing here?"

With a broad smile splitting her beautiful face, Maria opened her arms. "I keep the casa beautiful."

The casa. Her casa. Shyla wanted to order the beauty out of her kitchen, and out of her apartment. Her protective urge was nothing to do with Maria, it was about anyone being in her place.

Inhaling through her nose, Shyla held onto her calm. The long journey no doubt brought out her cranky side. The last few days had been stressful; she wasn't in the most diplomatic mood. Taking a moment to breathe, she fought to quell the urge to shout.

"Where is Mr. McDade?"

Maria's gaze turned quizzical. "I do not know. Would you like me to cook something for you?"

Shyla held up a hand and backed away. "No, thank you." Food was the last thing on her mind. Retreating to put the bags in the foyer closet, she closed the door. "I'll just go…"

She pointed to the hallway, but Maria leaped into her path. "Señor does not allow—"

"I'll take the punishment," she said, noting the worry in Maria's eyes. "Excuse me."

Though Maria was reluctant, she did step aside. Shyla could've gone around her but didn't want to make a scene, especially since she'd returned for a solemn reason.

While heading down the hallway, Shyla's confidence rose. She didn't need to convince herself it was real. Something about approaching Score's bedroom inspired her. Yes, she was nervous about the outcome, but she wasn't nervous about the man.

Opening his bedroom door, she went inside and glanced around. The terrace doors were closed. No one was in the shower area, though the masculine scent in the lingering steam suggested it had been used not so long ago.

A noise attracted her attention, though it snagged on the bed without following the sound to its source. From how the covers were arranged, the bed was made… sort of. It didn't quite reach her standard, so she assumed Maria's was lower, or the woman wasn't allowed in Score's bedroom.

Movement in the closet behind the headboard stole her focus from the sheets.

Wearing only a towel around his hips, Score must have heard her too because he was looking her way.

"You replaced me?" she asked, trying a half smile. His brow lowered. "Your new housekeeper is afraid of you."

"She's smarter than you were."

Her smile became more genuine, but it faltered when he turned his back to retrieve clothes. Being with someone was supposed to make communication easier, not more difficult.

Giving him his privacy, Shyla went to let the afternoon air in by opening the terrace doors. The last thing she wanted was to leave the apartment for good. Losing Score would hurt more than sacrificing any material possession. But the apartment was a symbol of them, of their unity at home. Being away while visiting Wyatt represented more than just physical distance. Their emotional distance had grown too.

Score didn't talk much about his feelings, his pragmatism was probably both nature and nurture. Though without knowing his family, she couldn't be sure. Shyla didn't need him to change, she needed him to be honest.

As he approached, she twisted to look over her shoulder for a second, then returned to the view. "It's beautiful. I missed it."

"It's been here. Waiting for you," he said, stopping next to her.

No one had asked her to leave, she'd done that on her own. His tone didn't really give her a clue as to his emotions, but she did wonder if her abrupt departure hurt him.

Turning away from the view, Shyla set her sight on

him. "I'm sorry I walked out."

"You have to protect yourself," he said, still focused straight ahead. "I understand that."

"You wanted honesty," she said, releasing her tension to truth. "That was your number one. You said this had to be more than sex, that it had to be different or it wasn't worth your time. I agreed to that. I wanted that. Can you blame me for being hurt when I learned you were lying to me?"

"I never lied," he said, his attention snapping down to hers. "I did not lie to you."

Which was obviously a point of contention for him. "You want to argue semantics? To debate whether an omission is a lie or not? I don't. I don't care about picking everything apart. I don't want to argue at all. I want to be with you. But I want you to trust me." Saying the words brought her new clarity. "All these times you've asked me to trust you, you have never put your trust in me." He said nothing. "Have you?"

Much as her urge was to keep talking, to keep the silence filled, Shyla controlled herself. If she didn't give him the time to process and express himself, then she'd never know what he felt about anything.

Rather than speak, he raised a hand. But as it approached her face, she dipped back and closed her eyes. "Don't," she said in a whisper of a plea. "Please don't touch me. You do that and I'll…" When her eyes opened, all she read in his was dismay. "If you touch me, I'll forget. I'll want you to keep touching me. I'll want you to take me to bed… We have to be able to talk, Phoenix. Not just about me or about facts and details, but about what's inside us too."

"I told you I love you," he snapped before spinning around to march away. "What is it you want, Shyla?"

She swallowed. "I want you to get that anger out. I want you to stop seeing me as your enemy. You think that you have to keep everything a secret. That you're an island, capable of taking care of yourself. I don't doubt that you can. Being with me is your choice. If you choose to be an island, I'll walk out of here and never bother you again." Talking to his back was difficult, especially with so much space between them, but she had to stay strong, to be confident. "Or you choose to trust me and I'll swear to always be yours. To never leave you again. Not for anything."

"You shouldn't be here," he said in a growl that didn't direct any anger at her. "I should never have let myself—"

"If you think I wasn't crazy attracted to you since the minute I laid eyes on you, you're nuts."

He spun around. "I should've been in control. Kept you away."

Shyla shrugged. "I told you, I don't want to pick everything apart. This is where we are, where everything has got us to. I love you and want to be with you. That's my choice." She licked her lips. "Now make your choice."

Reducing the complexity of their personalities and their relationship to a single choice was incredibly simplistic. To her, it really was as easy as that. She wanted him to choose her, to promise they'd forge their way ahead together. But if he wasn't willing to trust her and try, there was no point in them going any further.

"Making that choice could cost you your life."

She ventured closer, taking small steps to narrow the distance between them. "You told me on the phone that it didn't matter whether I was right here or on the other side of the planet. You care about me, which means if someone wants to hurt you, McDade or otherwise, they will hurt me. I am your liability."

Opening her hands at her sides, she stopped within a foot of him. For a score of seconds, he examined her. His strong brow and intent eyes gave her the impression he was processing. Maybe that was why he was so comfortable with silence, it gave him time to think.

Allowing him to pause for as long as he needed, Shyla learned it wasn't always such a bad thing to drink each other in.

"I can't make you any guarantees."

She smiled. "No one can guarantee anything. If falling in love with you has taught me anything, it's that the unexpected lurks around every corner." When his frown deepened, she smiled and grabbed one of his hands in both of hers. "I wouldn't change it. Not a thing. Being with you makes me happy. You make me happy... But I know that if you can't trust me, I'll always feel..." She searched for the word. "Inferior... I don't have the same experience as you and I'm not from your world. Anything I imagine about the way you grew up fills me with sadness. The boy you were deserved more, you deserved to be given options."

Despite her desire to name Burl as the main offender in that injustice, Shyla couldn't take another warning about bad mouthing the man whom she already didn't like. In the past, dislike wasn't something she often felt. For the likes of Mick maybe, but not toward a person she'd never met.

"I can't change the way I was raised."

"I wouldn't ask you to change anything about who you are. Maybe you could start by telling me why you don't trust me. Is it because of Siobhan?"

"I do trust you," he said. "This is nothing to do with her... nothing to do with that."

A psychologist may say different; Shyla could only take him at his word. "So what is it about? Why can't you tell me your big secret?"

Before Beeks discovered her in Score's bed, Shyla was aware that she didn't yet know every little thing about the man who'd taken her virginity. Back then, she'd looked forward to learning the details as they became relevant. Beeks' question about her knowledge altered that perspective. Not knowing something because it hadn't come up was different to not knowing something relevant to the present.

Beyond that, when Beeks had raised it to Score, he'd been clear that she wasn't allowed to know. It wasn't just that he hadn't looped her in, he'd chosen to keep her out.

"It's complicated."

She sat on the end of the bed and crossed her legs. "I'm not going anywhere. I'll sit here and listen as long as it takes. As long as you need me to listen."

Score could tell her that he trusted her and could tell Beeks he did too. The only way to know it for sure was for him to open himself up. Revealing the truth he'd kept hidden was the best way to start. If he trusted her with that, there would be light at the end of the tunnel.

It would take a leap of faith on his side, just as she'd had to take one for him. Whatever it was, she vowed not to judge. Listening was what Shyla offered and that was exactly what she planned to do.

THIRTY

"I DON'T KNOW where to begin," Score said, drifting toward the full-height window opposite where she sat. "You want honesty? You should know I never planned to tell you any of this… I wasn't even sure I was gonna go through with it."

"Through with what?" she asked, trying to encourage him on and show that she would exercise patience while he figured out what he wanted to say.

Score's chin moved toward his shoulder. "Do you know why they call me Score?"

"Yes," she said because Fish told her. "You were known for settling scores. Fixing the messes Biz made."

That she managed not to spit his name with disgust was an achievement to be proud of. His attention went to the window again.

"It's what I always did. What I was good at."

That and fucking, which he'd once told her was his specialty. Although the memory brought a smile to her face, Shyla chose not to break the atmosphere by mentioning it.

"I understand."

She understood that he used to do that, though she wasn't clear on why that was relevant.

"No," he said on an exhale as he turned. "You don't. If you did, you would've taken the hint to stop screaming about Biz any chance you got." Confused, she didn't know how to respond. "If you got it, you'd know that I was never just gonna walk away and pretend it was all over."

Stunned, her lips moved, but no sound came out. For some reason, Shyla hadn't put the two together, which actually worked out for him. If she'd connected his previous McDade responsibility with what he'd been through and settling down without payback, then she would probably have pointed that out with the same vigor he was complaining about.

"You…" Shyla eventually got her voice to work. "You're not done with them."

"Not by a long shot," he said, folding his arms. "Keeping the details from you protects you."

She heard his words, but it took a second to interpret them. Once they'd filtered through, she shot to her feet to close the meter or so of space between them.

Shyla rested her hands on his forearms. "I don't want you to protect me," Shyla said, earning herself a frown. "I mean, I understand why you didn't tell me before. But I'm asking you now. I don't want you to keep the details from me. I want the truth."

"Why?" he asked. "Because you don't trust me?"

"I trust you. You know that I do."

"This is how you want me to prove that I trust you?"

Shyla thought she'd made that clear and didn't like the hint of suspicion in his gaze. A confrontation would push him away, Score was stubborn like that.

Shyla took a deep breath. "The club is a front," she said, choosing to share what she'd figured out… or been told by her brother. "You're not interested in the nightclub business. You're using it as a way to launder money." He leaned back like he intended to walk away, so she tightened her grip. "I don't care about that. Maybe instead of letting me jump to my own conclusions, you fill me in. Is it drugs? Is that what you're selling? Does Burl know you're running something? Is that your payback? To take his business? His money?"

When his arms loosened, her hands fell away. "You're not cut out for that life," he said, his fingers drifting up her cheek. "I couldn't drag you into it."

Raising her hand to his, she linked their fingers and took it from her face. "Don't assume I wouldn't want it. I know I want to be with you, that is my choice. The only thing that will change it is if you don't reciprocate. If you tell me to leave—"

"You left," he said. "That was your choice."

"Coming back was my choice too."

His head began to move in a slow, shallow shake. "Your life is worth more than this. Your children's lives—"

"If we go back to Burl, we won't have kids," she said. "That saves us ever having to witness them walking in his shoes… I think maybe Nicole has made the same choice. Maybe she doesn't want to see her children live that life either."

"You shouldn't deprive yourself of what you want."

Sliding her hands onto his waist, Shyla edged closer. "The only thing I want is you. I need you, Phoenix… Are you working with your father?"

"Why would you think that?"

"You still talk to him," she said and smiled. "And because it's been mentioned to me that going out on your own without your father's approval could be dangerous." He still seemed hesitant. Shyla wanted to put him at ease. "That is the life you know, returning to it after all you've been through was probably a comfort. I understand."

"No, you don't," he said again.

If the only way to get to the truth was by her asking a million questions and throwing out random theories, they could be there all week.

"Spell it out for me, my love."

"I do run money for Burl," he said.

Shyla nodded, doing her best not to show any hint of judgement. "How does that relate to you getting payback and Burl wanting to kill me?"

Instead of answering the question, he cupped her head in both hands and raised her chin as he bowed lower.

Score pressed his mouth to hers in a long, slow kiss that lingered just long enough to weaken her.

The moment his lips left hers, his hands fell away too. For a few seconds, she just hung there in midair, forgetting all about revenge and retribution. He'd just proved her right. With just that kiss, Shyla's mind wandered away from answers and toward the bed not far behind them.

"There is no payback."

Snapping from her daze, she opened her eyes to find he was at the window with his back to her again.

"No payback?"

"I gave it up," he said.

Even more confused, Shyla couldn't figure out what his payback had been or why he'd sacrificed it.

"Why?" she asked. "Why did you give up on getting justice for yourself?"

His justice wasn't the type found in a court, but that made it no less real. "Risking my life was worth it. Risking yours wasn't."

As the truth filtered through, she couldn't decide whether to be angry or overwhelmed by his show of love. "You gave up on it because of me… That's why you thought Burl would want to hurt me… If you got your payback on him or Biz or whatever it was, Burl would've come for me."

"Probably not himself, but, yeah."

"And you didn't think you'd be able to protect me?"

"I wouldn't take that chance."

"I didn't ask you to do that," she said.

While sacrificing his revenge proved the depth of his love, it also had the potential to foster resentment. Giving up on it now during the early part of their burgeoning relationship would be easier than coming to terms with that sacrifice in the later years. If it was only going to tear them apart in the end, then it wasn't worth giving it up.

"Shyla, I…" he started, but stopped to release a long breath.

Though she couldn't see his face, she did note the tick in the back of his jaw that suggested frustration gritted his teeth.

"Talk to me," she said, approaching to slide her hands onto his waist again. "Whatever it is you have to say—"

"I'm new to this, I don't... Before you I didn't consider the future. I did what I needed to do."

That attitude may have come from his upbringing. Acting in the moment rather than considering the future was probably what kept a lot of wise-guys and criminals alive. Focusing too much on consequences could lead to hesitation.

Prison couldn't have helped either. Going through every day in the same routine forever over and over with no end in sight, had the potential to drive a man insane. Living on death row didn't exactly have a lot of prospects.

His release, whether it was expected or not, could've led to him thinking about what might be, about what he wanted for himself. His decisions had taken him to one point, he needed payback.

"Did you think about it in prison?" she asked. "About what you'd do to Biz if you ever got out."

"I thought about ripping him to shreds. Thought about working slow and forcing him to endure all kindsa pain."

If all he planned to do was attack and murder his brother, he could've done that already.

"Violence isn't your plan," she said, sliding her hands further around him until both were flat on his torso and her cheek rested against his spine. "You'd have killed him by now if that was your plan."

"Biz is a cocky asshole," he said. "Sure I wanted to hurt him, damn right I did. I expected the double cross from him... Everything's fair game with him."

"Your father's betrayal hurt more," she said.

Score always said that Burl was the head of the family, that he made the decisions. If that was true, either he'd sanctioned what Biz did, or he'd let his eldest son's actions go by without repercussions. Dangerous for a man like Parker McDade to start thinking he had carte blanche, even over his own father's authority.

"I don't give a damn about hurt. He let Biz bend him over and give it to him in the ass," he snarled. "I'm supposed to respect that? Respect a family who can't even control its own?"

"It's Burl. You want to take Burl down."

Grabbing her wrists, he opened her arms to free himself and turned to face her, the passion of vengeance burning from within him. "Him and his fucking lieutenant… Though I don't know which way's which."

She frowned. "You think Parker is calling the shots? Why? Why would your father let him—"

"I don't give a damn," he snapped, then took a breath and ran his palm from his forehead up over his hair.

Going past her, he stalked toward the door, but just paused there. His silence was his processing time. Shyla took advantage of it too. All of that anger, that craving to even the score, hadn't gone away. Yet, he'd given up on his plan to keep her safe.

Shaking her head, although he couldn't see her, Shyla's own wrath began to heat. "I won't let you," she said, filled with determination. "I won't let you give up on this, whatever it is. I won't let you do it, Phoenix." He turned around. "You need to do this. For us, for me. You're right, I did open my big mouth and I didn't take the hint. I'm sorry if that screwed anything up. I only voiced those views when you were around, nowhere else. Even if Burl did hear of my outbursts that should only help your cause."

"Help it?"

She nodded. "If no one even ever mentioned it around you, that would be more suspicious than me banging my drum. It gives credibility to whatever you're doing. Keeps him thinking that you're toeing the family line."

"But puts you in the firing line."

Licking her lips, she could feel her muscles begin to tense as her resolve grew. "If he's focused on me, that gives you the time to do whatever you need to do. It's misdirection."

"It doesn't matter," he said with a slight shake of his head. "It's over. I'm done."

"You are not," she said in a stern tone that surprised him. "I will not let you give this up for me."

"You don't even know what *it* is."

"I don't have to know the details to believe in you," she said. "I trust you. You know what you're doing. I know you do."

Again, he shook his head. "I won't."

"So what?" she asked. "You'll just keep running his money forever? That had to be part of your plan, or you were using it to prove to him that you were still on his side, that all was forgiven?" His confidence hadn't taken a knock. It wasn't that Score didn't think he could follow through, he was giving it up for her. Shyla had to get through to him, one way or another. "I love you, Phoenix. I love who you are. I want to know that man better. I want to know everything about you. You taught me about physical intimacy… now help me understand the mental and emotional too. I want every part of you, Love. Choose not to be the island. Choose to let me in… to let me be a part of you."

THIRTY-ONE

WHAT SHYLA WAS ASKING may be too much. Learning how to trust and rely on someone else overnight was no easy request. Score trusted Beeks, and must, at least to an extent, trust Fish too.

As she stood there waiting, trying not to give in to her urge to fill the silence, she caught her thumb nail. Rubbing and squeezing the nail with her opposite forefinger and thumb, it wasn't easy to be discreet. Her anxiety was creeping in again. Nothing he had planned for his family would change how she felt about him. But he could still choose to tell her to leave, to end the relationship that she so wanted to depend on.

"Come here," he said in a calmer, much more neutral tone.

Going to him, she garnered all of her courage and swallowed hard at the moment of stopping in front of him.

"You vowed to follow my command," he said and she nodded once, seeking his intent gaze. "But I also said that you were in charge. You have the power to end this at any time. To finish what we started."

"Tell me, Phoenix," she murmured, pleading with his good sense.

Shyla could let it go and continue to be with him. Like

she'd said, that could mean her always feeling inferior to the men. The trio would know something and she would be the only person in the dark. That could breed her own resentment. Unless Score could be honest with her and they came to some conclusion together, their relationship was doomed.

His brow lowered as his gaze probed deeper into her. "You decided to be with me even if it meant you could never have a family of your own."

"You are what I need," she said. "I made that choice. All I need is for you to be honest with me. To prove that any sacrifice I make is worth it."

"You shouldn't have to make any sacrifice."

"If you give me your word our children would never be handed over to that life, I'll believe you."

Any time the notion of refusing Burl had come up in the past, Score always asserted his father's word was law. Yet, if he'd planned some notion of payback, he couldn't be steadfast about that view. Maybe it was misdirection, just like she'd suggested. Being fervent about his support of his family would underline his commitment to them. That way, they'd never suspect him of double crossing them.

"There are three ways I can make that happen."

Hope. That was good. Though she tried not to appear too eager, Shyla's eyes grew wide in anticipation. "Yes? What are they?"

"Best way for you, I tell you to get the hell out of here to go procreate with some other guy."

Disappointed, the tension left her shoulders. She didn't want that and hadn't considered it an option. If Score broke off their relationship, Shyla would have to leave. But she couldn't imagine ever wanting another man in the way she wanted Score.

With a finger under her chin, he raised it up to link their eyes again. "I don't want to be with another man, Phoenix," she said, compelled by instinct to offer him honesty.

"Option two is I kill him."

Nothing about that statement wrung any emotion from him. Shyla was shocked. Score just seemed apathetic both to the act and to his own father being gone from the earth.

"Your own father?"

"I'd have to take Biz too… and anyone else who got in the way."

Resting her hands on his body, Shyla stepped nearer. "Let's call that plan B," she said. "You've already spent enough time in prison. I want my children's father to be present. There's more to it than just impregnating me."

"You know I won't make much of a parent."

Her lips curled until they formed a grin. "I disagree. I think you'd be the most incredible father. Tough and protective. Honest and patient… I couldn't imagine a better man for the job." Dubious as he looked, Shyla was absolutely certain. "What's the third option? You said there were three."

For a moment, he hesitated. His mouth stayed closed as he examined her. Shyla didn't know what he was looking for but said nothing during his quest.

Eventually, he relented. "I put them away."

"Away?" she asked, not following his meaning. "Them? Including Razer and Play?"

"Not them, but I can't trust them on the inside," he said. "I'm not supposed to discuss it."

With a frown, she shook her head once. "I don't follow. The inside of what? What aren't you supposed to discuss? Putting them away is…"

His expression hadn't changed, but hers did. The idea that silenced her was so fantastic, as in so unbelievable, that she couldn't bring herself to say it out loud.

He tucked her hair back behind her ear. "Maybe now you understand why I didn't burden you with it."

For at least half a minute, she stood there gaping at him. It hadn't even occurred to her, not even for a split second that he would… If she didn't consider it, no one else would, which made him perfect for the job.

"Baby," she breathed, moving right up against him. "You're talking about prison."

The words came out quietly, like she feared someone could be listening. Carrying this kind of secret brought new understanding to why Score was always so vehement about badmouthing the family. If someone heard negative talk and took that back to Burl, he could grow suspicious. That could make him clam up or cut ties, which would make Score's job more difficult.

"You don't have to worry about it."

"I am worried," she said. "Why wouldn't I be? Burl would kill you if he…" Her focus sharpened. "You think he would kill me… Beeks knows about this." He confirmed that suspicion with a slight movement of his brow. "He thinks that Burl would come for me if I knew…" Her clarity picked up pace. "Which means this is more than an idea… this is a plan. You have a plan."

"We *had* a plan," he said, glancing around at the floor. "I told you, it's over. Where is your shit?"

"I didn't leave with anything except my purse. That and the bag of stuff I bought is in the foyer closet. Phoenix," she said, grabbing his wrist when he began to turn away. "It's not over."

"You're home," he said, then came back around to her wearing a frown. "I was honest with you, where the fuck do you think you're going?"

"Baby," she said. Directing his arm around her, she leaned on him, reaching up to stroke his face. "I'm not going anywhere, but you are not giving up on this for me. Did you have a contact? Did you approach someone?"

"Someone approached me. While back."

"And…"

"Doesn't matter," he said. "We're through with it."

"Phoenix," Shyla said, holding her patience as best she could. "You said we had to do this if we wanted to be free. If we wanted to have a family."

"We?" he repeated. "No we."

"I want to talk to Beeks."

His scowl snapped back into place. "No."

"Beeks isn't emotionally invested. He'll give it to me straight."

"You think I'm lying to you?" he asked, both offended and pissed off.

Sliding her hands from his chest around to his back, she pulled herself tight against him. "I don't warm Beeks' bed."

Although Shyla had meant to loosen him up with a tease, it didn't work out that way. "I don't have to lie to get you into my bed," he said, his voice a low grumble. Tormenting her, he came lower. In her eagerness, Shyla pushed onto her tiptoes, begging his mouth with the pout of hers. "I just have to pick you up and put you there."

The prospect of such a reality curled her fingers until her nails dug into his tee-shirt. "Have you reached for me in bed?"

Shyla had sought him in the night. Half a sleep, still in a drowsy daze, she'd tried to get closer to a man who wasn't there.

Instead of answering, Score picked her up and carried her over to the bed. After he laid her down, he stood to slip off her mules and unbuckle his own belt. Envious of his fingers doing her job, she wanted to sit up and take over. Short of being allowed to undress him, the next best thing was getting naked *for* him. Shyla eased down the cotton straps of her dress and raised her hips to wriggle out of it. Score took over from there, ridding her body of both her dress and her panties as she cast off her bra.

He'd revealed her body, got her naked for his personal enjoyment. Shyla wanted to enjoy him in return and wasn't disappointed. Score pulled his tee-shirt off over his head before dropping his jeans and underwear.

Joining her on the bed, he lay over her, covering her form with his. "How's it been for you?" he murmured, holding his lips just out of reach of hers. "Alone, without me… Your pussy so far from my cock."

"Torture," she yelped, throwing both arms around his neck.

"Good."

That he enjoyed her torment was nothing new. The man had admitted how good he was at restraint. Shyla had admitted the opposite in the past. Even if he hadn't been sure of it, her wriggling and panting had to be giving her eagerness away.

Coiling both legs around his hips, she used his shoulders as leverage to push herself down. Score thwarted those efforts by dropping his pelvis to pin her in place.

"You're doing it again," she said, raising her head to kiss any part of his skin within reach. "Driving me crazy."

"You walked out on me."

The statement was matter of fact, yet his mention of it again reinforced her suspicion that she'd hurt him. "I'm sorry," she said. "So sorry, baby… I was lost and confused and I… I believed in us so much… The idea that we could be over—"

"We'll never be over, Lamb."

The gravity of his words relaxed her neck, so she could meet his eye. Just minutes ago, Shyla hadn't been so sure of that. He'd even suggested sending her off to be with another man. Somehow, physically being with him or away from him didn't change what they were. Like he'd said, she was his liability whether she was at home or far from his side.

"Promise me, Phoenix," she breathed. "Promise me you love me."

"I love you," he said. "I promise I love you. All of you. Only you."

The simple words uttered in the intimate moment touched her soul, they snaked deep into her, embedding themselves in her essence. They were together and he didn't want to lose her, just like she didn't want to lose him.

Languishing in the security of his bed, Shyla was more relaxed than she could ever remember being. Her revere was snapped away when Score surged up and forced himself into her with one thrust.

Her mouth opened wide, matching her eyes that found only satisfaction in his. He'd meant to do that, to change the mood of the moment in an instant. The man knew what he was doing, knew how to work her.

Retreating and advancing at a slower pace, he reminded her body of how much it enjoyed his intrusion. Heat and contentment swirled around her on the route to gratification.

"Phoenix," she whispered his name, her hips moving with his, her hands clinging to him. "Yes…"

He sped up, but switched his angle, pushing up and down against her body. Shyla smiled as the friction raised the temperature between them. He wasn't finished tormenting her, but focused in on that one spot, the sweet spot he knew just how to pleasure.

The sparks of ecstasy began to shimmer from her clit up into her belly just moments before the weight of orgasm pushed her hips upward. Bucking against him, she cried out and dug her nails in, gripping him almost as tight as the muscles of her pussy were gripping his cock. Desperate for him to stay, she tried to pull his upper body down, but he was speeding up, racing toward his own end.

Shyla wanted him to have it and struggled to breathe through the aftershocks of her own delectable climax. She panted, grabbing for oxygen just like she'd grabbed for him, sucking it in and huffing it out. Gritting her teeth against the clash of a second wave, she was only half aware of his growl of satisfaction. He pushed up into her, hard and deep, then stalled.

Through her daze, she met his eye. Her smile was weak, his expression discerning. Whatever was on his mind, he kept it to himself and moved to push her onto the far side of the bed while he lay next to her.

THIRTY-TWO

"CAN I ASK you something?" Shyla asked into the silence that had hung around them both for a while.

On his side next to her, Score was running his fingertips up and down her body. If she didn't say something to take her mind off his torment, she'd beg him for more before he was ready to give it.

"I don't want to talk about it in bed."

"No," she said, shifting onto her side to face him. "Not that."

Talking about his family and the plan intended to send them to jail wasn't exactly the most romantic pillow talk. Being in bed with him, enjoying their proximity and the warmth of their lingering passion, was just about as perfect a moment as Shyla could ever have imagined.

He rested his hand on her waist. "What?"

"Why did you break up with me?" He frowned. "When you found out I hadn't had sex before. You didn't even think about it, you just dropped me in a second."

"I didn't expect it," he said. "I don't like to be surprised."

"I know," she said, flattening her hand against his chest to enjoy him as he'd enjoyed her. "But you got really angry. It really upset you. Don't most guys prefer their girlfriend to have fewer partners rather than more? You said it was okay if I'd sold my body. If I'd been a hooker, I would've slept with a zillion guys. You'd really have preferred that over knowing you're the only one who's been inside me?"

"I like it now," he said, sliding his hand around to her ass to pull her closer. "At the time, it…"

It wasn't like Score to hesitate.

Concern took her palm to his cheek. "It what, baby?"

"Growing up there were women all over. Being McDades, we got our pick… We didn't always treat women the best, any of us."

A lot of young guys, especially guys jeered on by admiring friends and aware of their family reputation, could act in irresponsible ways. For a McDade male that expectation was probably multiplied by a dozen.

"You didn't have the best role model," she muttered. He surprised her by raising her chin with a curled finger. Just the look in his eye told her what he was thinking. "Sorry, I won't do it again."

"You will," he said. "You can't seem to help yourself."

Though Shyla smiled, she was sorry. "It hurts me the way they treated you. I get this… this physical reaction inside me whenever I think about it."

Bowing down, he used his body to ease hers back so he could kiss her lips. "Don't think about it."

"I like thinking about you," she said, studying his face as he watched his hand trail down her body. "That doesn't tell me why… Why didn't you want to be with me?"

"We're different. From different worlds."

"And my virginity reminded you of—"

"I didn't want to be the guy who broke you. The guy who changed you, made you cynical. Women where I'm from are dumb or bitter. I didn't want to be the one to show you how the world really works."

"Because you thought we'd only have a sexual relationship."

"Because I don't do romance. If you were expecting

some sweet, tender Prince Charming…"

"You didn't want to be the one to show me life isn't like the movies."

"If you'd been around the block, you'd understand that sometimes a fuck is just a fuck."

Tucking herself closer, she ran her fingers up his arm and into his hair. "You didn't think we'd last."

His fingers opened to run through her hair. "Nothing ever has," he murmured.

"Before," she said, folding her arms between them. "Nothing has ever lasted before. This will last."

His attention hopped from her hair to her eyes. "You're so sure," he said, his discerning gaze narrowing. "How can you be sure?"

"You said I was in charge," she said. "I might not be the only woman you've been intimate with, but I will be the last."

Something about her certainty must have spoken to him. The question left his gaze and he pushed her onto her back with his next powerful kiss. Anticipating the progression of their passion, Shyla's hormones tingled even before his hands began to explore her body.

The sharp squawk of his phone startled her. Inhaling deepened his kiss, but only for a fraction of a second. Score pulled away to flip onto his back. Reaching across to his nightstand, he grabbed the handset.

"Your father?"

"Beeks," he said, answering the phone. "Yeah?" Shyla lay there, stroking him, waiting for his return. "Thirty seconds."

Score hung up and vaulted onto his feet.

"Baby?"

Grabbing his jeans from the floor, he pulled them on. "Your phone is in the drawer," he said, nodding to the nightstand on her side of the bed.

His haste worried her. Sitting up, she frowned at him. "What did Beeks say? What's going on?"

"Something we don't need to talk about in bed," he said, dropping a fist to the mattress to plant a quick kiss on her lips.

Shyla was still recovering from his sudden departure from their passion. The moment his lips left hers, he turned and strode from the room. She heard the door open, but was still trying to figure out what was going on.

Determined to be in the loop, rather than be sidelined again, Shyla leaped out of bed and grabbed his tee-shirt from the floor. As she crossed the bedroom threshold, she used Score's shirt to cover herself. Wasting no time, she hurried along the hallway to find the trio of men were standing next to the dining table.

"Shyla!" Fish exclaimed, apparently thrilled to see her.

He scooped both arms around her and hugged her tight. While in his embrace, she glanced around, expecting to find the new housekeeper somewhere.

"What happened to Maria?" she asked when Fish let her go.

"Sent her away," Beeks said. "She was only a temp." His head ducked back as he frowned. "Unless you're not planning to stay."

"I'm planning to stay," she said, going to Score's side. "What's going on?"

Beeks looked at Score. Obviously no one planned to loop her in without his approval.

"News from home," Score said, his attention still on Beeks.

"Good news? Bad news?"

"Score seems to think it's a disaster waiting to happen," Beeks said.

Tipping her chin up, Shyla waited in hope that he would be honest with her. "Phoenix?"

He inhaled and looked at her. "My brother got married."

Though that was apparently a fact, Shyla was none the wiser as to why it was relevant or what would prompt Score to believe it a bad thing.

"Shouldn't you be happy about that?" she asked, knowing Biz couldn't be the groom because he was already hitched to Nicole. "A wedding is a good thing… Are you disappointed you weren't invited?"

"We wouldn't have gone even if I was."

Leaving her side, he went around the dining table to stare out at the ocean.

Shyla appealed to the non-brooding males. "I don't understand," she said. "Why is he mad?" Various possibilities ran through her mind. Maybe he knew the bride, maybe she was an ex. Shyla gasped. "He didn't marry Siobhan, did he?"

"Worse," Score said, proving he was still listening, even if he wasn't in their physical circle.

Trying to figure out who could be worse than the woman he'd gone to death row for, Shyla blinked at Beeks.

"It's complicated, Shyla," the lawyer said. "The McDade family are—"

"A Doherty," Score said, turning to zero in on her. "Raze married a Doherty."

"I… I don't understand," she said. "You said it was kill or be killed."

"And I stand behind that," he said. "If he doesn't kill her first, she'll take him down."

"So what do we… I mean how do we…"

Score looked to Beeks. "We need to step up the timetable."

"The timetable?" he asked. "You said we were out."

Both Beeks and Fish glanced her way, anxiety and shock written across their faces.

"Shy says we're in," Score said.

"You… you told her?"

Instead of answering the lawyer, Score sought her. "Are you sure about this, baby?"

"Am I sure that I want us to be free of them? Am I sure that I want to be by your side and bear your children?" A grin curved her lips. "Damn straight."

Taking another breath, Score's shoulders relaxed as he exhaled. "The only way to keep my brother alive is to get him out from under the Doherty."

"*The Doherty.*" Just the way he said it revealed his disgust. His brother was married to an enemy of a McDade.

Shyla couldn't begin to figure out how that had happened or why Razer would've fallen for a nemesis of his family.

Much as she wanted to believe it was love, her relationship with Score had shown her just how complex the McDade men were. Stoic, fierce, and true in their own way, McDade men shouldn't be underestimated.

If "The Doherty" was gullible and innocent, she could believe that Razer loved her. But knowing how the McDades were brought up in the shadow of horror and debauchery, Shyla struggled to believe the Dohertys would've had it any better.

Something was going on under the surface. Neither family could trust the other, so why would the couple join their families in matrimony?

Shyla wanted some time to enjoy her own man. Time to plan their future. But love them or not, the McDades actions would always influence theirs, at least until they were off the streets and behind bars.

Going around to Score, Shyla stood in front of him, resting her forearms on his bare torso. "I love you, Phoenix. Whatever it takes, that's our only priority. We are our only priority."

"Could get messy."

She almost laughed. "I don't doubt it will. But I'm under your command and protection, my love. Nothing can harm me… Nothing would dare."

One side of his mouth rose as he dipped down to kiss her. They were together and being honest with each other. Shyla had come to the residence desperate and alone. With her love and her man burning strong, she'd never have to worry about being either ever again.

TO BE CONTINUED…

Thank you for reading this tale!
If you can, please take the time to review.

~

Ask your local library for more Scarlett Finn novels!

~

For all things Scarlett Finn
check out:

www.scarlettfinn.com

BOOK TWO

OUT NOW!